Daâh:
The First Human

FROM THE SAME AUTHOR

Illusions of Immortality

Daâh:
The First Human

by
Edmond Haraucourt

translated, annotated and introduced by
Brian Stableford

A Black Coat Press Book

Edited by Peter Gabbani

English adaptation and introduction Copyright © 2014 by Brian Stableford.
Cover illustration Copyright © 2014 Juan Miguel Aguilera.

Visit our website at www.blackcoatpress.com

ISBN 978-1-61227-355-6. First Printing. December 2014. Published by Black Coat Press, an imprint of Hollywood Comics.com, LLC, P.O. Box 17270, Encino, CA 91416. All rights reserved. The stories and characters depicted in this novel are entirely fictional. Printed in the United States of America.

Introduction

The sketches making up Edmond Haraucourt's saga of Daâh first appeared in the Parisian daily newspaper *Le Journal* in 1912-14. They were initially reprinted, in an expanded version, as the book *Daâh, le premier homme*, published by Ernest Flammarion in the summer of 1914, a few weeks before the outbreak of the Great War. The book was somewhat eclipsed in consequence, and might be far better known today had it had the time and space to create more discussion and controversy after its publication. The contents of the Flammarion volume were eventually reproduced in 1988, together with some supplementary materials external to the text, by Arléa, Libraire des Fruits du Congo.[1] That version was reprinted in 1996. It is the book version that is here translated as *Daâh: the First Human*.

The sketches in *Le Journal* did not follow the chronological order in which their materials were arranged in the book version, and were offered as two distinct sequences. The first sequence began with "La Première larme" (corresponding to the section forming chapters XIII-XV in the book version) in the 26 December 1912 issue of the newspaper and concluded with "Le Flambeau" (corresponding to the final chapters of the book version) in the 10 April 1913 issue. The second sequence bore the collective title "Daâh, le premier homme: Scènes de la vie préhistorique" and began on 5 May 1914 with an episode corresponding to sections of chapters I-VI of the book version, continuing until 4 June 1914, when it concluded with

---

[1] The odd name of the publisher in question derives from an *avant garde* novel, *Les Fruits du Congo* (1951) by the journalist Alexandre Vialatte (1901-1971), most of whose fiction was only published posthumously, including several novels issued by Arléa.

5

an episode corresponding to chapters LXIII and LXIV in the book version—those dealing with "L'Amour."

As noted in the introduction to the previous Black Coat press volume of works by Haraucourt, *Illusions of Immortality* (2012)[2]—which also contains a biography of the author and an overview of his career, the details of which do not need to be repeated here—Haraucourt was a frequent contributor for many years to the regular feuilleton slot employed in *Le Journal* for short stories, although many of the items he contributed to it were too long to be presented in their entirety and thus appeared as short serials of between two and half a dozen episodes. Because of the heavier burden of explanation required by speculative fiction, all of the items of speculative fiction that he produced for the slot were serialized in that fashion, and even the naturalistic *contes cruels* that he produced for it in some abundance were often split up, in contrast to those produced by other regulars, including Octave Mirbeau and Jules Richepin, who became past masters at the art of stripping stories down to the typical length of a feuilleton episode (1400-1700 words).

The Daâh series was, in effect, a curious kind of compromise, easily permitting the author to work in slices of the requisite length, but also enabling him to stack up those slices gradually into something far richer and more complex. It is arguable, in fact, that the episodic narrative form forced on *Daâh* by its initial adaptation to the feuilleton format is ideally suited to a story whose innate continuity is essentially problematic. Because it is an account of the early evolution of thought and technical discovery, *Daâh* is necessarily an account of a series of loosely-connected incidents and sub-climactic leaps, and although something is definitely gained by collecting the episodes together in a book, there is also an element of loss as well. The account of the early development of sexual mores—which was ground-breaking and extremely daring at the time—is slightly reduced in its impact by its in-

[2] ISBN 978-1-61227-075-3.

termediate location in the book version, whereas it must have provided an appropriately startling and highly provocative conclusion to the sequence of newspaper stories.

Although other writers for *Le Journal*'s slot and the similar ones featured in *Le Matin* and *La Lanterne*'s weekly fiction supplement occasionally constructed series by using the same central character repeatedly, those series usually remained haphazard and "segmental," but the Daâh series is a cumulative endeavor with a much more complicated narrative arc. Although the sum total is not quite a novel, just as the original versions were not quite a serial, the ultimate work has a coherency that renders it very distinctive, not only among Haraucourt's works and the multitudinous products of *Le Journal*'s fiction slots, but also within the subgenre of prehistoric fantasy. Although some of the author's contemporaries, who thought of him as a neo-Naturalist writer, regarded it as an item of eccentricity ineligible for consideration as a major work, Haraucourt thought very highly of it, and he was not wrong to do so; it is certainly one of the masterpieces of its subgenre, quite unique in its method and its achievements, and it is definitely one of the finest works of a highly distinctive and greatly underrated writer.

The subgenre of prehistoric fantasy developed alongside the burgeoning of the science of physical anthropology, based on hominid remains discovered by paleontologists, popularized in such non-fictional works as John Lubbock's *Prehistoric Times* (1865; tr. into French as *L'Homme préhistorique*, 1876), Nicolas Joly's *L'Homme avant les métaux* [Humans Before Metals] (1879) and Gabriel de Mortillet's *Le préhistorique* [Prehistory] (1882). These non-fictional works inevitably contained a strong narrative component, and it was only natural that works taking that narrative element a step further, adding characterization and plot, should appear in parallel with them. The first substantial exercise in the subgenre was an exercise in the popularization of science aimed at a juvenile audience by S. Henry Berthoud, "Les Premiers habit-ants de Paris" (in *L'Homme depuis cinq mille ans*, 1865; tr. as "The First Inhabitants of Paris")[3].

The subject matter was controversial and sensitive at the time because many believers in the Biblical account of human origins, whose commitment of faith was all the more fervent because they were defending a ridiculous myth against steadily-accumulating evidence, resented its contradiction. Jules Verne, who inserted a brief vision of an exotic hominid into the second version of *Voyage au centre de la Terre* (1867; tr. as *Journey to the Centre of the Earth*) in response to the publication of a revised edition of the book he had employed as a primary source for the first edition in 1864, Louis Figuier's *La Terre avant le deluge* (1863; revised 1867; tr. as *The World Before the Deluge*)—in which Figuier decisively rejected the Biblical chronology he had treated with diplomatic respect in the first edition—carefully left the passage as a possibly-hallucinatory vision, in order to conserve "potential deniability" of any challenge to religious faith. There was, therefore, a certain amount of courage involved in a popular feuilletonist like Elie Berthet tackling the theme robustly in *Le Monde inconnu* (1876; rev. as *Paris avant l'histoire*, 1879; tr. as *The Prehistoric World.*)

Although that controversy had weakened considerably by 1912, by which time the Biblical account of human origins was no longer defensible except by the willfully stupid, the broader Disraeliesque question of whether man ought to be reckoned, in essence, as an ape or an angel had not gone away, and still remained sharply contentious—as, indeed, it still does. It is partly for that reason that there was, and is, no other field of advancing scientific discovery that not only invites but requires narrativization. Although the discoveries of hominid remains in various places became steadily more prolific in the half-century separating Berthoud's pioneering science-fictional endeavor from Haraucourt's, the items were inevita-

---

[3] Included in the Black Coat press collection *Martyrs of Science*, ISBN 978-1-61227-229-0.

bly fragmentary and difficult to relate to one another, especially in the absence of any reliable chronology. Scientists were obliged to leave a wide margin of uncertainty as they attempted to build up their own stories of the prehistory of humankind, and inevitably disagreed as to the manner in which the jigsaw of the data ought to be fitted together. Novelists interested in producing elaborate accounts of the life of prehistoric humans, employing them as viewpoint characters, and superimposing a hypothetical sociology and psychology on the paleontological data, thus had more than one scientific account from which to choose, and great deal of latitude in the matter of its extrapolative embroidery.

Of the writers who tackled the challenge before Haraucourt, the one who did so most assiduously and most effectively was J.-H. Rosny Aîné, beginning with *Vamireh* (1892) and *Eyrimah* (1893)—both translated in the Black Coat Press collection *Vamireh and Other Prehistoric Fantasies* (2010)[4]—and continuing, after a considerable gap, with *La Guerre du feu* (serialized 1909; book 1911; tr.—very inadequately—as *The Quest for Fire*). The considerable success of the latter-named work encouraged Rosny to produce two more novels of a similar kind in 1918 and 1930, and was surely responsible for prompting Haraucourt to produce his own account of early human evolution, or at least for opening up hospitable market space for its publication. Although not compatible with Rosny's account of prehistory, *Daâh* is not really a rival to it, because it deliberately takes the exercise further back toward its fundamentals, not only temporally but philosophically.

All of Rosny's prehistoric fantasies, along with Berthoud's pioneering novella and other works in the same subgenre, deal with human societies that are already formulated and already possessed of a considerable assembly of mores, even if their technological resources and languages are re-

---

[4] ISBN 978-1-935558-38-5. See also *Helgvor of the Blue River*, ISBN 978-1-93558-46-0.

stricted. The same is true of the earliest English-language exercises in the subgenre, which include Stanley Waterloo's *The Story of Ab: A Tale of the time of the Cave Man* (1897), H. G. Wells' episodic "A Story of the Stone Age" (1897) and Jack London's *Before Adam* (1906). Haraucourt, however, deliberately goes back to a supposed earlier phase in human development, commenting more than once that Daâh is living before the time of "cave men," when the ancestors of humankind were allegedly still forest-dwellers.

Haraucourt's account of human prehistory begins with its hypothetical proto-humans living a solitary existence, having not yet begun to form societies, and his account is as much an account of the origins of living in association as it is of technological discoveries and the development of language. In parallel with that, and as a connected aspect of the same process, it offers an account of the primal evolution of consciousness—a much more difficult endeavor in narrative terms. In consequence, as well as being a substantial work of fiction, *Daâh* is an authentic exercise in existential philosophy: a conscientious and fascinating attempt to strip human consciousness down to its fundamental elements, and to explain the dynamics of its origins. That is what made the story of Daâh unique at the time, and establishes it as the masterpiece it is. It is, in fact, highly improbable that our ancestors ever lived the kind of solitary forest-dwelling existence initially credited to Daâh, and it must have seemed unlikely even in 1912, but its adoption as a hypothesis favors the philosophical aspects of Haraucourt's account of the elements of consciousness, and is justifiable on those grounds.

The enterprise did not meet with universal approval at the time, either in its results or its method. The 1988 edition of *Daâh* includes a letter from Haraucourt to "Waldeck-Rousseau"—presumably a son or grandson of the famous statesman who had died in 1904—replying to several harsh criticisms of *Daâh*, one of which was "the perils of the inductive method and my pretention to logic." The perils are, of course, real, and the precise pattern of logic employed in *Daâh* is certainly open to debate in the light of subsequent discoveries in physical anthropology, but Waldeck-Rousseau's complaint that such intellectual endeavor is illegitimate in itself in a literary work is clearly absurd. He seems to have suggested, snidely, that Haraucourt was like his hero in taking it upon himself to explain the world, and Haraucourt replies to that accusation at length in his own letter, admitting that he is, indeed, like Daâh, because we all are, and that that is the whole point of the exercise: to analyze the fundamentals of human nature, that being interesting and worthwhile not just as an abstract intellectual exercise but because we are still possessed of them, even though we might have spent hundreds of thousands of years trying to modify and suppress them. Haraucourt is rightly unashamed of the fact that his attempt to strip human nature back to its original essence has involved intense introspection as well as reference to paleontological evidence, and that the logic of the endeavor involved the ingenious combination of the two.

Haraucourt was, of course, correct in arguing in response to his critic that we still have reason to be interested in the origins of human nature, and that there is still something for us to learn and gain by thinking about it seriously. It is partly for that reason that his account of human prehistory has not become "obsolete," even though we now have a much clearer picture, based on more elaborate geological evidence, of the actual pattern and time-scale of proto-human evolution. Perhaps ironically, however, the point on which Haraucourt's account differed most obviously from the then-conventional scientific account—another object of Waldeck-Rousseau's criticism—still remains debatable, and it is by no means established that Haraucourt's unorthodox contention was mistaken. That point is the relationship between the two kinds of skeletons then identified as "Neanderthal Man" and "Cro-Magnon Man," which the conventional account represented as competing species, the former of which was superseded—and perhaps wiped out—by the latter, so that the "Cro-Magnons" became ancestral to contemporary humankind. Haraucourt takes the view that contemporary humankind is the result of interbreeding between the two types, and hypothesizes that the critical evolutionary advances were made by the Neanderthal Daâh with assistance from the children he has with the Cro-Magnon female Ta, and other progeny of their cross-breeding with those born to him by the Neanderthal female Hock.

Waldeck-Rousseau's other specific criticism, that it is implausible to collapse such an elaborate history of change into the lifetime of a single individual and the adventures of a single "horde," is obviously rational, but Haraucourt's dismissal of it on the grounds of poetic license and narrative convenience is perfectly legitimate; *Daâh* is a work of fiction, no more intended to be taken in a crudely literal sense than the story of Adam and Eve, but nevertheless aspiring to a kind of truthfulness in its depiction of the psychological and social processes involved in the pattern of change and discovery. Daâh is a kind of archetype of primordial human being, and his story is not so much the hypothetical life-story of a particular individual as a distillation of the "collective biography" of a nascent species. As such it is deliberately provocative—Haraucourt was not a man to let conventional opinion go unchallenged, and was possessed of considerable artistry in devising such teasing arguments as the reason why the notion of property would have proceeded logically from the invention of the loincloth—and it is all the more compelling, as well as more entertaining, in consequence.

As a "collective biography," *Daâh* is highly effective, and if individual readers find much therein with which to quarrel, and a certain amount at which to take offense—the incestuous sexual communism and carefree cannibalism were blithely calculated to ruffle feathers—that is part and parcel of the exercise, and perhaps its true literary essence. The narrative does not intend or aspire to produce final and definitive answers to enigmas of human nature and human evolution, but to undertake the much more reasonable and far more necessary task of dramatizing the questions in such a way as to reveal their sharpness and their complexity. In that it succeeds, in no uncertain terms, and that is why the endeavor remains a *tour de force*, still highly provocative and still well worth reading.

This translation has been made from a copy of the Arléa edition of 1988.

Brian Stableford

DAÂH: THE FIRST HUMAN

PART ONE: THE NOMAD

I. Her

At the top of the chalky cliff, the branches of the thicket parted. A brutal and bronzed face appeared amid the foliage, and then the flesh of a shoulder, an arm and a breast—and the crawling woman stood up, naked and hairy.

She was a short, thickset female with a massive torso and sturdy limbs; everything about her was broad and abrupt except the pelvis: the height of an adolescent and the amplitude of a street-porter; short legs, low-set knees, flat feet, thick hands and spatulate fingers; her muscles, as knotty as an oak, clinging to a rocky skeleton, and her belly protruding; on the ruddy blackcloth of her skin, a flexuous fleece was designed in a symmetrical décor, the point of which narrowed over the sternum and descended in two curves from the throat all the way to the crease of the groin, while from behind two other volutes departed from the armpits to join up with the dorsal spine and slide over the loins, where they broadened out like a fan.

A mane of coarser hair, which garnished the skull with tresses and hanks, framed the face with a somber russet-tinted halo, the last flames of which reached the nascence of the shoulders. Within that thicket, the neck was even more massive, beneath a solid jaw. The vast mouth, with fleshy lips, projected its redoubtable dentition forwards, and it was as if the entire face was crushed beneath the slab of a sloping forehead; the nose, squat and broad, stood up level with the cheekbones and extended the double flare of the mobile nostrils to spire the revelations of the wind.

In the shelter of the low forehead, consumed by the hair, the violently emphatic eyebrows were indented to form two grottoes, in the depths of which the eyes were agitating like skittish animals. Those eyes were brown and narrow between the wrinkled eyelids, which only allowed a narrow stripe of cornea to be seen; by virtue of the habit of watching for multiple and incessant perils, they expressed anxiety, and moved restlessly.

Standing on the edge of the cliff, the woman lowered her gaze stupidly into the gulf, and the images entered into her: in the location where Paris would one day be built, the Seine, four leagues broad and yellow between the green forests, flowed beneath the stormy sky. From the depths of the horizon the river was racing furiously, and it covered the whole region like a tumultuous lake; on the shore of its waves, the woman saw the black dots of hippopotamuses and rhinoceroses moving, and in places, emerging from long grass, the round backs of elephants marching in single file. Over that morose immensity, the rain was falling hard.

She did not gaze for long. Accustomed to the narrow spectacles of the forest, she experienced vertigo before the excessively vast and mobile gulf. In the semicircle of those extremely distant horizons, which seemed to her to be shifting, like the river, her head was already dizzy; her eyelids blinked.

She tried to raise her face toward the sky, but the clouds were moving too rapidly; quickly, she closed her eyes. She shook her shoulders, and her mane streamed; then, slowly, she recoiled until she sensed the tickling of twigs on her back. On making contact with them, she pivoted with an abrupt movement; flexing her legs and tilting her upper body forwards, with one arm projected to part the branches and the other leaning on the ground, head down, she plunged into the wood.

For one more moment her voluminous rump stood out clearly against the dark background of the thicket, and then the curtain of foliage closed behind her.

II. Genesis

It was the first days of the human species, long before the bitterness of the temperature obliged our ancestors to seek shelter in the depths of caverns—and yet it was yesterday, or very nearly, since it was only one or two thousand centuries ago.[5]

By then, our planet, after so many successive revolutions, had already taken on the form whose broad outlines were scarcely to be modified again before our day. The envelope of the earth, gradually cooled, had wrinkled like the rind of a ripe fruit, and had been punctured by volcanoes; then, as it shrank, the globe, having become tetrahedral, had pushed outwards the ridges of its quadruple fracture; those wounds had scarred into long chains of mountains, at the feet of which the continents were stacked; on the unexpected crests, the hu-

---

[5] It was not until the late 1940s that the invention of radiocarbon dating provided a reliable yardstick for measuring the antiquity of human remains excavated by paleontologists, although radiometric dating had begun to provide information about the age of rocks, which led to the geometric time-scale, in 1907. Haraucourt's assumption that Neanderthal and Cro-Magnon remains implied a time-scale of between 100,000 and 200,000 years turned out to be broadly correct, but his attempt to accommodate that to the time scale of the Pliocene-Quaternary glaciations, which had been debated since the mid-19th century, is inevitably awkward. Although James Croll's *Climate and Time in their Geological Relations* (1875), following up the work of the Alpinists Louis Agassiz and Karl Schimper, can now be seen as a brilliant analysis of the causes of periodic glaciations, it was neither well-known nor orthodox in 1912, so Haraucourt's analysis of climate change is understandably primitive and over-simplified, but it was not lacking in enterprise at the time.

midity of the atmosphere learned to condense, inventing the snow and ice that were previously unknown.

The Alpine creases now bristled their refrigerant summits, but at the same time as that enormous freezer had surged forth, a cauldron had been hollowed out in parallel; to the west of Europe, a broader ocean displayed its immense surfaces of evaporation under the topics. Between that nucleus of heat and that nucleus of chill, the air current carried with it a tide of clouds. Untiringly, for centuries, the swell of clouds flowed from the marine region toward the mountainous regions. Through such a thick envelope, the sun almost never shone any longer; in the year devoid of summer, autumn prolonged the spring; in the day devoid of noon, twilight lasted from dawn until dusk; but the opaque mantle of vapors that stopped the sun's rays in passage also prevented the chilling of nights and winters, with the result that the variation in temperature of the hours and the seasons was scarcely sensible.

Centuries-long rains fell upon the plains, while snow accumulated on the heights; already, from time to time, a few excessively heavy glaciers were breaking up on the edges of the circles, and gently but formidably, dragged by their own weight, they set out in motion with an invincible slowness.

The ages of exuberance had long gone by for the earth; the last skeletons of the giant saurians were petrifying in the soil. A less furious era was inaugurated. The supreme logic from which all harmony is born, which regulates the simultaneous transformations of heavenly bodies and their parasites, had led progressively to the epoch over which the beautiful population of the Mammals would reign. With them, a more delicate life became manifest during the Tertiary age; by virtue of successive selections, forms diversified, organs were refined, senses became subtler; a more complex and better-organized nervous system tended to produce the brain...

A few millennia ago, those young conquerors had taken possession of the renovated world, but not all of them were able to tolerate the relative cooling that was beginning to shrink the atmosphere; already, races of animals were migrating or becoming extinct, while others varied in order to adapt themselves, and less cold-sensitive species appeared in the world.

The new-born humans moved discreetly among them, still rare and denuded of everything.

Here and there on the earth, variants of that naked biped were encountered; they resembled one another in their essential characteristics—for it is important to note that the climactic conditions, under the various latitudes of the globe, scarcely differed; such a production, when it became realizable at one point, became simultaneously realizable at another. On several continents, several races of humans appeared almost at the same time—which is to say, within twenty thousand years or so.[6]

---

[6] The rival theories of polygeny (that human races had been created, or had evolved, separately) and monogeny (that human races all had a single common point of origin) were still being hotly debated in 1912, especially in the context of anthropological racial theory. The modern synthesis of Darwinian evolutionary theory with genetic theory, which effectively killed off polygeny as a plausible thesis, had not yet been completed, although the trend was clearly inclined in that direction. The distinction between the two theses is not, however, as stark as it might seem, and Haraucourt's "compromise," assuming that anatomically different proto-human types separately evolved in different places would still have been capable of interbreeding—as modern "races" obviously are—when circumstances brought them together, is not scientifically implausible, although his grounds for espousing it doubtless had much to do with his philosophical agenda and his political ideology.

III. Eden

Seen from Mars, which shines ruddily, the Earth probably seemed green, so abundant was the vegetation. Throughout Western Europe, an uninterrupted forest was displayed, from the double massif of the mountains to the triple gulf of the seas; it was so dense that the branches of one tree were entangled with those of the next, and the plants killed one another like animals in order to earn their places to live.

The cadavers of the vanquished fattened the moist soil; the successive layers of leaves and branches had accumulated a spongy carpet soaked by the incessant downpour; the water that fell onto that putrescence as rain rose up above it again in mists or flowed beneath it as streams. A heavy and murky air, impregnated with vapors, stagnated over that bed of fermentations, and the foliage enclosed it beneath its vault.

In that nourishing atmosphere, the vegetables swelled up with sap, and insects seethed. The latter were already old; some of them dated from the carboniferous period, and they had prospered. Myriads of wings were buzzing over every pond; under every leaf, bellies crawled, mouths ate and feet scuttled.

Exuded from that water-saturated ground, springs flowed down the slopes of every hill; cascades roared in every gorge; in all the hollows of the mountains, lakes were born and grew, awaiting the moment when they could break their dykes to race into the lower regions. With every storm, the streams, transformed into torrents, dragged away soil, sand, rocks and uprooted trees pell-mell, along with animals drowned in their thousands.

The rivers received and absorbed everything, and carried it all away; the feeble watercourses that we call the Rhine, the Seine, the Loire, the Garonne and the Rhone no longer resemble what they were then; through the forest of the Occident, that quintuple surge of brutal water plowed a passage, opening five streaks of brightness in the verdure and the shadow; those sinuous avenues radiated from the center toward the shores like the tentacles of an octopus the color of the sky. Immeasurably swollen by the abundance of the rain, no less than by the melting of snows, the rivers progressively gained all the amplitude offered to the invasion of their waves; our plains were covered by them, our hills emerging as islets; only their heights were habitable.

The inhabitants of the marsh, the hippopotamus and the rhinoceros, accommodated themselves without difficulty to that inundation, which characterized the approach of the glacial ages, but a multitude of other beasts were driven back toward the plateaux, climbing up to seek their shelter and their nourishment under the trees; they found both in plenty, for the thick vegetation multiplied lairs, and there was no lack of prey for carnivores, just as there was no shortage of foliage for the herbivores.

Among the fauna and flora of that Eden, the humans of our days would not have felt much out of place; to begin with, they would recognize the plants and animals of modern Europe, and those of Asia and northern Africa. At the second glance, they would be astonished to find species from hot lands and those from temperate climates brought together as in a zoological garden. But if they looked harder, they would be alarmed to discover that the cats on the banks of the Seine were twice as large as the lions of the Atlas; that, compared to the ancestor of the caves, the Pyrenean bear is a mere cub; and that our elephants of the Ivory Coast could shelter under the abdomen of their ancestors of the Pliocene era.

Over that world of colossi, the troops of nimbus clouds sent forth by the sea flowed incessantly through a low and angry sky; storms burst without respite. At every moment, beneath the vaults of the forest, green holes illuminated by lightning lightened the gloom; to the din of the thunder distant rumbles responded; from the height of the punctured clouds, water fell in cataracts.

Sometimes, however, the rain stopped and the earth saw a few shreds of azure shining through. That was when a cold wind had risen from the Alpine moraines to descend toward the Occident, driving back its clouds and tearing apart its mists. Then the Great Apes, survivors of once-numerous species, shivered in the trees and wrapped their long arms around their breasts; the felines fled, skimming the ground and mewling in distress, horrified by the mortal blast that foreshadowed for them the glacial cataclysm in which they would perish.

Every evening, at the entrances to the caves that the giant Cats disputed with the Bears, the growl of their battles filled the misty air. The malign Elephants raised their trunks and trumpeted, satisfied to hear their enemies, the flesh-eaters, killing one another on the plateau, but the Ostriches and the Horses fled fearfully in groups, while the Hyenas, the Dogs and the Foxes crouched down in the grass and licked their chops, sure of finding the carcass of the Lion tomorrow, lying with its back broken and its breast devoured by the invincible Bear.

In that immense larder of the Pleistocene forest, no creature existed save to serve the hunger of another. The human omnivores maintained their place there, naked and gluttonous, eating until they could eat no more, and having no other function.

IV. The Solitaries

I am not inventing anything; I am trying to remember. You can remember, too, but you don't know it. Listen, in order that you might be helped. You carry in your fibers and young blood the indelible residuum of what you once were, in the person of your most distant ancestors. These are your dormant memories that I am awakening, in order to evoke in you the time when your ancestors conquered a soul for you...

They were wanderers; they lived in the woods.

Paleontology has difficulty recovering traces of those Tertiary ancestors. Evidence of a human presence was only able to subsist from the epoch when human remains were protected against the action of time, and the era had not yet come for us to conquer shelters; the caves remained in the possession of wild beasts, which scarcely lent themselves to that conquest; isolated humans were unable to claim them to capture them or to conserve them. The occupation of caves only became realizable for the already-numerous group of the clan, and it corresponded with the first social manifestations. In the meantime, the nomads fled such lairs and their vicinity, instead of seeking them out. They had neither shelters nor tombs; they lived and died outside, in the mud. Their remains, gnawed and scattered by wild beasts, excavated by insects, washed by the rain, and softened and pulverized by the centuries, have disappeared.

Like all beasts of prey, those humans lived in isolation.[7]

---

[7] In fact, very few beasts of prey, if any, live in isolation, but human beings obtained a very misleading impression of their lifestyle from the encounters they had with such impressive predators as lions and tigers. The science of ethology, and its subsidiary discipline of social biology, was still unknown in 1912, in spite of the seeds brilliantly sown by Charles Darwin in *The Expression of the Emotions in Man and Animals*

Alongside them, a few more prolific, more ancient species, notably families of insects, sketched out a commencement of society, which rendered life less precarious, but the nascent species saw those civilizations without understanding their benefit. Because of their small number, humans encountered one another rarely, and, on the other hand, because of their weakness, they retained more suspicion and had more difficulty in acquiring their subsistence, so they avoided one another instead of banding together.

The double egotism of hunger and fear kept them apart. Everyone was for themselves in a world outside of which nothing existed; the encounter of the sexes constituted a rapid accident, after which both parties went their separate ways and forgot one another.

It happened, however, that a couple was formed.

(1872), elaborating the arguments broached in *The Descent of Man* (1871). The seeds in question unfortunately fell on stony ground.

V. An Encounter

The young woman, on quitting the cliff, had moved on cautiously. Although it was not her goal, she moved in an almost straight line, only deviating in one direction or the other if the tangle of branches, creepers and brushwood blocked her path. Stopped continually by the multiplicity of obstacles, she only advanced slowly, always bent over, brushing the grass with her left hand, which she swung at knee-height, stretching out her right arm to bring it back thereafter, and then to raise it again. Her upper body obliquely angled, her neck extended and her face upright, she paddled through the verdure.

That crouching stance, which the exuberance of the vegetation rendered necessary and constant, had made her knees and heels enormous, as with all those of her race. At the same time the muscles of the hindquarters, having to lift the weight of that inclined torso incessantly, had generously developed, while those of the nape of the neck were hypertrophied by the continuous effort of holding the head up; thus, she did not carry her head on her shoulders but thrust forward, and her face went first, her eyes squinting and her nostrils wide open.

Her belly, heavy with undigested food, was bulging under its own weight; her breasts were beginning to hang down beneath her inclined chest, even though she had never given birth and was still a virgin.

At the slightest rustle in the foliage, she stood still in order to watch out; then, her narrow eyes, her wide nose and her ample ears shifted in the direction of the danger; as soon as it became precise she reached for the nearest solid branch, gripped it and hoisted herself up into the tree in order to seek refuge there. When she thought that she no longer had anything to fear, she slid down to the ground and resumed walking.

She had been alive for thirteen or fourteen years. One day, she had been born to a wandering female who had breast-fed her and carried her under her arm. Another day had come when that mother, finding herself weary, or being hunted, had thrown her into the grass—or perhaps some wild animal had devoured the mother and disdained the child. Over the centuries similar adventures had arrived, in due course, to thousands of others who had not taken long to perish, and that is why the race, so endangered and so sparsely fecund, only multiplied with extreme slowness. That daughter had succeeded in not dying, but she remained in the notion of no longer having more than a moment to endure.

Again she started; something had moved beneath the leaves; dead wood had cracked under a weight. Briskly, she launched her right hand upwards and seized a branch; with one leap she disappeared into the canopy. Only one leg still hung down, covered with coarse muddy hair. Profound wrinkles striped the sole of the foot; the big toe, separated from the others, groped in search of a branch to grip.

She howled; something had seized her foot. In vain she scrambled, around her ankle the grip of jaws or a fist tightened, and pulled her down. As she leaned over, she saw a face beneath her in which eyes were gleaming. Flatter and less hairy that those of other beasts, that mouth clenched its teeth rather than opening them toward the prey, and grimaced furiously.

The young female had never seen a being of her own race at close range, and only knew her own image vaguely, having glimpsed it in the mirror of pools, but animal intuition informed her of a lesser danger. That it was an enemy, however, she had no doubt, since everything was an enemy. Feeling that she was caught, she uttered shrill screams, trying to crush the face extended toward her with a blow of her heel—but the fist held her firmly; an increasingly furious shaking dislodged her from her tree, and she fell into the grass.

From then on, she did not cry out any more; with the hope of escape, her fear came to an end; she accepted the battle. Scarcely had she touched the ground, and before her aggressor had time to fall upon her, she rebounded and attacked with her fingernails, knees and teeth. A punch in the face stunned her without defeating her, and she returned to the attack. She sank her teeth into the shoulder of the male, who had seized her around the waist; he howled in his turn; picking up a stone, he brought it down on the top of her head, with a blow so hard that she collapsed; circles of light spun before her, and confusedly, she thought she felt a violent mass descend upon her back.

When she opened her eyes again, the victor was still holding onto her, and not devouring her. A strange dolor burned her, and a languor also retained her there, without the idea occurring to her of recommencing her self-defense. She was not even astonished to find the enemy so close and not to experience either fear or hatred. When he stood up, she did not take advantage of the moment to flee. Bewildered, she turned her head to the right and the left, as if she were searching for an explanation of what was happening within her; every time, her gaze paused on the man.

Now he was standing up, two paces away, breathing heavily. She saw him stretch his limbs, stick out his chest and extend his neck; then, abruptly, he struck his ribs with both fists. He lowered his eyes toward his victim, and their gazes met for the first time.

VI. Him

Hairier than her and even more thickset, he was, like her, short in stature but redoubtable in appearance. He was, in truth, a sort of monster, very different from all the beasts one encounters in the forest. As if he were only in the world to mark a phase in the development of his species, he bore the disgrace of beings in the course of transformation, which are seeking their equilibrium and will not remain for long in their present condition.

Rather precisely, he had the appearance of what he was in reality: a colossal fetus. A child prematurely born that suddenly acquires the musculature of Hercules and gesticulates furiously might give an idea of that silhouette, simultaneously grotesque and formidable.

As in the new-born, two organs were predominant in him: the stomach and the brain, the seats of the two functions that would be prevalent, one today and the other tomorrow: for the present, an abdomen, for it was merely a matter of eating; for the future, an encephalum, since there would be a matter of thinking. But that acquired monstrosity, the brain, did not yet serve the latter function; while awaiting the future, the disproportionate skull encumbered the rest of the beast with its size, and the human embryo was curbed beneath its futile weight.

The dumpy individual had the head of a giant; that oblong mass accentuated his bestiality instead of attenuating it. By means of the effort that he was making to stand upright, he only succeeded imperfectly in obtaining a vertical position, and as soon as he started walking, his torso swayed forward, like a lever alternately raising its burden and falling back again, dragged down by it.

That was, however, only a stance; the biped's upper body, coarsely sculpted, was solid and capable of supporting much heavier loads; the feeble curvature of the ribs made for a broad, flat chest; his vertebral column, instead of bulging in the lumbar region, was concave, like the beams of a vault; in his narrow pelvis, less elevated than that of apes but more elongated than ours, two powerful thighs were planted, terminated by enormous kneecaps like those of a gorilla and continued by tibias that seemed truncated. The legs, already so short and massive, aggravated their inelegance by the habitual flexion of the hamstrings; they curved inwards like parentheses, and the man, thus gathered on them, was further reduced in his meager height.

That curvature of the inferior limbs, that flexion of the hamstrings and the excessive development of the joints denounced a climber who was endeavoring to walk. The climatic conditions of the epoch, by obliging him to live in an environment that maintained ancestral heredities within him, only permitted him to disengage himself from them slowly.

In the inextricable virgin forest, he only rarely encountered an opportunity to walk straight ahead. He was not yet able to place his foot flat on the ground; he leaned on the external edge in the manner of quadrumanes;[8] and that foot, because of its free and prehensile big toe, bore some resemblance to a hand, while the hand, on the contrary, with its short and scarcely detached thumb, remembered having once walked.

But the most notable strangeness of that transitory type was the form of his head, so voluminous, and whose muzzle projected forward without a forehead or a chin. The depressed cranial cavity pushed the sinciput down all the way to the brows; it descended thereto in a gentle slope; there, abruptly, the frontal bone reared up like an embankment, leaving behind it a kind of ditch and deploying over the face the cushion of a continuous visor. Sheltered by that awning and separated from it by an abrupt furrow, the bridge of the nose jutted out; to

---

[8] "Quadrumane" (i.e. four-handed) was the term employed by the Comte de Buffon in his encyclopedic classification of natural species to distinguish the remainder of the primates from the "bimane" (two-handed) hominids.

either side of it, the orbits of the eyes were sunk in funnels of shadow.

The eyes, thus framed by bony spectacles, were less forward-facing than ours, and more widely separated, as if the nose, flattened out between them, had pushed them outwards; the two holes of the nasal fosses pierced the mask in which no depression was modeled and was supported by a ferocious mandible. Seen face on, that mask was vaguely trapezoid, and seen in profile, triangular; a pair of ears, amply splayed, enlarged it further; in the guise of tresses, a leonine mane enveloped it entirely; born on the forehead above the eyebrows, bushy at the temples, it reached the cheekbones with no discontinuity and became a beard on the cheeks; coarse, bushy, tangled and sticky hairs, the color of mud, hung down at the edges of the eyes and nostrils, and in front of the eyes and ears; grass was adhering to them, and drool glued them together at the corners of the mouth.

And yet...

In spite of his bestiality, his hybrid forms and his ambiguous awkwardness, in spite of his defects—or because of them—that brute affirmed himself to be human. He was not an ape but the sketch of a new being, prohibited for the moment, suffering from being without being able to be, hesitating before itself, clumsy and pitiful, condemned to search without knowing what it was searching for, hampered in its future even more than in its past, chastised less by its weakness than its latent strength, and the victim of the ensemble of the two.

Gleams of mystery were trembling in his eyes, and through that double prison window, behind the solid wall of that forehead, captive energies could be sensed quivering in the darkness. When a growl emerged from that mouth, it was like the plaint of a strength ashamed of its own impotence.

Standing in front of the female, he yawned. Through the enormous bay of his mouth, she could see his palate, as red as a wound, whose vault was very high; thirty-two huge teeth garnished his jaws, and the molars at the back resembled white rocks.

He closed his mouth again, picked up his club, and moved off.

VII. Their Patrimony

No individual, animal or plant is the first of its race; there always exists some similar form that preceded it, in a continuum; when any being brings a new element into the world, it is for other beings that it is preparing the seed, and to which it will bequeath that seed; it is itself merely the variation, ameliorated or deteriorated, of the precursors from which it has emerged.

Human beings, the dissident siblings of Apes, are not descended from the Anthropoids, but arrived in parallel with them, better endowed than them, and inherited, like them, what their common ancestors had conquered. Recent as they were upon the earth, they were an aristocracy, the descendants of something, and they possessed an entire patrimony of acquisitions. The obscure endeavor of their descendants was totalized in them; there was already a human machine, provided with its essential elements, ready to function in a human fashion, which was trying to do so while grating, entirely clogged up by mud and darkness.

After the Semnopithecus[9] and the Orangutans, after the Chimpanzees and Gorillas, life simulated its normal movement: an effect of which the slow evolution of species had been the cause intervened in the family of Primates to produce the privileged being to whom the unconscious phenomenon was leading, and was henceforth possible; with its still-rudimentary brain, already a prodigious enormity, it inaugurated the faculty of refining sensation to the point of extracting, first sentiment and then thought.

Humans' familial patrimony, to tell the truth, was still meager; it was reduced to a few notions regarding themselves

---

[9] The genus of langurs, of Hanuman monkeys, which most taxonomists consider to consist of the single species *Semnopithecus entellus*.

and the surrounding world, all of them tending simply to the preservation of the individual or the species. There were appetites, with the means to satisfy them, or suspicions, with the means of averting them. The latter only offered vague warnings regarding toxic vegetables, but denounced dangerous animals with greater precision, their fashion of striking and the manner in which to flee or combat them. That heritage of memories revealed itself in the form of instincts; certain self-preservative actions were suggested thus, without having to be invented, because others had found them previously.

For, if one examines it closely, instinct is an ancient intelligence that has lost consciousness of itself; the result being known in advance, the effort of research has become unnecessary, and the animal has gradually dispensed with it; the instrument, too expert in its work, continues to function of its own accord. In sum, the heredities of a species are the reservoir of ethnic experience, a total of superimposed educations and crystallized habits. Instinct is the memory of races, the patrimonial science and the accumulation of practical advice: the manual of the past for the usage of the future.

Of those materials, stored in the cells of their generators, new-born humans benefited. In their turn, they hoarded on behalf of future times. Fabricating instincts in their turn, they had to endow their descendants with the actions that would later be required of them; with difficulty, they enriched with their emotions and their efforts the undivided patrimony on which the community would found the unity of a race.

VIII. The Wedding-Feast

After the fortuitous embrace, the woman, exhausted by the efforts of her vain defense, had remained lying on the moss, her eyes wide open, dazed and slightly dreamy; for the first time, she took note of her solitude, which had previously appeared to be normal or necessary. She experienced a kind of anguish in consequence, somewhat comparable to that of hunger—and it was, indeed, a hunger of the soul that was beginning to awaken in her.

She got up, plaintively. Then she walked, going to the right, the left or straight ahead, aimlessly and with no plan, but also without fear and without prudence, because, suddenly, her life was no longer of any concern to her: the attack of a wild beast would have found her indifferent and almost incapable of uttering a cry. She no longer had any fears, any cares or any needs, as if she no longer lacked anything, because she had just discovered an emptiness within her and around her that was larger than usual, in which everything was lacking at the same time.

For several days she wandered around the vicinity looking for the man who had taken her. She found his trail and followed it through the wood; sometimes creeping up behind him and sometimes charting a curve around him in order to post herself in his probable passage, she watched from the height of a branch, waiting for an opportunity. In order to provoke that chance, at the risk of her life, she sometimes uttered a long guttural cry, which she heard drifting away in the domes of the forest.

Finally, he encountered her again, and she did not resist him—but when he went away she marched after him, two paces behind him. When he wanted to rest and he crouched down, with his back to the trunk of a beech tree, she crouched down beside him in the same attitude, and imitated all his gestures in order to flatter him.

When evening came and he climbed into the crown of an oak in order to sleep, she climbed into the same tree, and took care to choose a branch below his, very close to the trunk, in order that the other could not climb down without her being aware of it.

That ingenuity did not require any great effort of thought on her part; the plan, clever as it was, only represented, in sum, a prudent action that was doubly familiar: the tactic of a hunter accustomed to tracking prey, and the cunning of an educated prey in not allowing retreat to be cut off.

All night long she watched, for fear that he might leave without her. In the morning she was still asleep when she saw, at the foot of the oak, a young wild boar that was digging in the soil. She woke the man by tugging on his foot. After starting in alarm, he recognized the hand that was touching him and his fear turned to anger, but as soon as he saw the pig, he forget the woman.

He continued to forget her when the animal was slain, and even growled at her when she dared to approach him. Not for a moment did the thought cross her mind that she had been useful to him and that he was being unjust, and much less did it cross his. The experiment made of that utility, however, deposited a memory in their two minds capable of germinating and expanding. By virtue of that fact, and by the repetition of analogous incidents, the possibility of cooperation was spontaneously demonstrated to them, and their alliance was prepared without either one of them being aware of it.

He ate without seeing her. She admired him enviously, and then lowered her eyes to the opened carcass, and she drooled with desire; at intervals, a piteous gurgle emerged from her mouth to implore him; he never made any reply. She slid a sly hand toward the prey and suddenly plunged her fingers into it; then, bringing them back to her mouth she began to lick them serenely, one after another, observing the male with a timid eye.

He pretended to ignore her, but she tried again, and this time he growled. After that, she remained quiet; with her palms flat on her knees, she waited, no longer budging, except to run her tongue over her lips when the temptation became too strong.

Meanwhile, he was chewing less vigorously. She saw him break a long bone between two stones, from which he sucked the marrow delightedly, and then another, and a third; his movements were becoming increasingly ponderous. She was patient for a little longer, and then took the risk.

The man followed her gestures with a drunken gaze, and no longer made any protest. She took possession of the carcass and finally, grunting with pleasure, sank her teeth into the profound meat.

For her, who had neither the swiftness nor the strength of a male, such a windfall was rare; less skillful in hunting, she usually nourished herself on wild fruits, and on insects or rodents more often than large prey. In her turn, she prolonged the feast; with a bone in her hand, she tore away the fragments of muscle, exerting the vice of her jaws; pink juice ran over her receding chin.

Her little brown eyes, whose corneas were scarcely visible between the irises and the corners of her eyelids, gleamed with joy and swiveled in their caves. Suddenly, her mouth opened wide, exposing the gums, and a burst of laughter reminiscent of a sneeze sprang forth between her oblique teeth. Sated, she, too, affirmed her bliss and gave thanks.

The somnolent male contemplated her with a dazed indulgence, and closed his eyes again. She lay down beside him, their backs applied to the trunk of the oak, and very gently, the first couple went to sleep under the rain.

IX. Honeymoon

She no longer left him. He tolerated her, at first obliging and then as a matter of custom, finding in the association a few conveniences and an occasional pleasure; thus habit made him a companion, and that companion was a servant.

She did not suffer from that role. Her relative debility, informing her more rapidly of their common distress, had immediately attached her to that temporary protector more than he was attached to her. She recognized in him a strength superior to her own, and a bravery superior to that strength; she admired him for it.

Many a time she saw him, in unequal struggles—he had neither fangs nor claws—stand up to the most powerful quadrupeds and vanquish them by means of an audacity reinforced with cunning. In the universal battle, they were unarmed, and she was even more aware of that than he was; she remembered that, before him, she had rarely eaten enough to appease her hunger, and she knew that, thanks to him, she would be able to delay much longer falling under the teeth of one of the giant Cats of the caves that roared in the dusk, or those of a stealthy hyena, or a growling bear. Her prolonged existence depended on the consent that the little colossus accorded to her presence; every peril avoided rooted more deeply within her an animal gratitude that bore some slight resemblance to tenderness.

She took refuge in that humble sentiment in order to calm the surges of her anger when the male had beaten her.

They ate incessantly. Their only aim, after the more urgent care of not allowing themselves to be eaten, was to capture something to eat. They did not wait for hunger, but for prey; the entire animal kingdom seemed to them only to exist for the sake of their insatiable appetite. Everything that could move, everything that could bleed, and everything that passed within range of rapid action, was seized and immediately ingurgitated.

While the hunter crept on the track of large herbivores, so difficult to catch, the women dug up the burrows of rodents and searched for them at an arm's length, or pursued snakes and lizards through the layers of dead leaves; she removed eggs from nests, crunched grasshoppers, savored ant-larvae, swallowed snails and caught mosquitoes on the wing, which she licked from the palm of her hand. For want of anything better, they pulled up tender roots or bulbous plants, knocked down nuts or acorns, or collected mushrooms, figs, apples and berries. At the whim of their voracity, everything was good; the summer was rich in insects, the autumn with fruits.

All the lives that one puts into oneself add to one's own life.

While they walk, the woman follows, as closely as possible; during halts, she establishes herself within arm's length; she immediately begins scratching herself, while he does the same, for they are riddled with vermin, and they notice that more when they stop.

They never sit down; their attitude of repose resembles that of a child in its mother's womb: crouched, with their buttocks on their feels, their knees up, their forearms against their thighs, their hands flat on their knee-caps or hooked around their ankles, they compact themselves, gathering themselves together and holding themselves in a solid block, as if they were afraid that one of their limbs might go astray. Their legs are too mobile for them to be able to endure a sitting position without irritation; as soon as they hang loosely they begin dancing in space, nervously; it is necessary to hold onto them to keep them in place. It is also necessary to watch over their security and not to leave a foot too long out of sight in the thick and living grass.

That crouching pose is, therefore, the only one that procures them a moment of tranquility; it gives them the sensation of being "at home"—or, to put it better, "within themselves," all the parts of the body living as a family, and savoring the wellbeing thereof in a temporary relaxation. For everyone only finds true refuge within themselves; no other contact is as agreeable and reassuring as one's own body; the sister flesh of one's flesh is one's own, and no one else's. The individual is as yet only organized for egotism, and that egotism is equipped with five keen senses that watch over the safety of the being.

Those warning organs, therefore, do not have the same aptitudes or the same aspects as ours: coarse, brutal, insensitive to nuances, education has not yet instructed them in the delicacies of subtle sensuality; they are not instruments of joy but tools of protection; they are lookouts, and, being powerfully conditioned for that role of vigilance, they possess the plenitude of their initial power. Three of them in particular are on the alert: sight, hearing and smell.

The last-named observes the immediate surroundings: *Alert!* and the high, broad, profound, hairy nostrils wrinkle in the direction of the danger or the prey whose presence they have sniffed.

Hearing perceives approaches from further away: *Alert!* and the two vast ears, sticking out from the skull, move toward the sound, as the nostrils move toward the reek.

Sight goes even further: *Alert!* It works relentlessly, forwards, to the right, to the left, upwards and downwards; the eye sees everything at once; under the eyebrow, which contracts or retracts, between the eyelids that blink or distend, it swivels, it focuses, it pierces; it gives the impression of wanting to leap out of its hole. With an untiring zeal it summarizes and revises the observation of the other senses; at close range or far away, nothing escapes it; it is the perfect guardian, but, at the same time, it is the translator of the internal anguish for which it functions and which it denounces by its uneasy mobility.

Thus the man and the woman, always in peril, collaborate simultaneously in the double task of their preservation, and profit from one another; together, they are four eyes, four ears and four nostrils; they are reciprocal and mutual; they live in parallel; they are a pair rather than a couple.

X. The First Words

Being two, they talked.

The need to communicate stimulated the normal exercise of a function that was possible; habit took hold of it without either of them having any notion of it. The cry that emerged from the beast, by virtue of being repeated identically, gained a precise meaning and became a word; four or five of those various cries, and the couple had, unwittingly, invented language.

The woman spoke first. Being the weaker, she was more often alarmed; the hunter, always in quest of some prey, forgot her. Lost in the dense thickets, she emitted a timid and prolonged bleat from the depths of her throat:

"Daâh…âh…"

That bleak cry of appeal remained the only word in the human language for some time:

"Daâh…"

The other sometimes heard it, but scarcely made any response, impatient with the clamor, which warned the prey and caused it to flee. Then she repeated:

"Daâh…"

And little by little, Daâh became the name of the first human.

When the latter consented to reveal his presence, he barked vigorously:

"Hock!"

The imperious monosyllable simply signified: "Here!"

More usual from day to day, however, that brutal announcement of advance ended up signifying the creature to whom it was addressed, with the result that they both had names, without even knowing that they had given them to one another, and in a time when their solitude dispensed them from differentiation.

"Hock!"

The name of the female sounded rudely, having been given by the man.

"Daâh..."

The name of the man, on the contrary, had an almost caressant music, being the invention of the woman.

Educated henceforth to listen to one another, they did not take long to express phonetically the two needs that constituted the double preoccupation of their life: the concerns of eating and of self-defense suggested the two onomatopoeias of mastication and alarm. To announce hunger or offer nourishment, they said:

"Mâh!"

To signal the approach of danger, they said:

"Heûh!"

To those four primordial sounds a fifth was subsequently added; they found it convenient to indicate something that was neither a food nor a threat:

"Ta!"

The word that served them, with a gesture of the hand or the finger, to indicate the location of things had the subsidiary indication of the things themselves; everything was called "Ta," without distinction, and by turns.

As for the male, he had two war cries of his own. When he launched himself into battle, in order to be more formidable and also to give himself courage, he howled:

"Haâh!"

As he landed his blow, he growled through his closed mouth:

"Han!"

That was all. In addition, they used gestures, and their tongues remained tied, as their thoughts remained obscure.

XI. Exodus

Through the immense virgin forest they plunged ahead, drowned in the verdure. The grass rose up to their necks, the branches scraped their foreheads or striped their breasts. The man cleared the path for them, ready to attack. When he raced away in pursuit of prey, the woman launched forward in her turn, maintaining the double swing of her long teats, and ran after the hunter, not so much to help him as for fear of losing him.

"Daâh... Daâh..."

Her cry of distress was drawn out lamentably between the boles of the trees, rising toward the arches of branches, and the frisson of a sacred fear filled the vaults of the solitude.

"Daâh... Daâh..."

The imprudence of shouting like that attracted malevolent beasts, but the woman preferred anything to the horror of finding herself alone again, as before and forever, in the hostility of the living wilderness.

"Daâh!"

When she had found him she laughed her abrupt laughter, which split the entire width of her face, and she blew heavily, straight ahead, as if to spit out the rest of her anguish.

There was nowhere they could rest; no refuge was durable. Sometimes, exhausted by fatigue or malady, they tried to crawl under some thick bush and shelter there; they twisted or broke branches, forming around their two bodies a kind of nest, the opening of which they sealed with interlaced branches, but as soon as dusk fell, the wild beasts scented the couple and came prowling around; it was necessary to leave. Furthermore, a fixed dwelling would not have contented those nomads, too nervous and too anxious, by dint of insecurity, they were too curious and too mobile to stay anywhere for long.

They set out once again under the perpetual downpour. They did not know that it could ever stop, except for rare brief intervals, and did not imagine that the world might be different, since they always saw it as their eyes gazed upon it. They accepted it without judging.

Always keeping to the heights of the plateaux, they went along the left bank of the Seine, pushing westwards, like the river they were imitating, or like the quotidian Suns.

Perhaps they hoped that, by following those successive stars, they would end up reaching the land where the disappeared globes assembled, along with light and warmth—the good light that reveals dangers and the good heat that aids one to live! Perhaps they were searching, without knowing what they were searching for, moved by a need to act and be elsewhere, by an appetite for wellbeing, carried away by an animal dream of encountering some region where the days were less difficult, the nights less tormented, the predators less numerous, the reptiles less perfidious and the insects less voracious. They did not know themselves. Their dream did not take comfort in any confidence or any expectation; on the other hand, nor did it involve any disillusionment.

Hock and Daâh were never disappointed, since they never counted on anything. They walked. When a tributary of the river blocked their path and obliged them to retrace their steps or veer southwards, they resigned themselves to it without annoyance, for experience had taught them that the downpours were the same everywhere and the dangers always similar. Daâh feared them all, but did not tremble before any of them. In accordance with their threat, he confronted them one after another, with varied tactics but with a constant solidity that was no longer even bravery, so tranquil did he remain.

By force of habit, combat had become his labor; he took it on like a valiant workman who does not shirk his task. Whether the adversary was more powerful than him or weaker, he worked on it with his club, like a woodcutter raising his ax and bringing it down on the trunk of a tree; injury or death being possible eventualities at every moment, risked at every step, he was wary of them without being disturbed by their menace, and he no longer thought about them once a battle was finished, since another battle was bound to recommence.

That energy was not, however, devoid of weaknesses; the man was afraid of mystery. The fury of a bison troubled him less than the sudden quiver of moss when it shifted underfoot. Although he walked straight toward a bear in broad daylight, he no longer knew anything but how to crawl in the twilight, when motionless forms became disquieting and seemed to move: shadows, tree trunks, deep water and viscous bodies frightened him without him being able, or even making the effort, to give him courage. Ancient heredities warned him to dread invisible traps; every abrupt appearance of life made him start. Less by virtue of reasoned prudence than nervous impressionability, he hesitated before unfamiliar forms; the enemies that he had not yet confronted seemed to him to be redoubtable; his anguish paralyzed him, if only momentarily, in the face of those adversaries whose means of defense and offensive weapons were unknown to him.

Most of all, he detested those enemies that entered into the body without one feeling it, and treacherously, patiently, sheltered from blows, gnawed away at the belly of their prey. He knew them only too well by the burning bite of their teeth. Very prone to stomach aches, he attributed his torture to the presence of beasts that had taken refuge inside him, and execrated them because there was nothing he could do against them. Raging and grinding his teeth, he hammered his abdomen with blows of his fist to chase away the Rat or the Serpent, and howled at it to frighten it.

XII. Sunshine

The woman's womb was enlarged. She became enormous. Daâh did not pay any attention to the phenomenon and probably did not even notice it. A variation in the volume of an animal that he would neither have to eat or fight was not of a nature to interest him. The sole particularity of which he deigned to take notice was the slowness of his companion in movement; that aggravation of incapacity augmented his disdain for the inferior creature. When Hock, lagging behind, began to bleat sadly in order to call him back, he returned ill-humoredly, almost angrily.

She began to appear to him to be a hindrance; many a time he nearly abandoned her and kept on walking. But always, when he found himself far enough away from her no longer to be able to hear her, he experienced a kind of nervous anxiety that was neither pity, nor remorse, nor tenderness, nor even the egotistical notion of a personal prejudice, but which probably participated in all those sentiments at once. It was necessary for him, reluctantly, to retrace his steps until he had found her again. Then, furious with her again as soon as he no longer had to worry about losing her, he insulted her with growls and grimaces. She moaned to explain her helplessness.

Often, too, she lowered her head toward her belly with an abrupt gesture, and looked at herself with a surprise mingled with anguish. The teasing beast that she was carrying there, heavier and livelier that all those whose invasion had tortured her previously, was moving too often and for too long. To tame it, she hammered her pelvis with furious punches, in a same manner as Daâh. The latter watched her do it, tranquil and indifferent, in the manner of a connoisseur who has experienced an evil, and cannot be moved on seeing it afflict another.

That summer, the north-eastern wind blew more frequently than usual; the downpour stopped from time to time, and the couple gazed with amazement at the furtive re-splendent holes of azure that appeared in the sky.

Hock took pleasure in perceiving them; every time they went across a clearing, she raised her face to the astonishing sky from which the rain was no longer pouring and extended her arms toward it in order to receive the rays of the sun on her breast. Under the warmth of that caress she laughed as she contemplated her illuminated flesh; she was happy about it, almost proud, and she showed herself off.

"Daâh..."

The man enjoyed that rare pleasure almost as much as the woman; in order to savor it more, they came to the edge of the cliff. Crouching in the grass, with their backs turned to the edge of their forest, they had before them the profound extent in which light played upon the river and the islets; the atmos-phere, laden with water vapor, vibrated all the way to the dis-tant hills; sheets of diaphanous shadow, alternating with sil-very gleams, galloped over the domes of the blue-tinted trees, and the rainbow appeared to them.

That formidable reptile that had suddenly sprung forth over the plain frightened them by virtue of its size; with one bound they recoiled under the trees, uttering cries of terror, but they fell silent immediately, for fear of attracted the monster's attention. Hidden under the foliage, they observed it, open-mouthed and trembling. The strangeness of its colors, so bright in a uniformly dull world, only rendered it more fright-ful. They had never contemplated such an enormous being; beneath the curve of its belly it enclosed mountains, forests, half of the river and clouds; compared with it, the rhinoceroses and hippopotamuses wandering on the bank resembled larvae. Its maw hovered over them; a massacre was about to begin...

The colossal serpent did not devour anyone; the round masses of the pachyderms continued to frolic in peace in the mud and the reeds. That lack of fear surprised Hock and Daâh greatly; gradually they were reassured. Their childish souls were mobile, contagious to everything, accessible to the infi-nite variety of moments; their fear mutated into gaiety when the hippopotamuses licked by the giant became as rosy as flowers, as green as trees, yellow, violet and blue...

Abruptly, their joy evaporated; the rainbow had disappeared. Hock called it back, her arms extended toward the gulf, appealing for it to take its place again.

"Ta...! Ta...!"

But they forgot it immediately, for at that moment, an immense, resplendent Sun whose like they had never seen, surrounded by crepitating points—an irritated sun, menacing and triumphant, was installed in the blue heights.

"Ta! Ta!"

The dazzled Hock pointed at it, blinking her eyes, as if the marvel that had just been revealed were as yet only visible to herself alone. Daâh had straightened up, moved by enthusiasm; with his war cry and his gestures of battle, with great thrusts of his club, he, too, labored to drive away the clouds.

"Haâh! Han!"

He encouraged the star, and shared its triumph.

When he had collaborated fully with that work of splendor, he stopped, streaming with sweat, and blew forwards. Then he resumed his place next to Hock, on the grass where droplets were shining.

In front of him, the enchantment of the joyful islets spread out all the way to the horizon; the sky danced, the earth sang, and the first human couple, side by side, motionless, squinted their little eyes, filled with vast light.

XIII. The Firstborn

Daâh, who could not remain in one place for long, set about roaming around and exploring the vicinity; he discovered a place that delighted him. Toward the tip of one of the peninsulas that formed the curls of the river, there was a shelter under a rock at the top of a steep slope; the rain, by cutting ravines in the humus, had laid the calcareous sediment bare; all the sun's rays plunged into that redoubt, orientated almost directly southwards; its wall defended it to the north against the cold winds, while the overhanging rock shielded it from downpours. The place was, moreover, relatively secure; the steepness of the cliff rendered it inaccessible from below, and to arrive there from above it was necessary to hang onto roots and the asperities of the cliff.

The shelter had once been occupied by a bear, whose prints the hunter recognized; they were, in any case, quite old, and since the departure of that inhabitant, brambles had obstructed the only passage. Proud of his discovery, he clamored in triumph to summon the woman, but she did not come, and in the distance he heard a lamentable voice imploring help.

"Heûh..."

He scaled the rock, suddenly electrified by the idea of battle, and ran; he thought he would find the bear.

Hock was alone and rolling on the ground. The spectacle annoyed him; the fury of the fighter, which he was bringing against a presumed enemy, turned against the woman. His muscles, full of blows, expended them on her.

"Haâh! Han!"

"Daâh... Heûh, Daâh..."

She begged, shielding herself from the fist that was hammering her head, her belly and her breast. Finally, he stood up; authoritarian, he pointed the way to the shelter; he gave her the order to march:

"Ta!"

She followed him, crawling. He deigned to help her to descend through the brambles. When they arrived under the rock she collapsed on the clay, and brought a son into the world.

Daâh contemplated that prodigy with bewilderment; his arms dangled in front of his leaning body, and his eyes squinted in his motionless face; alternately, he leaned toward the little being and recoiled to inspect the ensemble. The movement and cries of the living thing almost made him afraid. Torn between mistrust of the unknown and his curiosity, he turned round before the woman, two paces away from her, without taking his eyes off the disquieting animal she was holding in her lap.

Almost everything that moves is an enemy; his instinct to kill invited him to murder, but a bizarre doubt, an apprehension akin to that inspired by gelatinous substances, a carnal repugnance, prevented him from touching the unexpected monster.

Why was the woman holding it between her knees and her arms? Hock's attitude and his own disgust amazed him almost as much as the appearance of the dwarf. In order to concentrate all his effort in the labor of reflection, he stopped; beneath the double tuft of his eyebrows, his facial muscles moved, stirred by the interior work, and his perplexity caused him to stare with fixed pupils.

Suddenly, he remembered, and understood!

The invisible rodent that sometimes made the female howl by biting her in the entrails was that! The sly beast that had been slowing their progress for so many days because it was hiding inside Hock, the bloodsucking beast against which he had raged without knowing what it was, could now be seen! It had finally emerged—and it was him, Daâh, who had forced it out by beating it through the mother's skin.

"Heûh!"

Facing the woman, he showed her, with an arm extended to the left, the edge of the cliff; then, approaching with his arms open he mimed the gesture of throwing a mass into the gulf:

Throw it away!

Instead of obeying, the woman contemplated her little torturer as if she were admiring it. With the hollows of her palms and the flat of her tongue she cleaned it; she pressed it to her teat, and rubbed her cheek on the top of its skull, and hugged it so avidly that she almost seemed to want to put it back inside her.

That unconsciousness in the face of danger and that obstinacy in disobedience made the master indignant; they offended him twice over, in his scorned authority and in his knowledge of things, for he had an already-human pretention of thinking himself infallible; his ideas might only last a moment, but for as long as he had them, nothing could make him let go of them; he deemed them to be certainties. Not very numerous, and always suspicious, he fabricated them experimentally from day to day, in accordance with the hazards of life, and those difficult conquests were as precious to him as defensive weapons.

The belief in interior beasts counted among the most definite dogmas; since one of those enemies had finally showed itself, all the rancor of his flesh rose up against it. By refusing to destroy it, Hock was revealing herself to be dangerous; the repulsions he experienced at the mere sight of the new animal were redirected against the woman who was protecting it and caressing it. She horrified him.

His hands still extended, the fingers splayed as if for a strangulation, he darted a vengeful gaze at the group, but he did not draw any closer. Like a dog barking at a viper, which prudently keeps its distance, he howled from three paces away:

"Heûh!"

Throw it away!

His cry was brief, and he rapidly closed his mouth and clenched his teeth, for fear that the monster might penetrate into him that way.

He agitated in vain; the mother paid no attention to his gestures or his vociferations. She had forgotten him.

When the first-born took her breast and suckled, she no longer saw anything else in the world.

She did not even notice that Daâh, furious, was climbing the rock and abandoning her.

XIV. Mother and Father

In spite of the conviction that Daâh professed of being superior in all things to his companion, because he was superior to her in strength and in courage, one may suppose that certain faculties developed in her with more celerity and vigor than in him. Is it not probable, in particular, that she was the first in whom emotion awoke? Even if one assumes the initial parity of their two nervous organizations, and if one argues that, at first, one was no more impressionable than the other, one must recognize that the woman would receive, from the very start, a culture that was diminished in the man, or even absent; more than the man, she was educated to tremble, and sooner than the man, she learned to love. Two stimulants were working powerfully for the progress of her sensibility: fear, on which she fed more because she was the weaker, and maternity.

Without any doubt, maternal love constituted the first softening of the beast to endearment. Maternity was the educator of the woman, and the woman, thus educated by instinct, became in her turn the educator of humankind. The mother brought the invention of love to the surface of the globe. Quite naturally, she was able to understand what bonds attached her to the creature issued from her loins; the first manifestations of her love must have resembled an organic function rather than a psychic emotion. What she loved in her child was perhaps not him but an extension of her own flesh; she defended it as one defends one's arm.

Animal egotism is perpetuated in maternal attachment; it is, in a sense, an extension of gestation, which childbirth has modified without interrupting it entirely; the offspring, already expelled from the original body, still cleaves to it by suction, like the offspring of a marsupial; common circulation has ended, but the same blood continues to nourish the two beings, and for as long as that function remains necessary, the mother remains devoted to the exercise of her role, which is not yet for her either a duty or an act of love, but a physiological state.

As for the male, he was unaware and must have remained unaware for a long time that any parental relationship existed between him and the new-born. His animal individualism did not permit him to see, in that creature, anything but a spontaneous production. How could he suppose that a relationship of cause and effect linked his fugitive amusement to the appearance of a being? What connection could he imagine between his own play and the other's work? He had no more idea than a cock has, while handling hens roughly, that it is cooperating in the birth of chicks. The mystery of generation, which all the research of science has not yet succeeded in penetrating, did not even intrigue him. He simply observed a fact, independent of him, and turned away from it with indifference.

Daâh had gone. Hock found herself alone again.

She was not much distressed by that. She scarcely missed the absentee; she only thought about him intermittently. Her entire being was given over to the care of her little one; she had no thought but to watch over him, clean him, turn him over, change his location, feed him at the breast. For the first time in her life, she lingered over the lengthy contemplation of something, and took pleasure in it. A vibrant curiosity immobilized her before that fragile body, and when the gluttonous mouth attached itself to her breast, the eyes of the human female were impregnated with a softness that the world had not yet seen.

XV. The First Tear

She became anguished at the slightest sound. The shelter beneath the rock, however, procured her more security than she had known in the forest. In order to render the excavation more hospitable, she began scraping the wall with a stone; the debris constituted, in front, a sort of terrace that permitted her to move at her ease. To complete her work, she piled up heaps of ferns and balls of moss, with which she constituted a nest in the manner of birds. It was there that she laid her first-born; she crouched beside him, in her customary pose, her back to the cliff, and she watched, facing the plain, waiting for bright intervals.

Of the vast landscape she could not see anything, anxious and blissful by turns, and she listened for passing noises and received the rays that warmed her. Fortunately, the wind from the north-east persisted, and with it an exceptional seasonal splendor. Now, Hock liked the suns for her little one more than for herself. As soon as one of them began to shine, she held out her wriggling creature at arm's length, as if making and offering toward a god in the hope of a blessing. Vaguely, in the depths of her maternal solicitude, mute supplications rose up, directed at the beneficent star, and without knowing that she was beginning to pray, she invoked it in order that it might stay longer.

She only absented herself in order to go in search of her subsistence; she took advantage, in that escape, of moments when the nursling was asleep, for fear that he might attract wild beasts with his cries. Before leaving, she covered him carefully with ferns to hide him, and crushed aromatic plants on the ground to mask his odor. She remained in the woods for as short a time as possible: the time to drink from the stream and hastily gather beech-nuts, acorns and snails; she returned to her guard-post rapidly.

On the third day she had a terrible scare. She was playing with the child, lying in her lap, when she suddenly applied the palm of her hand to the nursling's mouth; she thought she had heard the sound of rustling foliage and stretching branches overhead. Her back was against the wall; in her chest cavity she distinctly felt the repercussion of a heavy impact resonate through the layer of the rock.

She picked up a shard of flint and stood up. The steps came closer and heavier, breaking branches. A hoarse voice called: "Hock!"

Reassured, but irritated by her recent fright, she did not reply. She did not trust the male; rancor was stagnating within her because of the abandonment, and above all, the fists extended the other evening toward her new-born.

The brambles on the edge of the overhanging rock stirred, and Daâh's coarse hand appeared, and then his face.

Hock looked up at him, fixedly, at a distance, not knowing whether the man was returning as a friend or an enemy. That face, seen from below in the midst of the brambles seemed devoid of anger, but curious and almost anxious; his sharp eyes paused on the infant, and nothing moved thereafter.

Finally, the head overlapping the ledge withdrew into the brambles and seemed to go back into the rock, like that of a tortoise into its shell; it disappeared, and footsteps drew away.

The following day, it came back again, and a lump of meat fell at Hock's feet.

Twice, the male believed that he had departed and continued his route, but each time, the same malaise as before had haunted him. Each time, on no longer hearing the accustomed footsteps behind him and the plaints of his companion, on no longer sensing close to his back the presence that assured him against surprise attacks by felines, a more clearly defined impression of solitude had urged him to return to the shelter—to the point that he had resigned himself to it and retraced his steps without having decided to do so.

He prowled around the vicinity. He hunted.

On the fifth day, when he leaned over the rock, he perceived the infant hidden under the ferns, but Hock was not there.

Then a desire took hold of him to examine the strange beast; it seemed less repugnant to him and more intriguing. A curiosity that no animal had ever inspired in him attracted him toward the monster; he wanted to touch it, sniff it and understand it. Slyly, as if creeping up on a prey, he slid between the brambles and descended onto the platform.

He lifted up the ferns; the awakened child opened his eyes and mouth, and Daâh burst out laughing: the wailing larva was like Hock! It had the same little mobile eyes, the scarcely hairy face and the gestures that beat the air...

He dared to pick it up in both hands; it was warm and soft; it moved between his fingers. He dropped the beast, which fell onto the bed of ferns, crying. The thing definitely did not frighten him anymore, but did not please him much, and still intrigued him.

Perplexed, he scaled the rock and went back into the wood.

A few moments later, the mother came back with her provision of old acorns and rotten walnuts. She had scarcely broken cover, and the foliage disturbed by her passage was still rustling behind her when she thought she observed a displacement of the branches with which she had obstructed her path a little while before. She snuffed; the solitude was suspect; an odor of living presence troubled the air...

In the shelter of the rock, something moved, and the cry of a child immediately erupted; with the piercing voice a dull flutter was mingled, like the sound of a great Bid flapping its wings in taking off.

Hock understood immediately; she launched herself forward and arrived at the edge of the cliff just in time to see the pink torso once again, almost within arm's reach, in the claws of an eagle that was flying away.

She saw the droplets of blood on the luminous flesh, the little legs hanging down into the void, the head tilted back, and the red mouth wide open, from which a kind of silent howl was emerging.

Then she saw, drawing away into the distance, the flapping of large brown wings, beneath which the prey was no more than a bright patch.

Quickly, quickly, quickly the double curved line of the wings became a somber dot moving down below, like dark star in the middle of a gray sky, and which plunged into the mist—and the mother no longer saw anything.

She remained standing there, motionless, her arms beside her body, her mouth agape. Slowly, two tears ran down her face and fell onto her nipples, and she looked at the incomprehensible droplets in amazement, thinking about the droplets of milk that had moistened the same place the day before and that same morning.

For the first time in the world, a creature wept.

XVI. Familial Mourning

The mother remembered. For three days, she remembered. At intervals, a stabbing regret shuddered in her oblique skull. When she looked at the gulf of the sky, into which the eagle had disappeared, a surge of anger creased the two tufts of russet hair above her eyes. But the interminable procession of clouds, gray after gray, soon made her eyelids blink, and with fatigue and time, her brief thought was lost in the clouds. Then, no longer knowing what she was searching for, but searching nevertheless for something, her gaze descended toward the river and the banks, wandering over the hippopotamuses that were wallowing in the reflections, and rose up again to the clouds that are the Elephants of the sky, and move in files like those of the earth...

Eventually, she turned her head, no longer remembering either what it was she had been contemplating, or what it was for which she had been searching.

But she retained in the depths of her being a racial resentment against the winged animals; when an Eagle passed in front of the cliff, she showed it her fist and howled at it. If, in the course of her incursions, she encountered any kind of nest hidden in a fissure in the rock or wedged in the angle of two branches, she broke the eggs angrily and crushed them under her heel, instead of eating them as before.

The man had come back and found her alone, near the nest of ferns.

He observed that solitude without it inducing him to inquire after the disappeared child. The little monster had been there, and was there no longer; Daâh registered the fact, and then, as the fact seemed agreeable to him, he burst out laughing, which was in him an involuntary act. In order better to express his contentment by means of a determined gesture, he danced in front of the woman.

He was astonished by the slowness with which she responded with similar laughter and agitations. He crouched down beside her, and for a long moment he fixed an immobile gaze upon her. He was visibly making an effort to divine things unknown; his sensed a strange new, ungraspable idea on the part of his companion, and his hunter's nostrils twitched before the mystery.

Then, suddenly, he renounced it; like a stone dropped into black water, his thoughts had disappeared. He no longer remembered Hock, who no longer remembered the child. They searched the clouds for the return of the sun.

But the Suns only passed by rarely now; those that were still perceptible were pale and cool. The wind from the mountains ceased to blow against the nimbus clouds, which began to pile up in flocks. Autumn was approaching. The river and its islets became dull; again the torrents of rain descended upon the bleak landscape.

In the meantime, a dispossessed Lioness decided to adopt for herself the shelter under the rock where the couple had made a long stay. Hock and Daâh found her installed there one evening, with her cub, and were obliged to seek another refuge. They went back into the forest and resumed their errant existence.

XVII. The Second Tear

One day, after a march, she had become drowsy; on waking up she found that he was no longer nearby. For a long time she waited, without daring to leave the spot, and when he did not come back, she lamented as dusk fell.

Finally, he reappeared, curbed beneath the burden of a russet mass. By dint of patience he had succeeded in surprising a Deer that was suckling a fawn, and killed it. Ordinarily, he butchered kills of that size on the spot, but this time, proud of his capture, Daâh had wanted to show off the entire animal.

He threw it down on the grass; it fell with a dull sound; the limp feet oscillated momentarily, then became still. But Hock did not admire it; exhausted by excessive anxiety, she was sulking, and turned her back. The hunter grabbed her by the shoulders and turned her around.

He laughed. With his arm extended, he indicated something moving behind him, which gradually emerged from the undergrowth into the open: a slender head with bright fur, a moist shiny nose and candid eyes. The Fawn had followed its mother, and it suddenly launched itself forward.

With one bound, it was between the hooves. The Deer was lying on her side; beneath her pale belly, her udders were swollen, push out by the weight of the haunch; her neck was stretched out on the moss and her tongue was hanging out, sticky with pink foam.

The Fawn was already paying no heed to the intimidating human couple. With its forehead, where two bumps announced the location of horns, it bumped the withers of the corpse with weak blows. Then it bent its knees, searching for the teats; and because they were cold, because nothing was animated beneath its caress, because the sleeper persisted in not moving, it began calling out to her in a discontented voice, which initially resembled a reproach but became, by degrees, very soft and very plaintive. Extending its neck and raising its head, it appealed to the empty air, to someone in the distance who did not respond—and it really was the discouraged supplication of an impotence aware of itself, for, in the end, no voice emerged any longer from the open mouth.

Hock watched that with a fixed, strangely attentive gaze. When she saw that poor, futile mouth agape, striving to exhale its cry, without being able to do so, she remembered a similar cry, also mute, that her child had uttered toward her as he was carried away by the eagle. She saw her new-born, similar to this one, in the raptor's clutch, all alone and frightened in the midst of flapping wings, bleating silently into the hole of the empty sky, like this one...

Vaguely hallucinated, she took a step forward, two steps, doubtless toward her own child; she put out her hand and caressed the spine with its jutting vertebrae; she patted the ribs, gently and maternally, and instinctively turned her head toward that of the other mother, as if to interrogate her or watch over her.

Without interrupting her mechanical caress, she contemplated by turns the corpse and the orphan, with the result that gradually, haunted as she was by having once again dreamed about her baby, she began to imagine, in that immobile being and those extinct eyes, a vision similar to her own, with an identical pain. She felt that the dead Deer could see her child's chagrin. She bent down toward the ground, picked up an armful of leaves, and threw them over the Deer's eyes.

Of what had happened then, no one knew. The man paid no attention to it, and the woman was barely conscious of it. But that simple gesture was the most august and memorable event that the planet Earth had produced since the advent of life; with it and by virtue of it, an unprecedented phenomenon was revealed, of which there had been no anticipation in the universal battle. For it was at that precise moment that in a parcel of nature, in an imperceptible fragment of innumerable substance, in some cell hidden beneath the cranium of a female, something new was realized: *one creature had felt the sadness of another.*

A kinship was inaugurated between beings; a path was connected from misery to commiseration; a link was forged between the one that was suffering and the one that was gazing; an equation was posited, between understanding and compassion.

Her gesture accomplished, Hock stood up tranquilly, as if nothing had happened—but a mysterious light was still trembling in the depths of her pupils, and two tears were running down her face.

The dawn of the human soul had just been prophesied.

XVIII. Fear

The human soul was born in fear. Fear was the cradle of human thought. The first whimpers of mind disengaging itself from matter were gasps of alarm. It was in fright and by fright that the first labor was produced, thanks to which the sensitive beast rose up dolorously to the glory of giving birth to an idea, and transmuted the commotion of its nerves into a mental conception.

In the menagerie of a plateau to which the inundation of the valleys had driven herbivores and carnivores pell-mell, death lay in wait for everything that moved. From every shelter, death was about to pounce; it leapt from the rock, it surged forth from the grass, and it fell from the trees; it was the predator lurking in the thicket, the snake coiled up under the leaves; a step provoked it, a gesture summoned it; one cry and it arrived; all the noises of the area, all the quivers of the surroundings, were announcements of death; nothing moved that was not a threat. In that ubiquity of peril, every minute, for every creature, was a conquest; to walk or to sleep was a victory; to succeed in enduring for more than one day was a long triumph; life was survival.

Daâh and Hock were alive. Fear had become their habit, their mode of existence, their condition, almost their reason for being, since it was solely by virtue of a vigilant anxiety that they escaped the entourage of dangers. Certainly, the man was brave, but his purely animal bravery, in which neither reason nor will participated, could do nothing to defend him against the repeated shocks of his incessantly agitated nerves. When an adversary loomed up in front of him, he was almost relieved at no longer having to dread its coming, and he threw himself boldly into combat: the battle was his deliverance, the moment of expansion when he ceased to be apprehensive of the unknown.

The woman did not benefit from that temporary release; it was not given to her, as it was to him, to acquire the renewals of energy inherent in battle, nor the fleeting moments of confidence procured by the pride of victory. She only knew the fear, and was saturated by it.

At the fall of dusk, when she took refuge in the branches of a tree in order to sleep, the tension of her overworked nerves was totalized in her sleep, and the memories of the day became demented within her, to haunt her with nightmares. Suddenly revealed by the crash of thunder or the roaring of predators, she heard below her the breath of great felines scenting their prey and demanding it by scratching the bark of the tree with their claws; by the glare of lightning flashes, she perceived creeping spines down below, and the phosphorescence of eyes, and clung hard to the branches.

So many reiterated efforts made her tremulous, and because her brain was the most apt of all to perceive the terrors of life with acuity, she was overloaded by anguish to a greater extent than any other creature; her nascent thought was impregnated by it; her nervous cells became reservoirs of accumulated fear; in the utmost depths of her being she stored away such a provision of fear that all her descendants would retain the memory imprinted in their flesh, and a thousand centuries later, the children of her race would not be able to go into the forest or venture forth in darkness without experiencing in their marrow the prolonged frisson of hereditary terror.

The male, although he was more solid, did not escape the contagion of that anguish. Without rest, his eyes rapidly began to swivel, his head pivoting, his nostrils flaring to sniff the odor of death—with the result that, by virtue of suspicion and alarm, he acquired the habit of moving without cause; his mobility became a muscular reflex, and he moved as one breathes, for the sake of movement.

At the same time, however, those endless vibrations had themselves developed the organs of sensitive life; by virtue of perpetual exercise, the nervous system gained in power, enriching itself even on its fatigue, and increasingly, from day to day, the emotion of their brains tended to develop thought.

XIX. The Soul of Things

They think fearfully. Everything takes on an aggressive character in their eyes; since they suffer from everything, since everything is harmful to them, naively, they credit everything with a desire to harm them. Incapable of informing themselves about the world other than by comparison with themselves, they judge everything as similar to themselves; so, as their own actions are the product of intention, all the actions surrounding them seem intentional. Nothing exists except enemies waiting to destroy them; the dangling vines endeavor to block their passage in order to deliver them to the predators; a thorn is a claw; when Daâh, in order to clear a path, massacres interlaced branches, he has a clear consciousness of battling against them, and insults the resistance of those negligible adversaries disdainfully.

"Han!"

The mud into which his feet sinks is a trap set by the hungry earth; a stone hides a snake in order that Daâh will be bitten, and when it is displaced underfoot it is in order to make Daâh fall. He hits the trunk of a tree into which he has bumped in passing with his club. To chastise the stone that wounds his toe, he stamps on it with his heel, and, when his heel is weary of that battle, he labors it with blows of his fist until his fist hurts; then he seizes the stone and bites it with all the force of his teeth. Woe to the root that hooks itself onto his foot in order to aid a prey that he is stalking! He turns on it and hacks at it furiously with the cutting edge of a flint, at the expense of bloodying his palms.

"Haâh!"

His anger turns to frenzy when his enemy persists in torturing him without him being able to reach it; he watches from the corner of his eye for the beast hidden beneath his skin, which is racking his muscles or clutching his entrails; when hunger gnaws at him and he has nothing to throw at it, he tries to stun the reptile that is tearing him apart.

Everything that makes one suffer is alive! Everything that moves is animate; everything is conscious, like Daâh, who is so slightly conscious himself, but who can nevertheless perceive his will to act.

That same instinct of assimilation, which leads him to identify himself with all the animals in turn, whose gestures he parodies, similarly invites him to identify with his own motives those of the world that surrounds him. Everything resembles him. The motility that activates him, he attributes to everything; his limited intelligence cannot imagine anything that is not a reproduction of what he finds in himself.

Animal, vegetable or mineral, everything coexists, and he knows nothing more; he is ignorant of the essence of creatures and things, and only knows about them what appears to his senses: their form, their color, the sounds they make, the odor they emit, the taste that they have. He does not hesitate to observe between himself and beasts a similitude of needs and means, nor does the idea ever occur to him to seek differences between vital phenomena and those of inert matter, which nothing reveals to him. How can he imagine that entities exist around him which are not beings, that some lack life while others possess it?

He knows no more of life that its constituents; he only knows movement, and everything moves, the Herb and the Branch, the Lizard and the Stream that flows between the mosses, the Leaf and the Bird that flies. If it were necessary for him to classify beings and to distinguish them in accordance with whether they are more or less alive, the measure of their existence would only be given to him by their ability to do him harm, and the Rain, the Wind and the Stone would have more life than a Hare or a Marmot. Everything is in conflict! Like Humans, the Trees fight, with blows of their branches; Thunder is the quarreling of Clouds, Lightning kills Rocks; Darkness is even worse; it aids the Felines by favoring their ambushes.

Daâh, however, has friends—a few of them. There are the Suns and the Moons, peaceful animals that come and go one by one. The Suns are beasts, too, evidently: round, monotonous beasts that always follow the same path, never hurrying, without ever attacking anyone; by day one only ever sees one, perpetually solitary; but sometimes, by night, between two downpours, one perceives them through a gap in the branches and the clouds, gathered in bands like Ants. Daâh has glimpsed them; he has seen them roaming, always faint and very slow, in the depths of the sky, so far away that one can scarcely make them out, like the white dots that shine in Hock's eyes...

As for supposing the existence of one unique Sun that returns every day, Daâh does not think of that for an instant; the Suns succeed one another like the downpours; every morning brings its own, more or less large, more or less pale, which marches until dusk; by night, they gather together; the Stars are Suns that have completed a stage of their journey and are resting in the blackness of the sky, like Daâh in the blackness of the tree.

For Daâh feels a need to explain the world; it is an appetite that he has inherited from his ancestors. He is extremely curious: a simian curiosity that is on the way to improvement, interested in everything it encounters; while he gazes and walks, his imagination agitates; the task is incumbent upon it of discovering the causes behind appearances; its searches are cursory and quickly concluded. If it were necessary to reflect, Daâh would renounce the task, but he is still at an age when one only understands on condition that one does not examine. He judges the universe by the means at his disposal; being simple, he simplifies it; being an expert assimilator, he sees nothing around him but assimilations.

But as nature is even simpler than he is, with rules that are even more simple, simultaneously regulating stars and microbes, it happens that the primate chances to encounter a few of the supreme verities; thus, quite tranquilly, with very little effort, he jumps to false conclusions, uncomplicated by any objection, but which his reason and his mystical pride will eventually repudiate: the unity of matter, the plurality of suns, universal life...

XX. The First Poet

It is necessary to recognize that Daâh does not always encounter definitive verities, but that, on the contrary, he usually settles for his preference on stupid hypotheses. Undoubtedly, what seduces him toward the truth, and what sometimes permits him to reach it, is the infantile character that it commonly presents. It often has the appearance of an implausible story, and gradually, one will discover that which it contains of the absurd; it is in that way that it allows itself to be approached by Daâh—for the conception of the Absurd is normally the first manifestation of intelligence, its initial conquest, and also its original taste.

The Absurd is full of charm; it is the infancy of the idea, and, because of that, it is dear to infants of all ages; it astonishes them and amuses them; it distracts and illuminates; it is the marvel of the world; it is the joy of naïve souls and their recompense, being the product of the least effort. It presents itself, and one likes it; disengaged from the accessories that encumber its visibility; it is plain, neat, clear and entire; it shines and it imposes; it is the verity that offers itself at a stroke, as a whole, in the sudden splendor of a dazzlement, in contrast to the slow verity that emerges from the depths and gradually emerges from a twilight. It displeases good sense, which has nothing to do in this instance, but it delights the imagination, which permits it to be mistaken for reason.

Right away, Daâh has understood that the Stars are distant Suns; he also knows that all those Suns have been born on earth, like him and the other beasts. In any case, he has seen nests of young suns; he has even failed to capture one that had just been born.

It was a mild and calm evening. At the fall of dusk, the two nomads, encountering one of the countless marshes that stagnate in the hollows of the plateau, had initially halted on its edge; they had climbed a tree, and the tranquil night had

71

thickened round them, blue-tinted, devoid of the voices of wild beasts; only frogs were croaking; the reeking breath of the marsh was floating in gray bands. They were about to go to sleep in that mephitic air when they suddenly saw strange soft luminous creatures rising over the pools, which had neither feet nor wings, but which nevertheless perched on the reeds, and then flew off, rising up a little, descending again, wandering this way and that, unhurriedly, stopping and swaying. Suddenly, they were no longer visible, and equally suddenly, they reappeared elsewhere; wherever they glided, a pale dawn colored the leaves, like the morning light filtering through the branches—and it was by that light that Daâh recognized the infants of Suns...

Imperiously, the decision sprang up within him to have a little Sun, to hold it, to look at it, to taste it, to warm himself, perhaps also to do nothing with it. He got down from the tree and crept toward the bulrushes; his feet sank into the mud; even so, he advanced toward the pretty prey. He was about to reach it; he stretched out his hands; the meteor immediately flew away; he tried to follow it, and sank up to his knees; irritated, he struggled, and the little Sun, furious in its turn, or frightened, danced violently in front of him, fled with a bound, and came back to assail him.

Daâh, thigh-deep in the mud, sensed that he was being swallowed alive by the earth, while the young Bird-Sun, in order to mock him, perhaps to eat him, rushed at his head.

"Heûh!"

When the hunter finally succeeded in freeing himself and running away, the flame ran after him; he stopped, and it stopped, too, and hopped teasingly, bobbing up and down, around its victim. He defended himself with his fists, and it circled around him. Suddenly, it disappeared.

Daâh was safe, but he had been scared. Never again did he risk chasing infant Suns over pools, and when he saw others, he hurled insults at them from a distance.

Thus, an idealist in his fashion, a dreamer educated by conflict and exasperated by fear, the Human became a poet before being able to reason, since he subjectivized the world. With the first effort of his idea, he invented life and poured it everywhere; before giving himself the soul that was his exclusive prerogative, he gave it to the universe, and already granted himself the role of administering the chastisement merited by the souls that only existed in him.

XXI. The-One-Who-Stands-Upright

In those times, when conflict constituted the unique function of creatures, brutal force was, logically, the sovereign of
the world; it alone was regal; no mental force seemed capable
of challenging its despotic power. In any case, intelligence
was scarcely manifest other than in the ruses of attack and
defense. Daâh knew all those of the other animals and had his
own, more numerous and more ingenious. He took no pride in
that; on the contrary, he experienced a kind of scorn, almost a
humiliation, in seeing himself obliged to have recourse, too
often, to cunning means in order to substitute for the inade-
quacy of his strength.

He would have preferred to owe his triumphs, like the
Cave-Bear, to the power of his muscles. When he had succeeded in felling some colossus of the forest, he planted himself on the vanquished individual, and almost immediately
struck his chest with blows of his fist to sound his victory;
then he flattered himself by attributing the success to his physical merits, and would have liked to attenuate or dissimulate,
especially in Hock's eyes, the importance of the assistance
that his mental planning had procured for him.

His intelligence, still too confused to have any notion of
itself, did not, therefore, reveal itself to him as a superiority,
but as an accessory of his inferiority, and it was not by that
means that he claimed to distinguish himself from his enemies. He did not know that he had an aptitude for thinking that
was greater than other animals, and derived no pride from the
fact.

Nevertheless, without really knowing why, he sensed
that he was different from the others, and he wanted to be,
with a vague scorn for all of them and a heavy esteem for himself. That sentiment was within him, profound and intuitive, as
necessary as a natural requirement. He experienced it and
maintained it, in spite of his weakness, as a protest against the

frequent proofs that he had of that weakness. He did not consent to be humble; the idea of his smallness and his nudity, his clawless feet and his fangless mouth, revolted him, not as an injustice but as a insult; in spite of all the demonstrations of life, it would not have taken much for him to believe that he was the strongest and the most beautiful, the universal victor, the master.

In order to justify that naïve presumption, he could discover nothing better than a physical advantage that was exclusive to him, and more ostensible than intelligence: among all the inhabitants of the forest, he was The-One-Who-Stands-Upright—and the only one! That faculty, no one disputed with him, the Orangutan no more than the others; even the Bear, in his awkward attempts to stand up on two feet momentarily, was merely suggestive of his impotence, and his supremacy, incontestable in other respects, had to cede on that point. Daâh, who admired that king of the world, rejoiced in being superior to him in something, and nothing else seemed to him to equal that advantage.

In fact, his vertical stance exercised a prestige on the plateau. There was no beast that did not seem troubled and intimidated by it, and anxious; all of them hesitated before the human being, with an evident effort to comprehend whether the spectacle of his gait might conceal some unknown danger, and several of them, although they were better armed, turned away from him prudently without attacking him.

"Haâh! Heûh!"

He clamored his challenge behind them, by striking his torso, in order to mock them, and laughed noisily at their rumps. Then he turned round to face Hock, and still beating his sonorous chest, showed himself to her as the vanquisher of beasts.

They rarely encountered other humans, and such encounters were awkward, never failing to cause them a complex emotion in which irritation and dread were mingled with a sympathetic interest. Daâh did not detest them deeply; on the contrary, he esteemed his own image in them, and approved of them for being similar to him—but by virtue of that very fact, he feared them, and their appearance constituted a provocation in itself.

No other animal excited him to conflict so much; he could not perceive one without experiencing a surge of anger, a very special need for violence and a desire to attack; at the sight of one of his peers, a warrior frenzy agitated his muscles and tensed his nerves; an instinctive jealousy and an appetite for triumph drove him to attack, for no reason other than for the love of battle and victory.

In confrontation with other enemies, he gathered himself compactly for the contest; in the presence of that rival, by contrast, he stood up straight, gripped his club and ground his teeth. The other did the same, and more often than not, they passed by, like two mastiffs that know they have nothing to gain and everything to lose if they come into conflict. But they only passed by slowly and reluctantly, and the temptation of bestial heroism sometimes dragged them back to fight.

More than anything else, Hock was apprehensive of those encounters, always furious, whose outcome was uncertain. As soon as she saw one becoming imminent, she became alarmed and gave evidence of it; with a fearful bleating, she raised supplicant eyes to her master, grabbing him by the elbow or the wrist, and pulled his hips with all her strength in order to drag him out of sight.

She did not always succeed in that; her very presence was the reason for more than one battle. Daâh was all the more reluctant to retreat because Hock was there to see it; as proud as a stag, he experienced an obscure sensation of being diminished by not fighting, and of diminishing in his female an admiration of which he was jealous, much more than of her possession. At the risk of his life, he wanted to be the strongest—and above all, to prove it.

XXII. Reversibility

He aspired to nothing more, for those duels were devoid of profit; he had known that for a long time, having observed many times, not without astonishment, the singular repugnance he experienced in eating the vanquished individual. He had often tried, habituated to nourish himself on whatever he killed, but as soon as he began to crush a fragment of that flesh between his jaws, however savory, the water of disgust sprang forth in his mouth; no other meat caused him a similar aversion, not even that of the hyena, which stank. He chewed the morsel for a long time without being able to swallow it, and ended up spitting it out between his feet. Then he looked at it on the grass, frowning in order to help himself to understand, and turned toward the dead man, whom he sniffed at a distance, with an interrogative expression.

No matter how brief the time was that he spent in that contemplation, it rarely failed to cut off his appetite entirely, and to engender a kind of malaise, or even anguish; two paces away from that body, too similar to his own, lying there at full length, he thought vaguely that he might end up like that; in that image he saw himself; before that ruin of his fellow, a sentiment of a broader egotism disturbed him. In sum, he was subject to the specific horror that is consecutive to the fear of death, which the superior animals feel in the presence of the cadaver of one of their own kind.

The human being, racked by a more active imagination, is doubtless one of those who find it hardest to escape the reflexes of that impression; he only succeeds in vanquishing them, his voracity triumphing over his repugnance, when he has been too long deprived of carnal nourishment. If that privation is perpetuated over a long enough period for several generations to suffer therefrom, anthropophagy can result, and end up being incorporated into mores or even rituals, but it is only produced as a result of education, and when a race has contrived, by hereditary custom, to forget the native horror and substitute an inveterate taste for it.

Those times had not yet come; there was a long and difficult road to travel toward the ages in which the animal kingdom, impoverished in places, would cease to finish a sufficiency to the carnivorous appetites of humans; cannibalism, not being a necessity, was not a temptation. The nomad hunter, whose jaws worked relentlessly, only found himself exceptionally in the stimulating state of famine that he would have needed to eat his fellow.

Not only did he no longer dig into it, but at the moment of abandoning the corpse, a kind of saddened sympathy retained him in proximity to the cadaver that would soon be shared between the Wolves and the Hyenas; a resentment took hold of him at having worked on behalf of stinking beasts; dully, he raged against them, and growled as he looked around for them. Finally, he went away, rolling his quarrelsome eyes, and always with regret.

Thus was denounced already, by a reversibility of animal egotism, the preliminary symptoms of a sensation that would be able in time to become a sentiment, and which would constitute human solidarity.

XXIII. The Dance and the Song

Once, in fact, the contest had been exceedingly fierce. Daâh stood next to the vanquished man and looked at him without hatred, for longer than usual. Finally, he went away.

Suddenly, he heard behind him, too close for his liking, suspect cracking sounds. He ran back. The carrion-eaters were, indeed, forming a circle, and their muzzles were already searching the belly and drawing out the warm entrails. Without worrying about their number, Daâh fell upon them; he had never rushed to an attack with so much fury; his agile club split skulls, broke ribs and smashed jaws, and the band dispersed.

He found himself alone again with that large naked body lying on its back. The dead man seemed immense, with his two arms widespread and his two legs outstretched; under the downpour, his belly was filling up with pink water which was running out of him, but his hand was clenched on his club in a supreme challenge, and his wide open eyes were still threatening empty space.

Daâh marveled at that attitude, bellicose even in death; he recognized himself in it; he sensed that the anger in question was not turned against him but against the filthy beasts, and clearly discerned that the cadaver had adopted a defensive stance against their bites. It was the rage of seeing them reach out for him with impunity and the horror of not being able to move under the insult of their contact that gave the defeated man that furious expression! And Daâh approved of it; with his familiar gesture, he struck his torso, to show the immobile man that he had dispersed the common enemy in his stead. In order that the other would admire him more, he leaned over his face.

A blue mist was floating in the circles of the fixed irises, and that mist was plaintive. Daâh gazed at it so intently that, little by little, it began to move, and he saw the dead man's thought; just as he had divined it, albeit indistinctly, in the blue mist, he perceived the silhouettes of the carnivores: the entire horde of cowards, coming back as dusk fell, and also a heavy Bear that was passing by, turning a thrust of its nose toward the body, and a disdainful Lion that scarcely stopped in order to sniff...

At the sequence of insults, Daâh frowned. His instinct of pride rebelled against the assault on the species; the insults that his fellow was suffering offended him in his own flesh, and a vague regret, which was not pity but rather egotism, informed him of their solidarity in the struggle.

Suddenly, he stood up; twigs cracked behind him; eyes, almost at ground level, shone in the covert of foliage; the flesh-eaters returned to the charge.

To frighten them, he uttered his battle cry: "Haâh! Heûh!"

Hock ran to the rescue. With the tip of his club he pointed to the fallen hunter, and with his left arm, he indicated the circle of flesh-eaters hidden in the undergrowth. Then, once again, he pointed at the man with the gaping belly and cried, with disgust:

"Mâh! Heûh!"

His mouth, opening and closing by turns, simulated the effort of chewing beasts. The woman understood that he did not want to abandon the other to the tribe of the scavengers.

To shelter the dead man, she proposed the earth, with the gesture of scratching; but the work would take too long and the claws of the quadrupeds would soon have undone what human fingernails had contrived with so much difficulty. Daâh proposed the tree, his ordinary refuge, and Hock, at that idea, opened her eyes wide, which brightened. Daâh, having made a decision, grabbed the corpse by the neck.

He threw the body onto his back; the head was tilted back, resting on his shoulder, and the bushy hair was near his mouth. He made a top-knot of it, which he gripped with his teeth, then opened his arms to embrace the trunk of an oak and started climbing.

Through the leafy branches, Hock could no longer see him, but she heard him breathing; broken twigs fell upon her along with the rain. He reappeared; she saw him wedge the dead man into the fork of a branch. He came back down, and with his nose in the air he searched the thickets for branches. Hock pointed her finger at the black, hairy head, like a large fruit, in its nest of damp leaves.

"Ta! Ta!"

He eventually discovered it, and immediately burst out laughing. The cadaver was truly inaccessible and the wild beasts could come back. He saw their disappointment in advance, their prowling around the oak, their mouths straining toward the prey and their futile leaps. To explain their disappointment and anger to Hock, he pranced like them, trotted in a circle, crouched down and leapt up, coming down again on all fours, stood up, shook his head, and projected his arms and legs. Soon, infected by the joyful humor, the woman also became demented; each in front of the other, to imitate the beasts, they danced.

When they were tired and covered in sweat, they stopped. Then, the same idea occurred to them both at the same time. They extended their necks toward the heights, and, standing at the foot of the tree in the fading twilight, still out of breath, both of them, with one lugubrious voice, started to parody the howling of the disappointed hyenas: they sang.

XXIV. The First Burden

Flouc... Flouf... Flou...

On the carpet of dead leaves heaped up for centuries by the luxuriant Pliocene vegetation, soaked with rainwater, their bare feet adhered to a warm mud.

Flouc... Flouf... Flou...

Always the same noise of a hole in the mud drawing in air like a mouth when the foot is removed; always the same sucker sticking to the soles of their feet, to their ankles, to their calves; always the same serpent of mud spurting up between their toes. Since they started walking, since they were born, they have been walking in the putrid and viscous mud. While they struggle with their arms against the beasts or the branches, they struggle with their legs against the living earth that pulls them down in order to eat them, aspire them, suck them in, as voracious as everything else that surrounds them.

Floc... Flac!

When the clay soil refuses to absorb the downpour that never ends, puddles are hidden under the leaves, and they sometimes sink into them hip-deep.

Flouhou...

They help one another to get out of the trap, and set off again. The indefatigable rain streams over their bodies, and claps of thunder burst without respite in a sky that they can only perceive at intervals through the bushy dome of the immense virgin forest.

They do not always go completely naked. Often, thrown over their shoulders and covering their backs, they wear an animal skin, from which the paws, tendons and muscle fibers still hang, in order to protect them from the rain more than from the cold. But at every moment it slips, irritating them, and they usually do not keep it for long; it is sufficient for them to be harassed on two or three occasions, or for it to hinder a necessary gesture, for it to be immediately thrown against a tree trunk or into the mud; it is even sufficient for it to fall off, and it remains on the ground unless it is of immediate utility.

If it happens that the hazards of the hunt have procured a large prey, they only take the trouble to remove the skin if the cold or the violence of the inundation invites them to cover themselves temporarily; if, on the contrary, the weather is warm or the tree under which they find themselves provides good shelter, neither hide nor fleece interests them.

Hock never thinks, any more than Daâh does, about exchanging her shred of stinking and ragged pelt for a better fur. That ingenuity would require preliminary reasoning, a comparison, foresight—which is to say, an intellectual labor that is too complicated, and also a material labor that is not imperative. They only have vigor for fatigues that impose themselves ferociously on their brutal strength; Daâh, who uses energy to the point of valor when it is a matter of marching or fighting, remains sluggish and idle before tranquil work; he turns away from it. Industrious toil would not tempt him and would put him to sleep. He only knows how to take trouble when enraged; he can only conceive of effort in violence.

They do not even carry a flint with them to strip the skin off felled beasts and cut the flesh; they make use of a stone they find nearby, or a branch that they plunge into the carcass and manipulate like a lever; they dislocate the joints, break the ribs, devour on the spot; then they sleep and digest, wake up, recommence consumption until they can swallow no more, and go away, leaving what remains behind, without taking a piece of meat for the following day. Concern for provisions assumes foresight; their ineptitude in presuming future moments results, for the best of reasons, in the incapability of providing for them.

If such an idea occurred to them, they would reject it without hesitation; having only two needs, their nourishment and their defense, they no longer count the first as soon as it is satisfied, and only the second exists; sated, they become incapable of evoking tomorrow's hunger, whereas the charge of a

83

burden is an immediate and obvious inconvenience. The future cannot prevail against the present; the present has instinct in its favor, the future only has reasoning; a brute cannot resign himself to sacrifice his present ease to the imagination of needs to come.

Will the meat that one has left because one can no longer eat, or the fur that one discards because one is warm, soon be lacking when one is hungry or cold again? It does not matter: they will not be regretted because they will no longer be remembered.

Thus, no baggage; hands free for battle! The only object that the man consents to carry is his club, of which he makes use continually.

And they go on.

They had been going on for months, when Hock had a second son, whose birth halted them for an entire day.

Daâh received this event with less surprise than on the preceding occasion, and most of all with less fear. He knew now that the screeching animal was not to be feared, that one could touch it without peril. He ventured to do so more deliberately, and Hock let him do it; he weighed the child in the hollows of his large palms, turning it over and sniffing it; he lifted it up by one foot, and his hilarity was immense on seeing it head down, opening a toothless mouth. This time, he thought that it resembled a frog, but also Hock, like the first one. He tried to stand it upright, like Hock, but the new-born collapsed into the grass, on its back, and struggled, waving its arms in the air, like Hock.

Daâh burst out laughing, for that was his custom when he had understood something, and he understood, now.

Yes, it's a little human. Humans have young, like Lions, like Deer; they grow them like Apples, like Walnuts, and then they fall, and then they go. The other went; this one will go.

And one day, perhaps he might grow a little man, too. Daâh was pleased to suppose so; it was impossible for him to conceive, as a first hypothesis, that such fruitfulness could be appropriate to his protégée and forbidden to himself. His irascible pride would have been offended to have to discover such a manifest inferiority in himself; he did not have to reject the supposition, because it did not occur to him.

Hock was tired; he consented to sleep there. As soon as morning came, however, he set off again and the mother followed; she carried her child under one arm, and then under the other, and on her shoulder and on her back, holding him by the wrists.

And that was the first burden: the human creature had just learned to charge herself with something; the mother invented the function that would later become incumbent on women in the nomadic horde; she was initiated into the role of bearer of burdens, behind the man who bears arms.

XXV. The Conquests of Mime

Although it was true that Daâh was proud to be, among all the animals, The-One-Who-Stands-Upright, the arrogance that he obtained from that privilege did not go as far as making him scornful of other animals. Between them and himself he perceived no essential difference, and did not reckon himself to be a singular animal, since he saw, indistinctly, the two primordial necessities of eating and self-defense imposed upon all of them, including him. Under the double urgency of that common law, he sensed naively that a bond of narrow kinship attached him to the rest of the animal kingdom, and he simply divided creatures into two groups: those that ate, and those that were eaten. On that scale of strength, he placed himself around the middle; he detested few species and did not love any, except as food, and his hatred of the strong was not exempt from an admiration that incorporated a certain deference, and even more envy.

However, he possessed a sort of faculty, or instinct, which served him greatly, and which would, by virtue of an imperceptible progress, day after day, serve him increasingly to remedy the indigence of his natural weaponry: he *recorded.* Involuntarily, but constantly, he received impressions of the external world through all his senses, and although is memory was short, those furtive and perpetually-renewed impressions ended up aggregating within him automatically and almost without his being aware of it, to the extent of constituting, in the mists of his mind, an entire little world of concrete images that resembled notions.

Forms, colors, sounds and odors repeatedly recorded cerebral imprints in him, which were classified as to their signification. He knew that Lions roar, that Vipers crawl, that Thunder rumbles and that Bears prance; he recognized the danger denounced by some glimpsed pelt, some perceived rustle under the leaves, or some whiff in the air; of each one he noticed the habits, the appearances, the tactics.

It was very little; but it was the commencement of everything. For that unreal world that he transported within him was as alive as the real world; Daâh positively felt it agitating inside his skull, like an interior force demanding to be exteriorized, and he experienced a malaise in not being able to project it outwardly. For want of words with which to express it, he had recourse to cries and gestures: gesture and exclamation were the double outlet of his mutism.

Suddenly, without any apparent reason, he started dancing like the Bear, growling like the Lion, mocking like the Hyena. For him, those mimicries were something more than a game; evidently, his perpetual mobility had suggested to him, in preference to any other, that means of translating himself, but they only procured the means, and the veritable cause of those imitations was an almost physiological need that he had to rid himself of a mental residue.

By that means the exonerated himself of his plethora; in the same way that he had nourished his body with meat and fruits, his rudimentary intellect had alimented itself with images, and that spiritual nutrition was accomplished in parallel with the other. Having absorbed and digested visions, he rendered imitations. He imitated everything.

Performing that comedy for Hock was his fashion of talking to her; performing them for himself was his way of thinking. By that means he sharpened his mind, meager as it was, although he was not aware of it—but above all, he augmented his resources and multiplied his means of subsistence, and the benefits of that practical enrichment did not escape him.

He observed it, always rejoicing in it, but always after the fact, and without having premeditated his enrichment. When his simian inclination had made him parody a gesture, and when that gesture produced its normal result, he marveled stupidly, but he registered the event in his storehouse of images, and the following day he recommenced, in order to provoke the opportunity to marvel again: he imitated Daâh imitating an animal.

The parody, many times repeated, became an assimilation, and the assimilation became a habit. What is habit, except a matter of self-imitation? Thus, he accommodated himself to unusual actions, customary to other species, which gradually became customary to him: aptitudes special to other animals, which he only possessed to the slightest degree, were developed in that fashion.

In all the ambient animality he found something to take; a shark of ideas, he swallowed everything; by dint of striving to simulate everything that was animated before him, he identified himself to some degree with everything that he had seen, and the multiple capacities of the animal world, more or less skillfully collected, were totalized in his own.

Those assimilations left him, however, utterly ingrate toward those from which they proceeded; he no more thought of conserving any gratitude to them on account of those imprints, than he did of conserving any to those he ate, on account of their more or less tasty flesh. His admiration for them even diminished as soon as he was able to imitate them; as soon as he had succeeded in amplifying his means by adopting those of another, he considered himself at least equal to his master, if not its superior, and did not deign to remember the origin of the gain. He flattered himself that it was a personal conquest, nothing more—and in that, he was not entirely wrong, for usage, hazard and the astonishments that hazard provoked in him, almost always had the result of revealing new possibilities to him that were totally unknown to their initiator; he recorded them, along with everything else.

XXVI. The Club

Frugivores, rodents, carnivores: he imitated all those that eat; he learned from felines the manner of creeping silently toward a prey in order to surprise it in its lair; he saw Snakes sealing Birds' eggs and did as the snakes did; insects taught him the patience of dissimulation, and he knew how to cover himself with earth or foliage, curling up on the ground like a rock to wait for a passing Hare or a small bird alighting.

The Wild Boar showed him how one unearths roots, but he mistrusted it, still having the instinct that turns beasts away from an unknown and possibly toxic nutriment. For a long time he contented himself, prudently, with remains in which he recognized the bite of the wild pig; he sniffed them, hesitated, risked a lick of the tongue, a nibble of the teeth, sucked and chewed, reassured himself and acquired a taste—but he lacked solid tusks for digging in the humus, and the brilliant invention of utilizing a stick, a horn or a stone for that purpose would have had to wait a few centuries more, but for the wily instructor to whom Daâh owed more lessons than any other: the Ape.

To that industrious elder, who drew by inheritance on an experience already centuries old, humans owed innumerable borrowings; it was from him that they had learned to sleep in the trees and to take refuge there from Lions, and from him, too, they obtained the subtle trick of breaking the hard envelope of a fruit between two rocks, and they had amplified that find by utilizing the stone to open long bones and such out the marrow. More useful still, it served for scraping, sawing and cutting. It was to the same inventor, again, that they owed the most precious artifice of all, without which they would have perished long ago: the Ape carried a stick!

Daâh picked up a stick in order to imitate the quadrumane. Since infancy he had gone about with a piece of wood in his fist, and his arms apart. Naturally, the branches he

89

chose were of large caliber—as large as possible; as his muscles grew with age he took pride in increasing the dimensions of his weapon. The heavier and more massive it was, the more he appreciated it; ordinarily, he selected one at the limit of his strength.

That size, generally exaggerated, obliged him to hold the weapon by its thinner extremity in order to grip it better. It appeared to him then that the branch became heavier. Stupefied by such a bizarrerie, he gazed at and sniffed the two ends; discovering nothing that could explain that aggravation of weight, he did not try to deny it, as a reasoner would have done, but had the genius to be astonished momentarily, very moderately: just enough to laugh at it but not enough to dispute it.

Laughter was, in him, the sign of adoption. He had only three ways of greeting the observations of his senses: for known phenomena, a manic, rapid recording designed to clear it away, followed by an immediate indifference; for unusual cases, a start of anxiety or a burst of laughter, according to whether he glimpsed a danger or a profit.

Before that stick, which had not changed and yet changed its weight, he remained open-mouthed and wide-eyed; he repeated the experiment of lifting the branch and brandishing it, sometimes by one extremity and sometimes by the other. Now the stick is lighter! Laughter. Now it is heavier! More laughter. He recorded the two facts, and, above all, a third: his blows struck more forcefully when the heavier was distant.

Daâh did not ask any more of it; he resigned himself to inventing the club and making use of it, without understanding it.

XXVII. The First Pact

That precious discovery went back to the days of his adolescence; it preceded the encounter with Hock by several years. The club had, therefore, been his first companion. He loved it. It flattered him. He was proud of it, as a badge by which he was distinguished from the quadrupeds, and he admired himself in it, as if it were an extension of his own being. He was nevertheless able to remember that it was neither him nor his, and to recognize what assistance that stranger brought to him in battle.

Long accustomed to attributing motives similar to his own to things, and a determination to harm him or serve him, he had less mistrust of them in this instance than any other; he had the very clear sentiment of receiving a consensual and faithful aid; the weapon that never betrayed him at difficult moments was not a tool, or even a servant, but rather an ally.

At the moment of going into combat, he gripped the hilt as one shakes the hand of a friend, shaking it with an abrupt gesture, and mentally stammered conjurations in order to give himself courage and renew their pact. After the battle, he caressed it in the manner of a hunter passing his hand over the back of his dog to compliment it; it was almost thanks; the harder it had struck, the more esteem he experienced for it. He did not quit it either to eat or sleep; when it was not in his hand during a halt, it rested by his side within the reach of his hand; while he slept in the tree, he held it against his breast.

That friend of the first hour, therefore, not only brought him the benefit of its material utility; it furnished him additionally with an item of social information, which seems to have been the first of all. It is to the club, in fact, that the role fell of initiating humans into the idea of a cooperation, and showing them the profit to be gained thereby.

Long before he had associated with his fellow, and even his female, a broken branch had revealed to the human male the possibility of uniting his strength with other strengths; thus was prepared in humans the notion that would determine their mental and mechanical superiority and ensure their triumph over the globe, since, thanks to the club they were able to enslave and devastate the world, exploiting for their usage the animals, the plants and the very entrails of the earth.

XXVIII. The Whirl

At length, the necessity of always brandishing the club in order to strike down the branches that barred the way ends up engendering in Daâh a mechanical gesture: his arm rises up and comes down without his being aware of it; as long as there is an obstacle in front of him, he strikes; when, by chance, there are no more of them, his arm becomes bored and, after a brief rest, it recommences striking empty air.

Then the free space permits a broader gesture, and the stick describes a semicircle, which ends up flattening out in the mud. Sometimes, however, it happens that the club, not encountering the ground, continues its circular course, and Daâh applies himself to perfecting that result, so well that he soon succeeds in obtaining a complete rotation. By means of further progress he becomes capable of realizing several successive rotations, and is able to turn the club with increasing force and increasing rapidity; he laughs at no longer being able to perceive it, so rapidly does it pass by; he laughs at hearing it whistling like a bird; he admires the transparent disk that it traces in whirling around the axis of his wrist.

"Haâh!"

In order to make Hock admire it, he calls her, and the woman approaches.

"Ta! Ta!"

She laughs in her turn, delighted by no longer being able to see the club that existed and seeing in its stead a great round object that did not exist. Curious, she advances her nose, sniffs, and felt a wind on her face that has no explanation. To listen to the whistling bird, she inclines her head sideways, and stays there, motionless, in the attitude of a fowl listening—but the temptation becomes too strong; Hock can no longer resist it. She puts a finger into the circle, and immediately utters a cry, withdrawing her bloodied hand.

93

Daâh cannot help laughing at the imprudent woman's surprise as she licks her wound and clutches the injured index finger of her right hand. Then, when he has laughed until he is satisfied, he wants to look at the wound—not out of pity, of course, but to convince himself of the damage he was able to inflict in that fashion.

He leans over the hand, examines it and turns it over. The flesh is well and truly torn, the blood streaming, the bone laid bare. The effect is good: Daâh asks no more of it, and he records it. He is content; he has gained something. He knows that one must not venture too close to him when he is whirling his club, and that behind the circle he is sheltered by a rampart.

"Haâh!"

He dances with joy in front of the patient, who continues to whimper and lick her finger.

In all the days that follow Daâh does not fail to take advantage of the clearings to practice the game that pleases him by virtue of its novelty. In doing so, he has little idea of multiplying his means; he does not even suspect that he is on the path of invention; he is simply amusing himself, and glad of the improvement that practice brings.

It is for that reason that the overly frequent impacts of the club against the ground suggest to him the idea of raising his wrist to shoulder level—but the club still hits the ground sometimes, and that is why he raises the wrist to the level of the face; the arm stretches, the fist is closer to the forehead, the circle that was once vertical becomes oblique. A little more, and now the wrist is above the cranium; the circle in which the club rotates becomes horizontal. It covers the man like a roof and protects his surroundings. The enemy can no longer approach him from the front or from behind. Daâh has just built around him a fortress that kills. When beasts in a pack attack him together, they will enter the circle of death of their own accord

"Haâh!... Han!"

Let the Wolves come, now, and the Hyenas! He would like them to be around him, to make the trial. He seeks them with his eyes, calls to them and provokes them with cries. Where are they, in order that he might teach them the master's discovery? He, who was the naked beast before, so feeble and unarmed, is now the one who can no longer be approached: he has eliminated the mortal body-to-body combat, the choking grip, the tearing claw, the biting mouth; from now on he will stop them at a distance.

He no longer fears anything. Because he feels stronger today than yesterday, he is ready to dream that henceforth he will be the strongest of all, and it would not take much, in the intoxication of his young imagination, for him to exaggerate confidence in his strength to the extent of believing himself to be invincible.

XXIX. Distress

Daâh knows days of depression. They are rare; life in the woods and constant peril keep energy alert, since a moment of forgetfulness is sufficient for one to die. There are, however, moments when death itself no longer causes a tremor, so weary does one become of being afraid. It can come from outside without one deigning to flee, because one already carries it within. Daâh is more subject to these crises than any other beast; his impressionability puts him at the mercy of influences exerted upon his nascent soul by the state of the atmosphere or that of his body. Often, too, these evil hours come to him on the days after his triumphs; when he has had a plethora of delight, confidence and spirit, and believes in himself, and overloaded his nerves or his poor encephalum, a reaction throws him down flat in the mud.

Flouc... Flouche...

He marches, and the rain drenches him, as it did yesterday, as it always does. Today, it bothers him. He has seen too much rain; it discourages him. Limply, in the murky depths of his being, a revolt attempts to rise up, and immediately collapses. He frowns and parades a vaguely hateful gaze around him. He execrates the world and effort, but even anger is too costly an expense for his sluggishness. He is exhausted. Her arms are slack, his club heavy and cumbersome; he no longer loves it. His feet drag, his hamstrings lack resilience.

Go to sleep between two branches of an oak? Yes...no...not even... The forks are too high; the mere idea of an ascent wearies him. He lets himself fall at the foot of a trunk, wedges himself with his back against the rough bark; his arm slides into the moss and he watches the downpour.

The water spills from the height of the clouds and streams from the tops of the trees in cataracts; it floats before him, a dull moving curtain shaken by gusts of wind; under the abrupt pressure of the gusts it goes crazy, whipping the branches, slashing the leaves, peppering the trunks, riddling the puddles, and its innumerable noises mingle in a tumult in which one might believe that all the voices of the forest can be heard.

It is as if thousands of animals were hurling their cries into the distance, which flow toward Daâh. He recognizes them: the Bear that growls, the Lion that roars, the Hyena that laughs. Monkeys chatter and Dogs bark; all his enemies are howling at him and assailing him simultaneously with their convergent menace. There are too many, and he is too alone!

He renounces the struggle. He can do no more. Let them eat him, and it will all be over, since it is necessary to be eaten sooner or later and he cannot escape the rule of existence. At intervals, thunderclaps stir the life in his depths, but as soon as he has started he collapses again.

Hock prowls around the vicinity. A little while ago, seeing him crouched down, she drew away to the far side of the clearing, and he watched her back moving away under the downpour. Is she looking for something to eat again? The idea of swallowing things disgusts him, and Hock, who breaks branches as she moves, irritates him.

Has she disappeared? He is annoyed. Can he see her again, over there? He perceives her through the veils of the downpour, like a creature of dream; he can only make her out vaguely; he has the impression of no longer knowing her, so indifferent is he to her and so barely does she seem to exist. So little! She resembles a void that walks...

Certainly, Daâh has not formulated that image, but a sensation of death, sudden and cold, has run through him, and in the penumbra of his mind he has glimpsed a mystery, a hole, blackness, the void: something frightful, like the gulfs of the mountain, with night in the background. *No longer to be...!*

He shivers. He opens his round eyes and his mouth remains agape. The woman comes back, however...

As she advances, he experiences the impression of coming back himself, and from far away, from a world that he did not suspect a little while ago, and which he is already forgetting.

Hock draws nearer; she is, as yet, only a being of vapors, mist in human form that totters in the haze; at every step that brings her closer she condenses more; it seems that the impact of her footfalls is solidifying her and that she is resuming existence...

Now she is in front of him. He stares at her with a bewildered gaze. Whether or not she is really alive, he does not know and does not care. She leans toward him; she looks him in the eyes; she sees the anguish there and divines it, for she knows that malaise; but when she suffers from it, he pays no heed to it. She remains motionless before those desert pupils, and their distress penetrates her in its turn. From the depths of her throat, a grave and feeble bleat is exhaled:

"Beûh..."

There is no response. Then, her plaint becomes a plea; breath against breath, she appeals to him:

"Daâh..."

He does not hear her; he does not see her; he remains stuck in the mud of his darkness. She resigns herself to it; she sits down to his left, and side by side, staring straight ahead, they both watch the rain falling; they can no longer even see it.

But they will always—still, in a hundred thousand years—remember the Deluge.

XXX. The Widow

As they moved further westwards they encountered humans with increasing frequency. Undoubtedly, guided by the same instinct, the others had been following the same direction, but some obstacle, perhaps insurmountable, stopping them one by one, had confined them in the same area. What the reason might be, Daâh did not care; he observed the fact, which was unwelcome. He had ended up becoming so accustomed to his companion that he was now apprehensive of losing her, and every approach by a male seemed to him to be that of an abductor.

He tried not to let that show, but he avoided his fellows even more carefully than predators; he took great care in examining their trails when he discovered them; then he changed his own, and tried to erase his tracks in order not to be followed. Hock helped him in that, with more subtle ruses, of which he knew her to be capable, and she applied herself loyally to that prudent work without any afterthought of sexual curiosity, dreading above all else the loss of her protector. Those precautions did not prevent alerts from becoming increasingly frequent.

One day, toward the end of summer, on emerging into a clearing, they saw a couple at the foot of a beech tree.

The man and the woman, crouching in the grass, were eating and looking straight ahead. An eviscerated ibex was lying in the grass. Instantly, they were on their feet, and the male took three steps forward.

His higher forehead, his less compacted face and his less massive body indicated another race, frailer and more delicate; his stance was straighter. Immediately, he was odious to Daâh, by virtue of his form and his bearing, by virtue of his eyes, the audacity of his gesture and the pretention of showing himself to women in a provocative attitude.

The man had taken three steps; Daâh took six, to affirm that he was the braver.

His valor had never had so many spectators; his appetite for glory was multiplied tenfold by that. He did not pause until he was in the middle of the clearing, where he planted himself, stiffly, his jaw raised and his weapon in his fist. Immediately, the other advanced.

The two women, on the edge of the wood, bleated like deer, calling back their men. But the latter could no longer hear them; one last bound brought them face to face and their clubs collided.

"Haâh!"

"Han!"

The duel was brief: a skull caved in, a double roar of pain and triumph; and a single shrill scream—the distant voice of the fearful woman.

Daâh, standing over his victim, finished crushing his face with thrusts of his heel. Then he bent down and plunged his hand into the pulp of blood and brain; he smeared his breast with it, and in the crimson of his victim he danced around the body, whirling around him the circles of his club.

Finally, he placed a foot on the torso of the vanquished man, turned toward the widow, and emitted a long howl.

She had remained under the beech, collapsed and devoid of strength; she was waiting for death. But when she saw the man start marching in her direction, fear lashed her and she tried to run away; head down, she sought an exit in order to plunge into the forest; always driven back by the tangle of brushwood, she ran one way and then the other, like a beast at bay. When he was able to catch her, she moaned plaintively. He grabbed her by the hair, knocked her to the ground, and took her there and then in order to attest his victory.

On the far side of the clearing, Hock watched them complacently. Tranquilized now, she deloused her child. She, too, had thought, a little while before, that the dead man's companion was about to be killed; when she was able to observe that the victor did not appear to have that intention, she became

100

disinterested in the rest; while running her fingers through the infant's bushy hair, she waited.

Suddenly, she remembered that at the moment of the encounter, the other couple had been eating under the beech tree. She tucked her son under her armpit and ran toward the tree. Having arrived at the foot of the trunk she checked the grass with her foot before setting the brat down; then she crouched down and, without paying any more attention to the couple, whose swoon left her free to choose the best morsels, she attacked the remains of the meal, chuckling greedily.

After a time, she saw the master coming back. He was walking slowly, with the air of serene majesty that he ordinarily adopted when returning from the most difficult battles; he thought that gait indispensable to the combatant returning victorious, as a conclusive testimony of his power and the minimum of effort that his victory had cost him.

He arrived. He was hungry. His face was rubicund, his thorax illuminated by blood, as was his right foot, up to the ankle and his right arm half way up to the elbow. Without crouching down he extended the ample gesture of his red hand along the ibex, took hold of the beast and broke its back over his knee. With a flick of his wrist, he tore away three ribs and, still dignified, waving that scarlet fragment in the air, he turned to the widow in order to give her a sign to approach. In an almost gentle voice, he invited her to come and eat with him.

"Mâh! Mâh!"

She hesitated, in the distance. Already impatient, be barked an order:

"Ta!"

His imperious finger designated a place beside him in the grass, where he threw the piece of meat.

She came then, tentatively; her breast, too, was stained with the blood that contact with the victor had imprinted on her; she bent her back as a sign of obedience, and her hands extended their palms at the level of her temples. She had not been hasty enough, however; the man reiterated his order.

101

"Ta!"

This time, Hock was discontented, because of the sharing of the food; her facial muscles swelled, hollowing out wrinkles in front of her hair. At the same time, with her arm and her head, she made the violent gesture to the right and the left of sweeping away something unwelcome, which, later, was to signify refusal.

No!

The male did not admit protests against his will. He growled, and tranquilly put the rebellion down with a blow of his fist. For the third time he repeated the injunction:

"Ta!"

The widow came closer, and when she had arrived before her new master, she bowed her head, moving it up and down, slightly more with each repetition, in the gesture of submission that offers the nape of the neck to a blow, and which was later to signify acquiescence.

Yes!

She took the place indicated. Then Daâh, with his bloody right hand, took hold of her by the hair in order to indicate that he had her. Then all three of them, in silence, a bone in hand, bit into the raw flesh.

When they had eaten, the nomadic hunter, faithful to his custom, perched the dead man in an oak. That done, he picked up his club, while Hock picked up her child. With a shove on the shoulder, he commanded his captive to start walking behind him and to follow.

"Ta!"

The trio went back into the forest, the man in the lead.

From that day forward, Daâh had two women.

XXXI. Bigamy

Daâh only knew one number: unity. The fleeting quality of his sensations prevented him from pausing on one thing long enough for it to leave a clear and permanent image in his memory; every object became as if dead as soon as he was no longer looking at it; the vision of the second effaced that of the first, and Daâh was incapable of counting as far as two. For him, every individual existed in isolation, being one Oak next to one Oak, one Bear and one Bear, and each one was designated by the location it occupied.

"Ta... Ta..."

It would, however, be unjust to say that the candidate for humanity was utterly deprived of any faculty of abstraction. By virtue of finding identical appearances endlessly and everywhere, he reached the point of storing in his depths vague but analogous images, whose analogy ended up becoming obvious; he thus succeeded, without any process of classification, in conceiving the idea of a resemblance between forms notoriously recorded in his brain. While continuing to be unaware that one oak and one oak make a pair, he knew that they were similar. In the same way, he learned that his companions resembled one another in certain particulars, and, without calculating that he had two women, he was pertinently aware that he had one and one.

"Ta... Ta..."

The newcomer was, at first, merely a "Ta" like everything else in the world: "Ta," the thing that is there; "Ta," which designated her place during the march or the halt; "Ta," which formulated the order to approach, to crouch down, to follow, to run or to stop.

"Ta," which prescribed immediate obedience, in all its forms, gradually became the exclamation to which the captive responded; and, just as had happened to the first woman, the frequency of appeals ended up constituting a personality and a name for the second:

"Ta!"

Sometimes, too, the master called her Hock, like the other, not in error but deliberately, because of their sexual analogy, and he only called her that in special circumstances, precisely when he substituted the second in the role that had until then been played by the first. When hunger did not oblige him to launch himself into the woods to search for food, when a location appeared to offer him a temporary security, when he had eaten and he was in a good mood, he played with one or the other, at the hazard of proximity, and according to the caprice of the moment:

"Hock!"

During the early days of that common life, it appeared that a whim attracted him toward the stranger more frequently than toward his former companion; doubtless the charm of novelty seduced him, and that possession flattered his pride, revivifying on each occasion the proof of his victory. But that memory of battle did not take long to attenuate, and he soon lost it completely in the mists of the past; nothing any longer remained of it. The widow, however, persisted in retaining a prestige of which she took no account, and to which Daâh himself was subject without being aware of it.

That physical preference was not based on a keener admiration. The male did not say to himself that one of the females was more beautiful than the other; his faculties of analysis were still far from permitting him any conception of beauty; he did not perceive any notable difference between the two creatures, distinguishing them simply as one distinguishes two animals of the same species whose pelts are dissimilar.

"Hock... Ta..."

It remained the case, nonetheless, that he experienced quite different sentiments in their regard: a more profound affinity attached him more sympathetically to Hock, because of their common past and similar tastes, whereas a more vibrant charm attracted him to Ta; he felt a strange pleasure in looking at her or touching her.

That diversity of impressions and appetites would appear to indicate that the instinct of the male, more alert than his intellect, had differentiated the women perfectly: one of the two was of his own race and the other of foreign stock. What his mind did not know, his flesh had divined: the flesh went toward the unfamiliar, and Daâh was perhaps obeying a law of his sex, if it is true that nature wishes the crossing of races, and obtains some advantage therefrom for the improvement of the species.[10]

---

[10] Although the scientific term "heterosis" had not yet been coined in 1912 (it first appeared in 1914) the notion of "hybrid vigor" had been understood and discussed—by Charles Darwin, among others—since the early 19th century.

XXXII. The Two Races

Daâh's two companions bore little resemblance to one another. Hock was, like him, short in stature and thickset; Ta was noticeably taller, with a slimmer torso and more ample hips on sleeker legs. It was, above all, in the construction of the skull and the face that the contrast between the two races was affirmed. Both were dolicocephalic, but instead of a crushed mask with a low forehead, a short nose, a receding chin and profound orbits hollowed out like grottos beneath the double arch of a bony brow-ridge, the latecomer presented a high and bulging forehead, a longer, less turned-up nose, and eyes almost on the surface of the head with more prominent cheekbones. No trace of the simian prognathism that gave Hock and Daâh such a bestial character appeared in her; her mouth, less distant from the nostrils, was much less vast, edged with less fleshy lips; not only was the chin not receding but, on the contrary, it projected slightly. That species of elegance was further accentuated by the slenderness of the neck, which detached the head from the shoulders and displayed it more.

When she walked, Hock held her upper body forward, letting her heavy hands swing in front of her thighs; Ta's stance was more upright.

They also differed in their instincts and their tastes. Having originated in another climate, and perhaps endowed with a more ancient heredity, the second spouse already showed a few refinements: she liked bright colors. One day, Hock and Daâh saw her, with amazement, pick a red flower, which she placed in her hair at the top of her head; they immediately set out in quest of similar flowers and did likewise. She appreciated scents, and occasionally plunged her nose between petals; when the odor was to her taste, she laughed; but if she presented the calyx to Hock or Daâh, they turned away indifferently, almost with displeasure.

No less irritable than her companion, but less valiant, she was more subject to nervous frights; her dreams, the memories of the day, made her jump every night with a strident cry; even more than Hock she was afraid of the dark, snakes, silence and solitude. She liked caresses. When they perched in a tree in the evening, Ta climbed up higher, in order to be better protected or to have more warning in case of an alarm. When the fortune of the route caused her to encounter the relatively dry layer of a shelter beneath a rock, she rejoiced in being able to huddle in the warmth against Daâh or against Hock, gurgling with pleasure.

At any rate, the two spouses lived on good terms; they were ignorant of jealousy, since they were ignorant of love, and when the master coupled with one of them, the other took no more umbrage than in watching them crack nuts. The only rivalry they knew was produced by the division of meat. When the hunter had brought down some item of prey, he kept the best part for himself; impatiently, their eyes gleaming with covetousness, they waited until he had exercised his right of choice; immediately after him, they disputed the rest with angry yelps.

They searched for their nourishment together, calling to one another for help when aid was necessary, or even inviting one another to participate in a windfall when the provender was sufficient for two.

Similarly, they became afraid together; they assisted one another in that instead of reassuring one another mutually. Since Ta's arrival, Hock had suffered the contagion of a more unhealthy impressionability than her own; by virtue of reciprocal reactions they exasperated their nervousness. Ta's reached its paroxysm at the approach of violent storms; then the young female, intractable and furious, could not bear any approach; the slightest contact triggered the gesture of beating, and Hock responded with the gesture of biting.

The autumn went by; the stranger became even more nervous than usual; soon she could only walk laboriously, racked as she was by the preliminary symptoms of her first childbirth. She had only been living with Daâh for three months, but neither she nor the others were aware of the conclusions that might appropriately be drawn from that short duration, since the appreciation of time escaped them, as well as the laws of generation.

It remained the case nonetheless that the pregnancy was about to import around Daâh the elements of an exotic race; by mingling the two progenitures and their disparate tendencies, it introduced a redoubtable factor into the first human group, the scourge of the future. To see it appear so soon is like a symbol of the evil to which all human societies are subject without suspecting its cause, for the complexity of origins would perpetuate, in peoples and even in families, a difference of heredity thanks to which the violence would be exasperated of two passions that were to make history bloody: sexual attraction and intellectual dissent; love and discord.

XXXIII. The Fruit of the Woman

The trio wandered for about four months, and winter became more evident, not so much by virtue of cold as famine. The animals disappeared, some dead and others in hiding; between the branches stripped of their leaves, the prey perceived the hunter at a greater distance, and the barer wood facilitated its flight. They knew hunger.

They rarely found anything but the occasional marmot asleep in its bifurcated hole. Even the roots were rotten, the leaves ligneous. The cadaver of a bison, disemboweled and putrefying on the bank of a stream procured them an abundant harvest of small crustaceans, with which they stuffed themselves during an entire day of idleness, but then the hunger recommenced.

The stranger appeared to suffer more than the others; she lamented in the rear, like Hock before. Suddenly, in the same manner as Hock, she brought a daughter into the world.

The prodigy of childbirth was occurring before Daâh for the third time; it no longer provoked any but a mild astonishment. The man was accustomed to the phenomenon, and if he still experienced some surprise, it was due less to the creature itself than its appearance from Ta.

He thought, quite distinctly:

Well! That one, too!

The resemblance between the two women was confirmed by a further detail; one more strangeness was added to the multiple differences already observed between himself and his protégées. By one distinction more they were separated from him, to constitute a group external to him, confronting him.

That further awareness did not displease his pride in the least, so inclined was he to consider himself as a being apart. The notion of "woman," completed and made precise by the attribute of fecundity, was installed within him, and a proposition was agreed:

A child falls from a woman like a fig from a fig tree.

He added that acquired fact to the host of anterior obser-vations, and did not take it any further. More serious concerns were calling to him: he was hungry; everyone was hungry. Leaving the mothers where they were, one lying down and the other crouching, he went out hunting.

He came back without having caught anything. The woman who had just given birth, still weak, had now pulled herself together on the moss, with her back to the trunk of a walnut tree; huddling beneath the downpour, undiverted by any foliage, she was warming her child between her breasts and thighs.

Standing two paces away, he gazed at her fixedly. His idea returned to him, already better generalized by a latent incubation:

A child falls from a woman like a fig from a fig tree.

The young mother looked up at him, plaintively, but he looked at her without seeing her; he was thinking with all his might.

The muscles of his forehead tensed above his eyes; he was visibly having difficulty linking together his still-disjointed ideas, which were stirring and intersecting without having the power to connect.

A child is the fruit of a woman as a walnut in that of a walnut tree. Encumbering fruit, useless fruit...unless one eats them? Daâh eats fruit when he is hungry...

The idea of eating that fruit did not arouse the repug-nance that Daâh experienced before the meat of his peer; that miserable thing bore too little resemblance to him: a reduced image of a man or a woman; a fruit..."

"Mâh!"

He opened his enormous mouth wide and closed it again noisily; the mills of his teeth ground together, crushing noth-ing. The mother looked up at him. She, too, was trying to un-derstand, and almost guessed. She raised her fists and stretched out her neck.

The male remained silent. His arms were dangling, still uncertain regarding the action, but the two suckers of his pupils were already devouring the infant. Suddenly, his eyebrows frowned more deeply and violently, this time, and imperiously, he uttered his cry of hunger:

"Mâh! Mâh!"

Two large ferocious hands, with their thick palms and their splayed fingers, advanced toward the tender flesh.

The mother leapt up; the infant fell, and at the same moment Daâh saw, level with his face, hooked claws that were reaching out for him, and behind those claws, two irises flamboyant with an anger so vehement that he had not yet confronted anything similar, either in the eyes of Lions or those of humans.

Instinctively, he closed his eyes, and he, who took pride in making predators hesitate before his human gaze, recoiled.

XXXIV. The Pocket

Peevishly, Daâh gives the order to resume marching.

But the stranger does not move; she is occupied with a task, and she continues with it, as if she has not heard the master's command. Her eyebrows contracted with attention, she applies herself: she stretches the bear-cub skin that provides her with a garment; with the aid of a sharp stone, she makes a rip in it, two rips.

Hock watches her do it, striving to understand, and the man approaches in his turn to see; he is so curious that, in the presence of new things, he forgets everything; he no longer remembers the order he has given, so intriguing are the stranger's gestures. They are, in fact, bizarre; now she is trying to insert her head into the two holes in the fur; but one of the rips is too narrow and Ta resumes work in order to enlarge that gap by sawing the skin of the bear-cub. Finally, the head passes through; the fur, suspended by its two ends from the woman's neck, hangs over her breast in the form of a pocket, furry in the interior. The young mother picks up her crying newborn, stuffs it inside, and gets up. She is ready to go.

Daâh contemplates her, bewildered, but Hock's eyes are shining with joyful admiration. Thus far, embarrassed by the burden of her child, she has been defenseless against animals and plants, while the stranger will remain free in her movements; henceforth, Hock will follow the example that has been given to her, and she laughs with joy.

But Ta, the woman with the straight forehead and the black hair, has not invented anything either. In the country from which she comes, she has seen mothers carrying their children in that fashion, and they do so because they have seen other women do it, having arrived from countries even more distant, where the ancestor of the Mammals hid its little marsupials in the warm pocket of its belly The stranger is imitating the Kangaroo, as Daâh has imitated the Ape, and the result is the first cradle.

During the days that followed the birth of her child, the young mother gave evidence of a nervous overexcitement that rendered her intolerant of everything; she uttered shrill and brief cries, abusing the trees or the puddles, and chewed angrily, as if to avenge herself. Suddenly, she laughed. She was seen alternately cajoling her nursling, licking its face, warming it in her lap, and then, abruptly aggravated, beating it or even biting it. The victim's screams only served to exasperate that unhealthy tension, and the smallness of the body that she had in her hands seemed to frighten her; she squeezed it, threw it up in the air; her fingers clenched on its fragile ribs, and her eyes lit up with red gleams.

That crisis did not last long. Now, Ta tolerates the approaches of Hock without hostility, permitting her to touch her child, but it is necessary for the male not to risk approaching her too closely, and not to reach out toward her with his large hands; immediately, she growls a threat, and if he persists even slightly, she slaps him; inevitably, he retaliates—for Daâh has never received a blow without returning it—but he goes away.

Meanwhile, winter has come to an end as the months succeed one another; Hock's son and Ta's daughter are growing side by side; they learn to crawl, and their hands are soon detached from the ground, their knees disengaged from the mud; increasingly, the torsos straighten and the faces are raised; the down on their cheeks thickens and darkens; along the spine and the thorax, brown hairs are already designing shading on an excessively red epidermis, inflamed by the bites of innumerable insects—for the living clouds that swarm in that marshy atmosphere have recognized a predestined pasture in the infants; darts and probosces labor that tender skin; the little victims writhe in a voracious fog that sucks their juices and poisons them; a perpetual cry emerges from their open mouths:

"Hi! Hi!"

It is as if their skin is clad in scabs; the leather pockets that they inhabit, constantly drenched by the rain, are soaked with their warmth and populated by vermin; an acrid mist emanates.

"Hi! Hi!"

Finally, the two brats are able to stand almost upright, not as well as their father but already better than an Ape. They play around their mothers, crouched against a tree; their movements are less awkward, their intelligence is awakening; they open keen eyes; one might think that they, too, are gazing at the world, and trying to understand things.

The first thing that they divine is peril; heredity has instructed them in that regard; they have been fearful from birth. At any moment, their play ceases, a gesture is suspended, their mobile ears are orientated toward a sound; at the same time, the unquiet skin of their scalp quivers, from the brow-ridge to the sinciput, and their hair bristles, as if traversed by a breath.

If the danger becomes precise, they move rapidly, each one trotting toward their mother and scaling her, climbing her side like a pink crab, going to hide in her bosom. When the alert has passed, a little shiny eye shows amid the intermingled hairs of the mane and the bear-cub skin, watchfully...

Sometimes, the father deigns to watch that scene, and the family, spontaneously, is constituted around the others, before the man has even glimpsed the idea of paternity.

XXV. The Sinister Side

The examination of the cranial cavity reveals, in Daâh as in us, a notable development of the left hemisphere; since the nervous bundles cross over, one can affirm that the human being of those days, like us, was right-handed. With the right hand, the male accomplished valiant acts, carried his club, reached out toward obstacles and struck. The left was devoted to subsidiary roles: warding off blows, serving for support, moving branches aside, assistance—a servant.

The right side was that of strength, good for attack; the left was that of least resistance, only good for parades. The danger that comes from the right runs into armed energy; that which reveals itself to the left is more redoubtable, since enemy force is redoubled by our weakness. That is the side half-vanquished in advance, and whoever knows that is not sure of himself and becomes fearful. By comparison with the heroic and superb dexter, it is the poor, timid half; from the sinister, nothing surges forth but bad things, and evil things, if they emerge from that direction, become even worse.

Daâh has no need to think of these axioms to sense their verity: an animal apprehension proposes them to him and an intuitive prudence remembers them on his behalf. When he is going to fight, he tries to work his way around the adversary so as to have him to his right. In the same way, when he walks, he raises his left shoulder—which remains the higher among us—and shelters behind that shield, his torso slightly oblique. It is always to the right that he leans, if he is in the plenitude of his means and his self-confidence; if, on the contrary, he leans to the left when walking, and if, before an obstacle he decides to turn that way, that is an evident sign in him of momentary weakness and probably defeat.

Not only do those actions come to him without him deliberating, but he carries them out without even noticing that he has done so; the experimental dread of that which threatens him from the left is already manifest in him with the surety of an instinct, and he experiences it like an animal.

The custom of that latent anxiety and that spontaneous gesture penetrate him ever more deeply, taking up residence in the depths of his being, and future ages will recall its obsession; already found within it, entirely ready and duly fashioned, are the elements of a superstition that seems to be the oldest in the world.

Religions collect those memories of the original forest, and when fate come to designate the side from which sinister presages came, they naturally indicate the left-hand side; when prophets want to divide up souls and separate the good from the evil, they know without hesitation that the right is for the elect, the left for the reproved.

XXXVI. The Thinking Machine

If one could explain to Daâh what superstitions are, he would deny that he has any; in all probability, he would take offense, as a human being, if any were attributed to him; he would not hesitate to affirm that his items of information have the character of undeniable verities, attested by the facts.

The notions he possesses and the prudence he practices having been suggested to him by experience, the veracity of the former and the utility of the latter are proven. He never suspects the authenticity of what he observes; he does not establish any demarcation between the plausible and the implausible; he refrains from challenging the testimony of his senses, since he owes them everything; his subsistence, his security and his life only endure by their grace. Pragmatic as a matter of urgency, he makes use of what they bring him, and thus he is a philosopher without being aware of it, with an exclusively empirical method, the relative wisdom of which consists of not being astonished by anything, and admitting everything without hesitation.

Furthermore, hesitation would be forbidden to him; if he never sways between two actions, much less does he oscillate between two hypotheses, incapable as he is of simultaneously envisaging two ways of action or two ways of feeling. The one that presents itself to him first prevents any other from appearing; he does not judge between them; he decides first—or, rather, he acts, and his action informs him of his decision.

All his notions come to him thus, mechanically and almost unknown to him; every minute deposits a residue that he does not analyze, of which he is scarcely aware, but which exists. That perpetual accretion of life accumulates from day to day, agglomerates, creates a bed; then that bed gains in consistency, becomes solid, becomes a soil; the Tree of Knowledge is able to grow there, and to flower, and to bear its fruit: Daâh possesses a belief. One fine morning, he discovers it.

His convictions are, therefore, like a spontaneous manifestation within him, due to a phenomenon of parthenogenesis: his thinking machine, which he cannot yet direct, works of its own accord in the darkness of the unconscious, and offers its products; he receives them exactly as he receives the children of his women, by observing their existence. His appetite is not to understand, but to give himself the illusion of it, without delay. He knows, and what he knows is sufficient for him. He has faith.

The result is that, along the way, he accumulates the materials of his future mysticism, but for the time being, he only credits them with a purely experimental origin. If he fears the threat that comes from the left, it is because he has experienced its importance many times; if he believes in the existence of numerous Suns, it is because he has seen them, just as he has seen numerous Lions; if he believes in the reality of something impalpable that might already be called his soul, his life or his double, it is because he has seen it marching by his side...

XXXVII. The Shadow and the Image

Daâh's life is his shadow.

He sees it very rarely—too rarely for his liking. The apparition is all the more welcome for that. As soon as it is manifest, he is glad; he dances in front of it in order to give it more life, and it dances with him; he bends down to caress it, and it gathers itself to come to him; in order to chase away the clouds, of which it is afraid and which put it to flight, he howls at the sky and brandishes his club; then it is effaced, he does not know whether it has flown away like a Bird or whether it goes underground like a Mole. He sometimes believes one and sometimes the other, and is chagrined by it. To console himself, and also to reassure himself, he searches for the other double of his life, the one he can rediscover at will in streams, ponds and puddles: his image.

The Shadow and the Image: he knows that both of them are his and only his; he considers them to be faithful and devoted, and is certain that when they quit him, they do not go to someone else. He is sure of them; he has always known them; he cannot remember the time when he discovered their existence; it was a long time ago, because he was very small. At first, he did not know that they were himself, but he observed that each of the two phantoms reproduced his gestures exactly, and he understood that a mysterious affinity existed between them and him.

Mentally, he distinguished them from one another as *Daâh in the water* and *Daâh on the ground*, but he only has one name for both of them: *Daâh-ta*—which is to say, "the Daâh here," the Daâh by his side. Both of them are dear to him, he loves them more than anything else, more than his women, more than his body, for he has a kind of veneration for his doubles that he does not profess with regard to his own flesh.

His Shadow, in particular, is sacred. He does not try to discern whether is it the consequence of his life or its cause; he simply identifies himself with it; and, as he observes his life outside himself, being able to conceive of the abstract idea of it, he represents it to himself in that visible but ungraspable form, which can be touched, struck and broken, which is fragile and fugitive, which he has under his safeguard.

What repercussion might an assault on his double have on him? He knows what he would suffer from a claw or a tooth, but he does not know what would result from a wound sustained by his Shadow. He would interpose himself, in order to receive the blow that might strike it!

To protect it, his egotism is ever on the alert; if a Serpent traverses it, he senses the cold of its scales in the depths of his abdomen. If Hock or Ta steps on it by mistake, he hits them, and they approve. When he is about to fight and he sees his Shadow beside him, he has more confidence and is sure of victory. He takes care to place himself between it and the adversary in order to prevent it being trampled or struck. If his Shadow died, surely he would die, too! He knows that. He has seen it; the dead have no shadow. He has had proof of that, on a beautiful sunlit day that he will never forget.

It was morning, and Daâh was on the edge of the cliff. A gust of wind blew the clouds away and the sky was briefly radiant. Rejoicing in the Sun and glad to see his double, the man was playing with it when, all of a sudden, a Bear emerged from a cave and headed toward him.

The enormous brute, standing up against the sun, advanced with its paws extended, and its giant Shadow arrived with it. Driven back to the edge of the gulf, Daâh watched them come. He had never felt that he was in such great peril.

However, he killed the Bear, and when the beast was on the ground, he saw to his amazement that it no longer had its Shadow. As he approached the cadaver, however, he discovered it, but so small and so meager that he could measure it merely with the width of his foot.

Before that spectacle, he thought with all his might. Gradually, a certainty came to him, and a ruse of battle, too...

As he saw his idea more clearly, he swayed his head like the bear, in order to approve of it. Suddenly, he laughed. He had decided. Already he was preparing to step over the monster, but for fear that the dead creature might seize his double in passing, he prudently went around it.

Slyly, he headed for the cave, making sure that his Shadow was going with him. In front of the entrance he turned round, went forward and back, seeking the best place for the Shadow to go in first—but no place was the best; the Shadow refused to go in, doubtless afraid. It escaped, sliding over the wall of rock.

Daâh got down on all fours and the Shadow went in beneath him. While he inspected the cave, the downpour began again, and Daâh came out alone. Hastily, he rolled a huge boulder into the gap, which he loaded with less weighty stones; he blocked up the openings with pebbles. In front of that wall he piled up a heap of brushwood; then he admired his work, and returned, without the Shadow, to the Bear, which no longer had a Shadow.

With a cheerful voice he summoned his women to share the meat; they came running and opened up the beast. When they plunged their arms into the warm breast and tore away strips of muscle in order to stuff them gluttonously into their mouths, the hunter let them do it without claiming his share. Suddenly, impetuous laughter burst forth above them. Raising their blood-splashed faces toward the master, they thought that he was proud of his victory, but he was no longer thinking about the Bear. He was thinking:

Daâh has hidden his life in a safe place; no one will any longer be able to kill Daâh. Daâh, the invulnerable, will always be the victor...

Weeks passed; then, at the first ray of sunlight he saw his Shadow beside him again.

"Heûh!"

Had it escaped, then? Did it not want Daâh to be invulnerable? Daâh had ceased to be immortal. Someone, someday, would kill him, and no prudence could prevent that day from coming!

In his anguish, he felt something like a dolorous beast twisting under his skull; it was trying to get out; by means of an urgent contention of all his might, he helped it—and a thought nearly emerged from the man.

Confusedly, for a second, he glimpsed that a fatality weighed upon all beings: to die, and to struggle for life until one died in the struggle.

XXXVIII. The Fear of the Void

To die? What idea of nothingness could Daâh have? No instinct, no ancestral experience, informs him of it; among the cells that compose him, none remembers its death; in the innumerable host of beings of which he is the issue, all have marched toward death but not a single part of him has entered into death before giving him life; his flesh cannot recall anything and his mind cannot conceive anything.

It is, however, the second time that an evocation of death has traversed the Human mind. Already it has revealed itself to him one morning, under the aspect of Hock half-lost in a mist; today it has gained a more precise, more troubling quality: *Not to feel the teeth that will devour me...*

That almost savant conception has surged forth and disappeared so rapidly that he has scarcely glimpsed it, and has retained nothing of it. But between that minute and the preceding one, fugitive as they might have been, an impression will remain within him, and it will be combined with all those that he has inherited from his race: anguish has become human; in the animal fear that a beast has before dying, intelligence has mingled and nothingness is beginning to become a mystery.

Daâh is prepared to conceive of the void. He has a fear of gulfs; the phobia of the hole is inherent within him; he has that from his most distant ancestors, for it goes back to the earliest ages when the first life forms were struggling against the chaos of the planet.

He remembers that: on the edge of a precipice above running water, vertigo makes him dizzy and he trembles like a child; one might think that his soul were fleeing through the holes of his pupils and going to drown in space; his empty head pivots slowly on his neck, his gaze seeks around him for some obstacle on which to rest and from which to draw support; the asperities reassure him; he suspends his eyes therefrom.

On the edge of a vast and excessively bare plain he suffers an analogous malaise; as closely as he can, he moves along the edge of the forest, after the fashion of our dogs, which hug the walls of a square; when circumstances oblige him to risk himself in the middle of those amplitudes, he beats his breast in order to give himself courage, and he only goes forward crawling, his head down, his eyes on the ground, not so much to hide himself as to forget the formidable space.

His body has a fear of the void, by virtue of heredity; he will instruct his soul with the same fear.

XXXIX. The Voice of the World

"Brouhouhou..."

That is Daâh amusing himself while marching, by imitating the gross voice of the thunder.

Once again, the man and his women have emerged onto the edge of the cliff; they can see the endless file-past of the cumulus and nimbus clouds that pursue one another behind the striated curtain of the rain. Sometimes, a patch of blue appears, a sunbeam trickles through, a sun sparkles, ephemeral and furtive, between the backs and bellies of the clouds, suddenly bleached, only to become black, brown and green-tinted again immediately; they growl as they go by, with a frightful voice; they threaten one another, they beat one another, and in order to kill one another they have a weapon that shines so forcefully! They are malevolent; they detest everything that is large. Daâh has seen them strike in passing a rock that rises toward them or an oak that surpassed all the others, and which they struck down with a bolt of their ardent club.

Daâh does not fear them overmuch, because he is small, and they will scarcely be able to discover him beneath the forest, but he prefers not to risk exposing himself to their sight when they are angry, and his women are even more afraid of them than he is. They throw themselves flat on the ground in order to make themselves even less visible, and quickly close their eyes when the club-of-light penetrates the underwood and strikes with a din that makes the earth tremble, the tree-trunks whimper and the mountains and their ravines bark.

"Brouhouhou...! Hôh!"

When the battle of the clouds becomes too furious, Daâh only imitates them discreetly; he is slightly fearful of exciting them against him, but in spite of everything, he feels a need to be proud and to affirm it; in order to prove that he is brave, and to prove it to his women, he rumbles a timid thunder in the depths of his throat, respectfully, and yet provocatively.

125

"Brouhou..."

Hock and Ta do not like that imprudent game; in order to make the male shut up, the nearer one taps him; he immediately ripostes with a slap, and immediately recommences more loudly:

"Hôhôh! Hôh... Brouh..."

Then his thunder dies away; Daâh's throat practices the nuances:

"Brou.... Hou..."

For his favorite game is to imitate all the clamors of the forest: the cries, the calls, the threats, the plaints, the growls of anger, the stridor of fears, the gasps of agony, the hoots of the wind and the hiss of the rain. To the tumult of furious or terrified life, every animal brings its voice; he, Daâh, has them all; at least, he wants them all. He has stored sounds along with images, and, just as he applies himself to miming what he has seen, he tries to repeat, with the instrument that he possesses, the vibrations of space.

In that parody of sounds, he finds even more pleasure than that of his gestures; it is more numerous and more various, and it satisfies not only his need to imitate the world but also a singular taste that he has for translating his emotions phonetically. As soon as he ceases temporarily to chew and his mouth is empty, he howls, yaps, sings, bays, bellows, whistles, mewls. The notes, generally baritone, are nevertheless modulated; they rise and fall, scraping the walls of his cheeks; they rasp the enormous vault of the palate and collide with the long teeth; his uvula quivers; his tongue dances in the red cavern, softening the air that passes through it. By means of that gymnastics he makes the organ more supple, without being aware of it, while enjoying himself.

His large mouth, his profound palate and his broad throat give him a powerful, sonorous and raucous voice, in which the As and Os snore and the diphthongs are rounded out, with the support of the Rs that rumble or the Hs that hiss. Vowels are accentuated, monosyllables become more pronounced; the animals earn their names, which are parodies of their cries: the

Dog is called Ouah; the Bison Meûh; the Bear Rêh; the Thunder Brouhou...

Speech germinates, the floating images are able to hook onto words, and, fixed henceforth, the images become ideas.

XL. The Blade

One day, he witnessed the superb spectacle of a combat between the Tiger and the Elephant; his heart beat forcefully and he expressed wishes on behalf of the eater of grass; he saw the feline crouch down as it circled the colossus, which pivoted to confront it; three times the pachyderm had the fangs in its throat; then, suddenly, Daâh perceived that the Tiger, pierced through in the middle of its belly, was hanging from the ivory branch like a huge fruit. He admired that greatly and was very satisfied, to such an extent that, in order to testify to his joy, he danced in imitation of the thrust of the head that had skewered a Tiger.

With a shake of its head, the Elephant got rid of the feline, which was gasping; then it set about trampling it with its voluminous feet, and then it went away. The man saw that tranquil back drawing away through the long grass, and the big Cat that was no longer moving. Opportunities to taste that kind of game were rare; he wanted to have his share. He went down onto the battleground. His women ran behind him.

The wild beast was butchered; the ribs were broken; everyone had their own and when the man was drunk on flesh, he started to stamp his feet in the bloody mud, on the very site of the duel. He parodied its phases, alternately playing the part of the Tiger crawling and bounding, and the Elephant chasing it with its head.

For the sake of more resemblance he picked up two fragments of rib stripped of flesh and, holding them in the corners of his mouth with his fists, he became the trumpeting victor. He ran at the women, who ran away, laughing, and pricked them in the lower back. He fell upon a cork-oak and sank the tip of the bone into the bark.

"Haâh! Han!"

Then, weary of bending his back and extending his head, he straightened up; a simulacrum of the battle was beginning to be no longer sufficient for him; he was overtaken by fury, he grabbed hold of one of the fragments of rib by the blunt end and violently, with all the strength of his arm, he stabbed the cork-oak with such a rude thrust of the point that the blade remained planted in the tree.

"Heuh!"

He had just invented the dagger, the sword, the blade— and, streaming with sweat, his eyes rounded in surprise, he contemplated that masterpiece.

XLI. The Pick and the Pike

He made use of his new weapon, initially against a Marmot that he transpierced in its burrow; the beast emerged
skewered; hilarious and triumphant, he displayed it at arm's
length; the women danced in admiration, and the jerks of their
leaps made their breasts bounce.

Another day, he saw a Wild Boar digging the ground
with its tusks at the foot of an oak and immediately began employing his bone to unearth tubers and roots; the pick was announced.

He made so much use of the rib that it snapped in two; at
first bewildered, then indignant at that abrupt decision no
longer to serve him, he insulted the thing, trampled it underfoot and forgot about it.

To replace it, he seized his club and made it into a lever;
and the club broke in the ground in its turn. The big baby was
already getting ready to punish it when he noticed the oblique
break and the sharp point that the piece of wood had acquired;
he understood that the weapon wanted to imitate the bone, as
Daâh imitated the beasts; that aptitude for parody and the intention to serve him did not astonish him in the least in his
faithful friend; in order to congratulate it for that he caressed it
as he did after a battle.

While his heavy palm was passing over the wood, he
perceived the broken end; he growled at it, and in order to
prove to it that he did not regret it he came to it with a severe
expression, his eyes charged with criticism, and leaned over it.
Point by point, he put the old weapon and the new weapon in
contact, as one brings two rivals into confrontation in order to
excite them against one another. For he already had a propensity in his puerile soul for solemn gestures, and his habit of
thinking in images rendered him an inclination toward symbols; very confusedly, the idea was in him of a rite that he was
performing; he was officiating, and he almost had the sensa-

tion, if not the sentiment, of accomplishing an act of magic. At least, he had that to a much greater extent than the intelligent notion of progress, and, at that moment, he scarcely suspected that he had just enlarged the domain of his strength and simultaneously acquired the stake, the pike and the spear...

He learned that a few weeks later, and truly, it was a very considerable day, being the one on which he killed the second Bear.

Backed up against a rock and incapable of fleeing, he thought that he was doomed, but before the invincible paws were able to seize him, he sank his stake into the monster's belly, as the Elephant had done.

"Haâh!"

Leaving the weapon in the wound, he skipped sideways with a bound; then, slowly, he moved to the left, step by step, facing the adversary with his back to the rock. The Bear was no longer paying any heed to him; uniquely occupied with the unknown enemy that had just entered into its flesh, the giant of the caves lowered its nose toward its wound, from which a flood of blood was escaping, and tried with impotent gesticulations to tear out the death that was plunged into it.

"Haâh! Heûh!"

The victor, henceforth out of range and almost offended that he was being excessively neglected, struck his breast to show off the author of the blow and claim his glory.

The Bear understood and came after him, but the tree hanging down from his belly stopped him in his tracks, and Daâh, who jumped for joy while miming the comical gestures of the wounded animal, was eventually obliged to stop, his hands splayed over his belly, so much was he laughing, from safety, at watching death work at a distance, of its own accord, on behalf of a Human Being.

XLII. The First Stone

A great racket amid the branches! Above the human family, the dome of foliage agitates, shaken by an interior tempest, and shrill howls spring forth.

Daâh has unleashed that hurricane of wrath. Having perceived a Macaque in a walnut tree suckling its young, and seeing that it was inconvenienced by its burden, he had decided to pursue it. Having succeeded in catching up with it, he snatched its baby away, breaking its back over his thigh with a twist of his wrists. With the prey in his teeth he descended to the ground again. At the foot of the tree he tore the animal apart, ripped the skin, dislocated the limbs, and bit into the teaming flesh. The mother, who had followed him, leapt from branch to branch above him, abusing him with piercing cries; in response to her voice, a band of Monkeys had gathered to form a chorus; nuts were raining down on Daâh, but he took no notice; he was chewing.

Hock and Ta, crouching a few paces away from him, are watching him eat, waiting for him to deign to grant them a bone or a fragment of lung. To pass the time, they pick up the nuts that the furious Macaques are throwing and tranquilly extract the fruits from their shells, which they break between two stones. But their impatience to bite in their turn into the good meat that they can see bleeding, and the strident racket that is going on over their heads are beginning to make them nervous; the rain of projectiles is inconveniencing them. They respond to the clamors of the Monkeys with similar vociferations, and to the hurled nuts with nuts that they also attempt to hurl. The anger in the trees turns against them, and a battle is engaged.

They figure in it without honor; they do not have the skill of their adversaries, which they require. They succeed well enough in parodying the swing of the arm folded over the shoulder, but they do not open their hands at the opportune movement, with the result that the projectiles sometimes crash down at their feet and sometimes go straight up in the air to fall on their backs.

Daâh, who is still chewing, observes the combat and the incapacity of the females; he is scornful of them. Surely he can do better! He does not stop at thinking it; the temptation to demonstrate his superiority once again and to offer a model, labors his mind. He forgets to savor the warm and tender meat whose juices are in his mouth.

Eventually, he can no longer resist. He stretches out his arm, and with his vast hand he picks up a nut from the ground, with a fistful of mud and grass, which he kneads; the paste oozes through his fingers. With all his strength he hurls that magma at a Macaque, and Ta utters a cry of pain, because the vigorous object has struck her in the temple.

Daâh is satisfied. That is how to throw! The women will know better from now on, thanks to him. However, he is only half-proud, because his vanity obliges him to be; he knows full well that he had no intention of wounding Ta. She is, however, bleeding, and that is a fact; he has obtained that result by means of the new procedure, and that is also a fact that merits being recorded. He records it. If he has struck her without meaning to, it was simply his will that was missing; on the next occasion, he will only have to do it deliberately.

He does precisely that, picking up a gnawed femur and throwing it, aiming at the woman.

The bone falls into a puddle half way to its target. The Monkeys do better than that, and the Human cannot account for it, but he cannot admit that anyone can do better than him; his disappointment turns to anger. He leaps to his feet, and quickly picks up nuts with both hands, furiously. Perhaps to help him to do as well as the Macaques, he imitates their whining and their grimaces. Now he is pummeling his women, albeit at point-blank range.

They retaliate; on either side, everyone grabs whatever they encounter in order to hurl it in the face; for want of fruits they pick up stones.

The game becomes crazy, blood flows, bumps bulge; the women flee, and the quadrumanes in the tree watch, stupefied. Abruptly, they fall silent, and immobilize themselves at the same time; their eyes wide, they lean through the foliage to admire beneath them the human family whose members have invented ballistics while enjoying aping the Apes.

XLIII. The-One-Who-Sees-a-Long-Way

The hunter only improved slowly in that simian art. His boasting was the reason for that; he wanted to do better than the Macaques right away, and that presumption slowed his progress. Because he was taller and stronger than his teacher, he thought that he ought to apply himself to blocks of stone that the latter could not move; and since, on the other hand, he possessed two hands, the thought it appropriate to use them both to launch larger stones. In spite of these mistakes, the opportunity to learn what a valuable weapon he had just acquired was not long delayed.

Dusk had surprised him on a rocky plateau; there was not a tree in sight in which to seek refuge for the night, only meager brushwood here and there trapped between the stones: no shelter. A few rocky outcrops jutted from the desert; Daâh chose the highest and steepest; for want of any protection against the wind and rain that had polished the granite ridges, or the lightning that had scored the summit, they would at least find security there against prowlers.

The ascent was difficult, especially for the mothers, because of the children, but finally, the group established themselves as best they could on a bed of pebbles.

The odor of humans, however, attracted Wolves in the middle of the night; their pack came to howl beneath the fortress; in bright intervals they could be seen circling it and attempting to scale it, but they slid down its smooth walls. From the height of their terrace, Daâh and the two women pelted the most audacious, pounding skulls and spines with boulders. Howls of pain rose up from the blue shadow; the man replied to them with his war cry. All those agonized voices encouraged him to murder; the odor of blood intoxicated his strength. He lifted blocks of stone in both hands which he raised above his head, and cheerfully sent death into the mob of wild beasts.

"Han!"

The battle lasted until morning; in the light of dawn the Wolves gave up and fled. The daylight rose on a carnage of crushed beasts. The man admired his work; never had he killed so many.

"Haâh!"

The spectacle of such success has immediately dispelled his fatigue. He stands up, and while the weary mothers crouch at his feet with their nurslings he contemplates the rout of the running Wolves; their brown patches diminish in the distance as they plunge into the rain and disappear. In order to affirm their defeat more fully, Daâh launches another stone; then he extends his large callused hand toward the plateau; with the great circle that his outstretched arm designs in the air, he indicates the void that he has been able to create around him, and his burst of vibrant laughter trumpets his victory.

He believes that he has only dispersed the Wolves; he does not suspect that he has just executed the first gesture of history, and that, with his extended hand, he has taken possession of the world on behalf of centuries to come. Standing beneath the stormy sky, with the mothers at his feet, Daâh the vanquisher is symbolic, and on his granite pedestal, the group displays a statue of triumphant humankind.

For it really was a solemn day, the one on which the first hand hurled the first stone! All the genius of future times is in the power of that action; the world is conquered in advance. From that new discovery, the perfectible bimane will draw consequences that the quadrumane will never see; no species, except for his own, will conceive the latent possibilities of that gesture: striking at a distance.

The Ape had been able to throw its stone before him, without that projection being a peril for the world. Things would be different from now on, because Humans have brains. With them, Nature has introduced a new faculty into the world: henceforth, the world possesses an imaginative beast who dreams, and whose dreams amplify action; now that the animal in question knows the power of acting outside himself, they will dream incessantly of means of enlarging the limits of their reach, endlessly.

Humans have found their way, their role and their destiny. They have appeared on the planet to represent The-One-Who-Sees-a-Long-Way: the one who will propagate beyond himself and will extend himself beyond his reach. They are the life that exalts itself, and will be the presumptuous animal—the only one.

Think beyond. Believe beyond.

In that prideful injunction the secret of human strength resides, in its entirety; in that hopeful injunction, so rich in aspirations, a race has gained its motto:

Always beyond!

The thinking being that has once shown itself to be capable of acting at a distance will not stop, and will look forward, ever further. Not only will humans soon invent the sling and the arrow, the string held taught by the bow, the spring that extends and unwinds the projectile, and the compressed gas that explodes, but they will project their thoughts even further than their missiles.

By means of mind, even more than matter, they will project themselves into the distance, and two prodigious forces will spring forth therefrom: Faith and Science, both of which have a common origin, the idea of action at a distance, and both of which have an identical goal: to go further, and always beyond. With a parallel thrust, the centuries of mystical ecstasy and the ages of scientific effort will aspire toward the beyond; by prayer and calculation they will scale the sky.

In their overweening desire to abolish distance and subjugate duration, Humans will march over the seas and over the clouds; they will send their voices from one continent to another, and across time, all the way to death; to encompass the inaccessible they will provide themselves with wings; to lodge themselves in the invisible, they will invent gods fashioned in their own resemblance, which will populate the empyrean with mages of themselves and the passions of their hearts. They will fill the azure with concern for their destiny.

137

Parading their dreams and their sway over the universe, they will be able, by turns to reach with their hands the divinities that they implore and the suns that they weigh. They are the One who has come to attempt infinity, and wishes, mortal in body, to be immortal in soul.

Beyond, always beyond, since the marvelous and symbolic moment when a first stone was projected into the distance by a hand: which, from that moment on, was a human hand.

XLIV. The Inaccessible

As was his custom, Daâh was whirling his club, when it escaped from his fingers. He saw it fly away, cut an ample curve through the air, slashing leaves and breaking branches, and fall into the mud, which it splashed all around it. He stood there in surprise, being perfectly sure that he had not thrown it; that act of independence seemed to him to be displeasing; when he picked up the club, he rebuked it with a growl. Not long thereafter, however, he renewed the experience of loosening his fingers while the club was whirling; the latter flew more fervently, and he became irritated for a second time. At the following attempt, he recorded the fact; he adopted it.

From then on, the flight of his club ceased to appear to him as a gesture of insubordination and became, on the contrary, a product of his will; as such, it pleased him. Immediately, he constituted a game, and as the game was new, there was nothing he enjoyed more.

That primitive human, who bore within him the host of future humans, was a crowd in himself, and he had a soul subject to crazes. He undertook ventures with passion, and without measure, doing everything with violence, taking delight in repeating an action on the condition of doing so with stubborn frenzy, incapable of perseverance unless it became a mania. As he had done before in making his club whirl, he delighted in seeing it carve broad parabolas through the air. He had no pretention to be doing something useful; he was amusing himself. In admiring the flight of the object emanating from him, he thought: *Bird-Stick!*—and the spectacle of such an anomaly could not have been more interesting. As soon as the free space of a clearing opened up before him, he took advantage of it to launch his cudgel into flight, and shouted to the women:

"Ta! Ta!"

By extending his arms upwards he showed them the piece of wood beating its wings and going a long way because Daâh wanted it to do so. They laughed with him. The longer the trajectory was, the prouder the male was of it.

"Haâh!"

When the weapon inflicted damage, that was a triumph. It also happened that it flushed out animals, and the hunter concluded that they had recognized Daâh's club and were running away. That incident, which was repeated, suggested the idea of aiming at a prey. Such attempts did not have any result for a long time; the human, by applying himself to it excessively, lost all his means and invariably missed the target.

However, informed by his wrist almost as much as by his brain, he began to glimpse that the distance traveled was proportional to the thrust imparted; he regulated his practice. As with a pebble, he was able to hit the object at which he aimed when it was large: a rock, a tree trunk or one of his women; but he refrained from trying it on a large prey, for fear of being without a club when battle was joined.

One day, he brought down a turtle dove.

That was one of the most violent gaieties of his career. When he saw the bird tumbling from branch to branch, he stood there mouth agape; the stupor of his visage expressed how unexpected that practical result was. He ran forward. With both hands he picked up the palpitating, fearful creature with little shining eyes. He devoured it with his gaze, but did not even think about eating it, as delightedly, he felt it struggling in that prison of human hands; he experienced an intoxication in which natural cruelty played no part. Those warm and living feathers, held for the first time, caused him a delirium; his emotion was so strong that he seemed to be going through a crisis of dementia, and he gave all the signs of it in his tremulous gestures, his contracted features and his shining eyes.

But was not that gleam of folly in the depths of his orbits, on the contrary, a flash of divination? Was not that flame in his pupils, perhaps, a dawn of reason striving to disengage itself from the darkness? In an event so novel, did Daâh not perceive the announcement of future conquests? The human was on the brink of understanding. At the very least, he sensed at that moment that there were things to admire that were too far out of reach.

Furtively, he had the notion of a formidable victory: he had caught the inaccessible! That warmth in the hollow of his palms was the sky conquered, space taken hostage, the air captured!

"Haâh!"

To make that strange joy last, to savor the impotent effort of the vanquished for longer, he refrained from tightening his grip around the fragile thorax—but his fingers clenched involuntarily; the turtle dove, as it cracked, closed its mauve eyelids. Then Daâh grabbed the bird by the foot and, raising it above his head, he danced frenziedly. Never, since the death of the Bear, had he testified to so much pride. Hock and Ta were astonished by such extravagant behavior to celebrate the capture of such small game.

The hunter did not consent to give anyone else the slightest morsel of his prey; he ate it on his own. Stuck to his bloody lips, a glory of plumes and down framed the hole of his mouth. When he had finished chewing, he planted the wings in his hair and resumed trundling along, waving his arms in the air, his face turned toward the sky, at which he launched clamors of provocation with all his might.

PART TWO: THE HORDE

XLV. The Offspring

Every year, Hock and Ta brought a child into the world. The first daughter issued from Ta, having been conceived of the man with the vertical forehead, resembled her father; several sons, among those she had of the man with the oblique forehead, resembled their older sister. But Daâh did not perceive any diversity among these products, and experienced an equal indifference for all of that progeniture, to which he believed himself to be unconnected.

He had ended up becoming accustomed to seeing the two women, in turn, produce a little human; when the event became manifest once again, he recorded it, like every other incident in his life, and immediately lost interest, since the mothers were decidedly opposed to their fruit being eaten.

All the ideas that Daâh had not realized immediately escaped him as water escapes from a sieve; on the other hand, the same thoughts came back to him in identical circumstances; every time one of the women gave birth in a time of famine, the temptations gripped him again to utilize the fresh flesh that arrived in such a timely fashion; his gesture inevitably provoked the same revolt and battle; he had then to defend himself against the two mothers, who each sided with the other. That struggle was sufficient to make him forget the initial cause of the dispute, and more often than not, the play of hands that was produced, not without anger but without hatred, terminated with a coupling, after which the ogre went away tranquilly to search for food elsewhere.

Nevertheless, the mothers distrusted him, and for several days thereafter they kept watch on the man, for fear that the desire to eat the child might recur. After a week had passed, they had nothing more to fear; habit had taken hold and the new-born was part of the horde, by the same entitlement as the others. Daâh protected them if necessary, not out of tenderness, but by imitation of that which he had seen done.

The great care that the women took of their children scarcely lasted beyond ten months, until another one arrived; they did not consent to breast-feed two at once for very long, and rudely pushed away the one that persisted in demanding the breast when its place had been taken. Neither tears nor pleas moved them, and, on the contrary, irritated them. They took pleasure in watching the contortions of those soft creatures, palpating their thin limbs, and exciting laughter on those round, scarcely hairy faces; suddenly, however, the game ceased to please them; they plunged the nursling into the sack and no longer gave it a thought.

They had very soon had the idea of throwing that pocket, which they had initially carried over the chest, onto the back. Their gestures gained more ease, and the burden seemed less heavy. That progress was virtually imposed on the day when a younger sibling followed its elder too closely, when the latter was not yet steady on its legs; it was necessary to lodge both of them in the same bag; the inconvenience that followed suggested the means of remedying it, and the Kangaroo's pocket became the Woman's backpack.

Usually, the two creatures lay in it together. At halts, it was unloaded by emptying it onto the moss, or it was suspended from a low branch. As soon as a child became capable of walking, it was allowed to run its risks; if, however, it got too far behind or wandered too far away, one of the mothers recalled it, whether or not it was her own, with the same protective instinct. That female solicitude, intermittent and often distracted, was exercised without distinction on all the little ones, as if their maternity were collective. Along the march, the same cry of appeal was heard in one voice or the other, monotonous and almost mechanical, reiterated in order to soften it:

"Ta, ta... Ta-ta..."

All the infants were called Tata.

Their father contemplated that increasing brood with a kind of pride, which, unable to be that of an author, was nevertheless that of a master. The sentiment of his importance was amplified by the number of beings that lived under his guard. He continued to march at the head of them all, as if he had claimed the honor of being the first to confront peril. When one of his sons, already growing up, dared to stray in front of him, he took umbrage and frowned; a tap of the club on his back invited the imprudent youngster to resume his place.

"Ta!"

The two mothers marched immediately behind the Chief; they had the right to do so, since they were accustomed to it; the rest swarmed in the rear, at hazard. When the daughters gave birth in their turn, their children followed them as they had followed their mothers. Thus the horde classified itself spontaneously by height; a kind of hierarchy was established, by affinities, between the three generations—and Daâh, who was then scarcely thirty years old, found himself, without being aware of it, simultaneously the grandfather and the father of that ample family.

XLVI. Multiply

The horde became considerable.

Although, among the mammals, females are ordinarily less numerous than males, they figured here in the greater number; perhaps that was one of the phenomena by which nature, as a consequence of logic, seems to manifest a consciousness of its work, with a determination to do it usefully: the nascent race had need of molds in order to multiply, and the molds arrived. As soon as the daughters reached their twelfth or thirteenth year, they began to give birth; no one was any more astonished by that than by seeing leaves appear on branches. Hock and Ta were not yet twenty-eight years old when they were already grandmothers; at forty, Daâh found himself a great-grandfather.

If all those creatures had lived, the family would soon have been formidable; indeed, among the twenty-five children that Daâh had of his two women in thirteen years, eleven of whom were boys, the fourteen girls, in a further thirteen years, could have brought a hundred offspring into the world, since they would not have failed to give birth once a year, like their mothers, who would have continued to produce in the interim. By the third generation, the Chief, still valid, would have grouped around him more than a thousand human heads.

There were scarcely thirty.

The majority had died; others had been lost on the way. A few had even quit the group voluntarily, in order to venture forth alone; the latter, fortunately rare, were always males. The daughters, with a more alert sense of their weakness, and less pride, understood the dangers of isolation more fully; independence did not tempt them. The adolescent males, by contrast, irritable and believing themselves to be strong, were at the mercy of abrupt determinations: a fit of anger, a dispute, a discontentment, even a simple whim or an accident on the way was sufficient for them to decide to leave; their impulsive

146

reflex prevented them from examining any of the reasons that ought to have retained them.

In any case, those defections passed unnoticed; not knowing how to count, they were ignorant of their number, and they only appreciated it in terms of the density of the group. When disappearances had been numerous, someone, after a time and by chance, darting a glance around during a halt, remarked vaguely that the mass had gaps, and that observation lasted exactly as long as the glance; it did not involve any sadness or anxiety, and no other concern with regard to the disappeared than for the interest of the horde, whose force had diminished.

The matter only became troubling in tragic circumstances. When a Hyena or a Wolf carried off an infant, when a Lion or a Bear took possession of a woman or a man, a great cry rose up, propagated from mouth to mouth.

"Heûh!"

Everyone understood, dispersing instantaneously in all directions, backs fleeing under the thickets, climbing trees, and anxious heads hanging down from the branches; by a reversibility of egotism, each one sensed that misfortune, because each one might have been the victim of it, and the little frisson of death ran from the nape of the neck to the loins.

For they know pertinently, like Daâh, that the peril of being devoured is the condition of every living creature; everyone is conscious of being, in the forest, a meal defending itself temporarily, a nutritious and coveted fragment of flesh; there is no other destiny than to fall, sooner or later, into the teeth of something stronger.

Death, therefore, is only constituted by the definitive accident of being ingurgitated by another; the sick and the debilitated are simply prey of less resilience, which were designated thereby for imminent sacrifice. Natural death does not exist; violent death is the only kind that anyone knows. The purely nominal distinction that we make between the two is prohibited, and rightly so, since violent death is no less natural than the other, and since it is, in this epoch, the only necessary one that there is in nature.

Everyone ends up in the tomb of a stomach. Everyone knows that, and no one is indignant about it.

XLVII. Comestible Death

Toward the middle of winter, the horde suddenly emerged on to a bare plateau. The vast plain extended, limited at the horizon by a dark blue line that indicated the recommencement of forests; in the interval, a short vegetation undulated in the colder wind; the keener air pricked the nostrils. The Chief stopped. Dazzled by a light no longer filtered by the vault of branches, and troubled by the horror of open space, he hesitated.

He opened his large hand above his eyes in order to examine the distance; a long way away, patches the color of chestnuts were moving placidly over the slope of a hill; he recognized Horses. His heart beat with joy and his mouth filled with water, for he had the winter hunger, having not killed anything for days; the Horse was a succulent but rapid prey, which hardly ever allowed one to get close, which could hear all sounds, and could scent the hunter...

Perhaps, though, if he crept through the grass, Daâh could hide long enough to reach the prey? A blow of the club would break a leg...

"Ta!"

With his finger, he traced a great circle in the air behind him: a gesture signifying an order to stay still, to gather the children together and hide in the undergrowth. Then he struck his chest and pointed at the herd.

"Mâh!"

By means of that new sign he expressed his desire to depart alone on the conquest of that nourishment. At the same moment, however, his joyful face became plaintive and irritated. An alert had just been produced in the equine band. One of them had leapt up.

All together, the brown patches took off at a run, gathering in a compact group, flank to flank, and, as if carrying one

149

another, the galloping solipeds flew through the grass that came up to their withers.

Now, that unique patch was growing from one moment to the next; instead of drawing away, it was coming closer. It was, therefore, not Daâh that the Horses feared. Another danger was driving the herd from behind, and it was bringing that danger with it. A Lion? A Tiger? From the hunter that he had been a moment before, the Human became prey.

"Heûh!"

Daâh uttered that alarm call and cocked an ear. The flight of the herd, having gone around a hillock, was directed straight toward him. Almost immediately, barking rang out.

Dogs! More terrible than the Lion because of their number, and irresistible because they fought as a pack, the courageous and voracious Dogs, inventors of armies, enemies of Humans and Bears, did not hesitate before anyone. They would cling on without distinction to the bellies of Bison or Tigers, and, when they did likewise to the great Deer of the peat-bogs, with its great horns, they made it resemble a tree laden with monstrous clusters of fruits!

"Ouah, ouah! Heûh!"

The terrified horde disperses toward the forest; the infants cry; rosy bodies worm their way through the red-tinted grass; trees are climbed.

The Horses draw nearer. The rhythmic impact of their hooves makes the soft soil rumble—but the barking bursts forth more forcefully, much closer.

Daâh brings up the rear, and does not deign to duck down as he walks; he knows that a Dog has no need to see its prey to know where it is and track it. He makes haste, however, and looks around.

He sees a Horse pass by that is in the lead; the herd follows; the ground trembles; in the place where Daâh was standing a little while ago there is a russet undulation of spines, extended necks and oblong heads, rushing like a muddy torrent under its foam of manes. A brief interval, and the Dogs emerge; erect tails stripe the landscape and volleys of barking rip through the air.

The bulk of the pack has passed by, but the laggards have caught the scent of the human and abandoned the pursuit of the Horses; noses down, they run toward the edge of the forest where the family has sought refuge. A child is howling at the foot of an oak.

Daâh extends his left arm toward the Dogs; they are less numerous than the fingers of his hand; it is possible to fight. The human prey becomes the hunter again; he launches himself forward. When he reaches the foot of the tree, one of the canines already has its fangs in the child's throat; another has seized its groin, the third has grabbed an ankle, and all three are growling, pulling in three directions, tails stiff and mouths streaming with blood.

Twice the club has whirled; one of the Dogs runs away, limping, but two others have rolled in the mud. The battle is won, since the horde will eat.

Human groups fall from the trees and run forward. Next to the little cadaver, the wounded Dogs are still moving; they are finished off by hammering their skulls with lumps of stone.

"Ouah! Ouah!"

But they are too hungry, today, to dance for long; they have been fasting for too many days. Two Ouah-ouahs for so many hungry mouths is very few; the Ouah-ouahs of winter are meager.

Everyone crowds around; they are opened up, frantic hands tear away the red strips; whoever is not the most agile risks having nothing.

However, the Chief is not there to take out the first share, as he is accustomed to do...

Daâh is, in fact, some distance away. Since the mothers have always refused to let him kill their offspring, even when food is in short supply, and since, this time, the Dogs have taken charge of that task, he has finally found an opportunity to realize his curious desire.

Squatting all alone against the trunk of a beech tree, Daâh is calmly eating his grandson.

XLVIII. The Climber Who Walks

By the mere fact of living in a group, the new generations are already indicating tastes and practicing customs that no longer resemble Daâh's, and which sometimes astonish him. While the Chief, in spite of the crowd that escorts him, remains fundamentally solitary, as in the time of his youth, and maintains his inveterate mannerisms of a beast of prey, the children he draws in his wake testify to a marked inclination for all forms of assembly; with the exception of the rare deserters driven away by an impulse, the members of the horde do not stray far from the others. During the march they advance in small groups; at every moment, the laggards run to rejoin the main body; at the halts they hasten to come together, and when dusk comes, they jostle at the foot of a trunk, because they all want to climb the same tree.

When, by chance, they encounter a shelter under a rock into which they can pile, the sons and daughters precipitate themselves into it avidly, and lie down pell-mell, pushing, growling, nudging with their elbows and knees, insinuating themselves into the heap and squeezing together, hugging one another in order to go to sleep. Then, like a nest of woodlice, the heap gradually immobilizes, and in the moisture that bathes them, the faces take on an expression of bestial bliss...

When they are heaped up like that, their mutual contact, their common warmth, and also their door, procures for those beings an impression of security and confidence. One might think that they remembered having lived in troops long ago, and that ancient heredities are resuscitating within them; the promptitude and facility with which they adapt to mores unknown to their father seems to indicate that they are simply recuperating ancestral habits; in solitude, the wandering individual had forgotten those customs, but as soon as the group was reconstituted, the race recollected its past and hung onto it without hesitation.

Might it not be the case that the condition of the solitary animal has only been, for the precursors of the species, a transient state imposed by circumstance, which occurred between the age when the inferior apes live in bands and the one when the human horde was formed? Might it not be the case that the branch from which humankind was about to emerge presented, at the outset, an abnormal particularity that induced or even obliged it to adopt unusual mores?

While all the simians, in spite of their canine teeth, remained frugivores, why did the members of that particular species begin to eat flesh? Did they adopt the habit because they encountered on the ground more numerous and more varied game, or, on the contrary, did they descend from the trees in order to find that fodder which they coveted in greater profusion? What motive led them to prefer a sojourn on the ground to that of the branches? What singularity of their anatomy: arms too short for aerial gymnastics; the form of dimension of the digestive canal; the nature of the gastric juices? Was one thing the cause of another, or vice versa?

Perhaps, some day, science will speak, if it discovers the remains of the Primate in the ice of the Austral Pole.

At any rate, in an era when its four limbs still presented the specific characteristics of a Climber, that hominid had become a Walker, and became increasingly accommodated to that new way of life. Its appetite for flesh, by making it a hunter, made it solitary; simultaneously, its nervous inquietude made it a nomad.

On the ground, however, a more complex existence excited its ingenuity; by virtue of multiple opportunities, it discovered latent resources within itself, and utilized them; its hand became more flexible along with its brain; it improved itself; gradually, the progressive development of its intelligence and the needs that were engendered in consequence, brought it a taste for sociability, into which it threw itself with the joy of a return.

Then, in a group, it talked, and from articulate speech, Humanity emerged.

XLIX. The Distant Brother

"Heûh!"

In the twilight, the cry of horror reverberates; the voice of the Chief is recognized. He has climbed into a tree to search for a shelter for the night, but has jumped down to the ground abruptly. To his sons, who have come running, he indicates a moving brown mass among the branches.

"Ta!"

They all look up. Amazement immobilizes them. Between two long hands that part the branches, there is an enormous head, which leans toward them, with angry grimaces. Beneath a pyramidal skull, the face has a large, flattened nose and almost human eyes, which are blinking. Its jowls are moving, as if to speak...

A Human? No. A Bear? Even less. A Monkey? Do any exist of such formidable size?

Suddenly, a thunderous growl emerges from the mouth, which opens; the brown mass laps down into the grass and raises itself to a semi-erect pose. Assuming a fighting stance, the colossus strikes its ribs with its left hand, like Daâh; in its right hand it holds a club, like Daâh—but the length of its arms is alarming, they hang down almost to the ground.

Before the frightened horde has had time to react, two sons roll on the ground, their skulls split. A daughter, seized, is already under the monster's arm, which is carrying her away. She howls. The women flee, yelping, and the men follow them; all their courage is paralyzed in confrontation with that disconcerting abduction, and the club of the abductor, who is not human.

Like his sons, Daâh beats a retreat, but is the last to do so, facing the enemy, continuing to extend his cudgel toward the Orangutan—and they growl at one another as they recoil from one another.

For Daâh recognizes it, although his children do not; he has not seen one for a long time, but he encountered one once, in his adolescence. The species is rare now; the climate has gradually decimated it, and it has disappeared from the region: a great good fortune, truly. Daâh execrates it.

The hatred he feels for the animal in question is very particular; it has nothing in common with the respectful fear that the large wild beasts inspire in him. It participates somewhat in the irritation that he feels at the sight of other humans; it is troubling, anxious, as sharp as a family discord, and also complicated by the sentiment of an insult.

Daâh, who imitates everything, resents the fact that he and that anthropoid both have the same gestures, almost the same appearance. He tolerates the small Monkeys, but not the big ones, which resemble him too much; he feels that they are too similar to him and is rancorous in consequence. He perceives an affinity that offends him, that lowers him: he is the parvenu that the return of a lower-class relative humiliates in his own eyes.

He cannot tolerate anyone being so similar to him! His nascent pride will not admit that insult. He loves himself; he admires himself. For what reason? He does not know yet, but he has the instinct of being alone, different from everything else, and the intelligence that he senses in advance gives him vanity before giving him reason. That appetite of pride will be of service to him, moreover, by inciting him to be better than others.

In the meantime, he recoils and he growls; he goes away to seek another tree. He is vexed; his entire race will remember that.

L. One After Another

In anger, they do not go pale, they go red. A corner of the skin turns crimson, between their little eyes and the hair on their cheeks. All are bearded, even the young; the fully-grown are protected by a more abundant fleece. Their pilous system is, however, less dense than it will become during the chill of the glacial period. The hairs, of unequal length on different parts of the body, are also not uniform in color; those on the face are not a dark as those of the chest and the abdomen; the mane is often tinted with red and brown.

The large knees, buttocks and the underside of the thighs are depilated by friction and by the frequency of the squatting posture. The back of the hand is hairy, but the palm is bare, callused and striated by profound wrinkles by the labor of the long brachial march through the forest. The fingers, which broaden out in spatulate fashion, bear short, flat nails, rough and horny, the color of stone; the toenails are even more eroded, especially on the big toe; its mission of searching incessantly in muddy ground or among foliage, for a solid point of support, that it must recognize, choose and grip, persists in making that adjudicator an active and reliable organ, as intelligent as a finger; it is so habituated to labor that it amuses itself by continuing to dance in moments of repose; one delights in watching it play by itself, and takes hold of it in the hand.

The mobility that pesters them is manifest throughout their person; their heads move without respite, rising, dipping, plunging; their arms dig in, their hands rummage. They take a keen interest in everything: a blade of grass, a leaf, a pebble, an insect, any shiny object, anything that moves or makes a noise.

That perpetual tension maintains them in a state of expectation that is eminently favorable to all kinds of receptivity; influences take effect on them abruptly and violently; any ex-

157

ternal agitation, when it is echoed within them, obtains its full effect of nervous commotion. A surprise frightens them; the unexpected makes them jump; a cry of alarm sprung from below, in the horde, the agony of a beast lamenting in the distance, and the funnel of their ear immediately swivels toward the sound, along with their eyes.

Their skin is perpetually itchy. A dead leaf or a twig disturbs them; in response to the tickle of an insect that is not an ordinary vermin, they bristle. When a beast of prey is stalking them, they sense its gaze entering into their flesh, and they are gripped by unease until they have discovered the hidden eye. At the slightest contact with a neighbor, believing themselves to be under attack, they lash out; radically incapable of overcoming their reflexes, they do not even suspect that one could succeed in that, or that it might be appropriate to try.

To that native incapacity is added the tyranny of atmospheric influences, which dominate them at all times and transform them without them being aware of it; alternately depressed beneath the weight of an invisible load or racked by quivering forces, they drag themselves along or are exasperated. They are automata of the weather, hyperesthetic barometers; and like the pressures of space in that period of age-old storms, varying continually, their poor souls rise and fall.

The influence of location acts upon them like all the others, sometimes to depress them further, sometimes to enable them to blossom; the place where they are suggests vague sadness to them, or energetic vigor, self-confidence, the desire for audacity, the need for intimacy or the discouragement of an irremediable impotence.

Thus manipulated by everything that surrounds them, they pass without transition from one sentiment to another, from alarm to joy, from anger to fear; none of them knows what kind of individual he will be in the next minute: furious, cheerful, lubricious, cowardly, valiant; all are latent possibilities that any action might release. They never premeditate anything; everything in them is brusque and unexpected; everything arrives in fits and everything is manifest to excess.

Their laughter, sudden and violent, is merely a manifestation of their psychological state, a spasm. The smile is unknown; when they are not laughing in bursts, they frown. Their faces only have four expressions: vague bewilderment, savage hilarity, fear and threat. Their most ordinary actions and simplest movements are jerky, just as their volitions are sudden. Man, woman or child, everyone decides and acts at the same moment, without contest or examination, with the abruptness of a released spring; they learn their intentions by observing their results, and when a hazard prevents them from realizing them immediately, they renounce them more often than not, unable to recall what they wanted.

Even reasoning is done automatically in the depths of the being, like subterranean rivers that flow with no one suspecting their existence but suddenly spurt out of a spring. Their minds are as incapable of dwelling on a thought as their bodies are of staying still. Everything calls to them but nothing retains them: tyrannical but furtive desires perpetually launch them toward everything, unexpectedly, and everything is a limit for them.

Hunters of everything, rejected everywhere, they retreat into themselves and set off again, with an ever-passionate surge, which carries them away with an irresistible violence toward an unavoidable letdown.

LI. The Unanimous

Of all the influences exercised on them, one of the most powerful, and perhaps the most constant, is that of the human example; as soon as a member of the horde receives an impression, it is propagated around them, perhaps magnetically, and passes from neighbor to neighbor; the most sensitive activate the others. To communicate their emotions or their desires, they have no need of speech; the tension of their nerves is sufficient to electrify them one after another, and to make them unanimous. They are subject to the contagion with an acuity so unhealthy that they cannot find any help within them to resist the impulse of panic; their evident interest, or even the concern of their self-preservation is unable to retain them.

That reciprocity of influences is the first condition of amorphous societies, and very quickly produces a result of capital importance: in the same way that imitation of oneself, frequently repeated, engenders personal habits in the individual, so the continual imitation of neighbor by neighbor institutes common habits in the group, which become in their turn generators of needs and common tastes, and then common ideas. When the progress of those social beings raises them to the point of a community of minds, the group will call itself a people: a community of interests, it will call a clan; a community of emotions is merely a horde.

At the present moment, it is not a matter of thinking but only of vibrating; mind does not yet divide them, and the beast is close to them. Only a slight diversity is manifest between the children of the two races: the descendants of Hock, the humans with the low brows, are more massive, heavier and stronger; the humans with the high foreheads, born of Ta or her first daughter, seem to bring a little more initiative and spontaneity to life; one might believe that they will be the first to succeed in the labor of intelligence. But the promise is vague and the settlement distant; for the moment, the two va-

160

rieties are only distinguished by the physical aspect, and the same causes operate in both in identical fashion.

As for the personal modalities that we would designate much later under the name of "character," which differentiate individuals, they have not yet appeared, or are only revealed imperceptibly. It is necessary, first, to constitute their elements, and it is precisely that preparation on which the horde is working, by means of its initial unanimity.

The permanence of the type is elaborated in the horde; every family will multiply in isolation, without emerging from itself, and, by a prolonged selection, will fix the particularities of the group; when that fixity is duly acquired, the clan will be outside the form of humanity that was appropriate to it, and from then on, the vestiges of that initial type will be able to perpetuate through the crossings; alternate and mixed, intermittent but irreducible, perhaps they will return one day in successive generations, under the aspect of distinct characters, which we believe to be individual but which are actually specific: in the qualities or vices of a human being there is a race that evokes the past, with its primordial soul.

Each of us is an ancestor resuscitated, a clan recalled, a revival, an ancient link reappearing in the uninterrupted chain; and if we sometimes astonish our entourage, by some unexpected and disconcerting propensity, it is because we are bringing back into their midst the heritage of an atavism too distant for them to have any part of it, and which amazes them because it brings them another.

LII. On the March

Their lack of individuality protects them from hatred. Denuded as they are of individual character, they have no profound reason to detest one another anymore than to love one another. Preferences are nevertheless manifest, and also antipathies, but they are limited to the pleasure or displeasure of marching side by side, of sleeping in the same tree, of hunting together; they also make one dispute a lump of meat with more or less anger. Generally, sympathies are produced between children of the same race; they never rise as high as affection, much less to amity; egotism is too vivacious, and no heredity has prepared in their hearts the need for tenderness, since the rare humans have lived thus far in a solitary state.

In any case, intimacies are purely occasional and their effect is scarcely prolonged; two adolescents fighting, crimson, their eyes flamboyant, howling in one another's faces, suddenly cease to want to kill one another in order to launch themselves together in pursuit of a rat that moved under a bush, or to climb to the conquest of an apple tree whose branches are red with fruit; tranquilly, they share the rodent or the apples, trying to steal the best morsels from one another, and they laugh unless they growl or start quarreling: chance decides.

Such quarrels are frequent along the route, and the spectacle of fisticuffs invariable provokes another fight in the audience, and then a third; the irascibility of the young males does not permit them to contemplate a battle without them immediately feeling a need to fight.

To associate is to rationalize egotism. They are not united but juxtaposed; they give one another little help. As soon as it is a matter of fighting a redoubtable beast or one that is good to eat, they cooperate; if it is only a question of individual peril, all are left to get out of it as best they can. A hand is not extended spontaneously to someone stuck in the mud, nor is it refused to anyone who asks for it; indifference needs to be

162

shaken by an appeal, which quickly awakens in the individual the memory of a similar danger, and brings back to mind the need that he had then for aid.

They do not act out of altruism, or even calculation; it is simply that an image is evoked in the helper; he sees himself in the painful situation in which another is struggling, and he goes, so to speak, to his own aid, toward the person of someone similar. It is important, too, that the eventual rescuer is momentarily unoccupied; if, unfortunately, he is in the process of hunting or eating, there is little chance that he will consent to sacrifice his pleasure to the imagination of an annoyance.

Obstacles irritate them; the difficulty they encounter inspires them, not with a calm determination to put an end to it, but with anger, and if that resistance persists the irritation turns to fury. While crossing a stream, they unleash cudgel-blows against the water whose current puts pressure on their legs; in a thicket, if a bramble catches them, they pull away, tearing their skin, instead of stepping back in order to extract the vegetal claw.

Those to whom the instinct of hunting and battle suggests, in confrontation with an animal, ingenious plans for flight, striking and parrying, are stupid in confrontation with things; if they are not facing the threat of an adversary that excites their faculties, they find nothing within them. Inanimate things, to which they nevertheless lend an intention to harm, do not have the power to reawaken them from mental sloth, and that is doubtless one of the most ancient manifestations of pride.

Obstacles are renewed incessantly. They go on even so; they always go on. In the forest that encloses them they are like escaping prisoners; just as the trees, thirty times their height, grow toward the light, climbing up above one another in order to conquer their life in the light, so they push forward, also toward the light.

Fortunately, clearings are not rare; in many places, tornadoes have hollowed out circles of devastation, which the violence of storms has progressively enlarged. They are salut-

163

ed with a clamor and the young males launch themselves forward, running in circles, chasing one another, knocking one another over, rolling in the grass or the mud.

Often, too, they encounter passages already frayed: thousands of tunnels run through the undergrowth in all directions; ordinarily, they convey a stream; sometimes they terminate at a lair. It is the daily path of some colossus; the height of the vault, its width, the imprints on the carpet of leaves and in the mud denounce the inhabitant of the abode. Daâh never hesitates; he recognizes immediately the avenues of the Lion, the Bear or the Tiger.

"Heûh..."

He growls and turns away. But in the home of the Elephant there is joy. The Elephant is a friend; it does not eat Humans, and hollows out pathways where felines rarely venture. Gaily, they move along the spacious path, following the Chief. It is not without risk, for the pachyderm might be irritated by the invasion. It does not matter; the pleasure of moving freely ahead blossoms in the turbulent and shrill population; its members renounce prudence and forget fear. The temporary release that they grant themselves is perhaps not legitimate, but it is beneficial; they need it badly; the overloaded nerves are no longer adequate for fright; the nervous animal saves itself from epilepsy by mental lightness and inconstancy.

As evening approaches, so does anguish; the accumulated fever of the day torments the blood in the veins and the penumbra is stifling. It is the unhealthy hour when everything is vague and everything is magnified, the hour of holes and mystery. They have the horror of uncertainty, the suspicion of trouble; something perceived through the layers of the rain or in the enigma of the mist does not appear to them as it is or will be; they deform and amplify it; a silhouette in the twilight is more redoubtable than in broad daylight.

As soon as dusk falls, a slow lamentation emerges from the women and children.

"Heûh... Heûh..."

The eyes search for the quotidian refuge. Finally, Daâh stops at the foot of a tree; he has chosen the shelter.

"Ta!"

Egotistically, he climbs up first. In order to climb after him they jostle one another around the trunk. Hock and Ta are the most ardent to follow him, but they do not always succeed in conserving their rank. Ordinarily, the young ones want to inhabit the tree where the Chief will sleep, but the adult males, no longer wanting anyone to protect them, go to shelter elsewhere; a few women follow them, and Daâh sulks; those groups displease him; their dissidence insults him.

The sick, down below, trail from one tree to another, imploring help. For a long time yet, movement agitates the leaves, for every occupied place seems to be the best; they are disputed and occupants are dislodged. Finally, the young mothers hang the animal-skin sacks in which they have placed the newborns on branches, and from them whimpering emerges. In the penumbra, cries and a few bursts of laughter, appeals and calls to order still leap from branch to branch.

Then the shadows become denser and the trees, darkening, fall silent, as the concert of nocturnal hunters begins out there in the darkness, yapping, mewling, roaring, in search of food, to the sound of thunder under the rain.

They go to sleep...

LIII. The Halt

But their morbid nervousness continues to torment them, even in sleep; dreaming that they are still marching or that they are fighting, they move their legs, their arms and their fingers; their muscles work beneath their skin, The night is also punctuated by awakenings; the howling of beasts and the crashing of thunder rip through it without respite; at every moment, the nightmare of a woman, the anguish of a child or the plaint of an invalid, tears through the torpor of others, and the disturbance reverberates.

After such a repose, the dawn is a deliverance; aggravated and tense, their nerves still taut, the skin prickling with the chill, they leap down onto the wet grass, stretching themselves, and feel hungry. The women whimper, the men growl, the children wail.

"Mâh! Mâh!"

To recommence life, all of them have found their need to eat; they rummage in the moss; acorns and beech nuts, mushrooms and snails, larvae and insects, everything is good. In quest of more solid nourishment they resume their route, harassed from the outset. In single file or in little groups, they hasten with certainty, as if they know where they are going. They scarcely feel their lassitude, so accustomed are they to it; they move mechanically. The monotony of endlessly going on, aimlessly, gives them an appearance of the serenity of livestock going to the stream to drink, harassed by flies, and fatigue makes them silent.

Then, souls warm up, in effort, in gaiety, in anger; the trees pass by, and the animals, and the time. The halt is called beside a stream, or around the first kill.

When the prey is large, they all assemble around it and prance in a circle before eating, to express their delight Daâh makes his selection, as in the time when they were still lying in their mothers' wombs; they have seen him, and they do likewise. The frequent repetition of the same game has ended up engendering a custom, the exercise of which is almost necessary and will become indispensable. It is already a rule that those movements around the large cadaver parody the actions of the felled beast, and are accompanied by howls that imitate its particular cry.

That comedy charms them; for those who can only see it and only comprehend it by sight, the evocative power of the spectacle affirms their victory and demonstrates it to every spy hiding in the depths of the undergrowth; it is suggestive of future victories; it sketches a threat to others, a promise to themselves.

Furthermore, they slake their universal hatred, for, in truth, they detest everything that lives, even the inoffensive animals; the vanquished is always, for them, an enemy against whom they bear a grudge, whether because of its resistance, its flight or the difficulty it costs them. By insulting this one, they scorn the entire race; and by dancing in front of that conquered flesh, they are taking revenge on the entire world that renders their existence so harsh. They rage before devouring it.

But Daâh extends his hand; he advances, not without dignity. They draw apart to let him through. He bends over the victim; with a thrust of his crooked index finger, he plucks out the eye. They do not know yet that the heart is an essential organ; only later will they tear it out of the breast and watch it palpitate in the hollow of their hand before biting into it. Presently, what they consider to be the seat of life is the eye: the protective eye that watches out for peril; the shining eye that is the little sun of the beast; the eye that declares the thoughts for want to speech, which threatens in battle, which is extinguished after defeat...

To make himself understood to all those who are preparing to absorb the strength of the vanquished, Daâh shows them in his fingertips the bloody globe that gazes at them one last time, and then he swallows it.

A howl salutes the Chief's action and that clamor of the Unanimous rolls beneath the domes of verdure to announce to the forest something new and redoubtable: young Humanity is beginning to find Symbols! In honor of them, they will soon bloody the world. And thus are initiated the rites of the holocaust.

LIV. The Siesta

As soon as Daâh has swallowed the eye, the women and children hurl themselves on the prey; with sharp stones and wooden levers, they dig into it and skin it; those who succeed in tearing away a good morsel draw away in order to devour it at their ease. They drool. They break the bones in order to pump out the marrow. The vociferations are soon succeeded by the noise of chomping jaws and gurgling throats. Laughter bursts out intermittently.

Gradually, the process of digestion numbs one's will, memory and all energy, even fear. No one thinks about the prowling death that might be nearby. Torsos collapse into the grass. No one has the idea of posting a sentinel who will watch over the safety of the horde; In any case, if that service were demanded of anyone, the notion of duty required to keep him alert is lacking.

Very close to one another, they lie down, not on their backs but on their sides; with a swiveling of the shoulders they have hollowed out heir hole in the elastic soil, and limply, with a mechanical gesture, they pull leaves and branches over them, as much to shield them from the rain as to hide them from gazes. Arms that beat the air fall back on a neighbor, who grunts; heads find support, at random, on a flank or a breast. A snore emerges from the heap and floats with the flies.

That siesta after the feast reposes the fatigues of the nocturnal sleep. They wake up; they stretch; the soul is indulgent; fingernails slowly scratch the skin, tracing long furrows; the hands make limp gestures to pick up a trotting beetle or catch a damsel fly that alights, and the lazy fingers amuse themselves by pulling the legs, wings and wing cases off, one after another, like the petals of a flower, while the eye of the torturer, still vague, widens without malevolence over the diminishing insect.

Leisure is dangerous among all impulsive beings; the instrument that is not being used works at hazard. This one comes back to life with a reserve of nervous energy and a need to utilize it. Beneath its deceptive calm, the animal is in its plenitude, it is entirely itself, an exaggeration of itself, and its very tranquility is preparing for actions that trivia unleash. It searches: in that head which turns to the right and the left there is the betrayal of a feline; in the eye that blinks as it inspects the surroundings, a sly gleam ignites and fades away; the muscles are getting ready for bounding. The best that the future might bring is that a young male might throw himself on a female, or run off to play games.

The latter are scarcely less violent than brawls. They most often consist of hunting scenes, or the competitors imitate animals, those pursued and those tracked. These mimes, which begin in a good humor, unfailingly terminate in a battle, with each of the players having quickly forgotten that he is playing a role, especially if others are watching them compete. They cannot resist the temptation of having themselves admired; before an audience, their ardor for combat turns into a frenzy.

Suddenly, the games are interrupted; all faces turn toward the same point, with interrogative expressions.

That is because Daâh has just stood up; he is weary of the location and of immobility; he has been looking at the same trees for too long, and they are annoying him. He wants to go elsewhere; he goes.

Sometimes, he utters a rallying cry; as often as not, he does not even make a gesture; the others have only to observe him and follow him; he does not care; he does not deign to do anything more.

And the horde does, indeed, follow; some, who would have preferred to stay longer, start grumbling, but they march even so. For they have, in matters of authority, vague but intimate notions that bear no resemblance to precepts but which act in their depths with the vigor of instinct: notions that are rather singular and somewhat contradictory, which will nevertheless remain approximate to those of all humanity.

The Chief is strongly imbued with the sentiment of his power and the rights that it confers on him; he is a despot out of pride. As for the others, they have both a taste for independence and a need to be led; they are ungovernable, and yet they only aspire to follow a master; they will not tolerate shackles, and suffer from receiving orders, only obeying reluctantly; they dream of emancipation—and yet, they are ever avid to substitute a foreign will for their own; as soon as they no longer feel it weighing upon them, they miss it, and immediately start searching for another in order to regiment themselves within it. They need a tyranny, a prescription, a suggestion, an example.

That double appetite for fictitious liberty and mental servitude is the result of an antagonism between their two heredities: the soul of solitude, that one history has bequeathed them, and the soul of the herd.

The former is responsible for human pride, and the latter for the instinct of imitation.

LV. Mah-Mah

"Mâh... Mâh..."

A new vocable has been introduced into the human family; as the number of little humans multiplies, their repetitive cry becomes more obsessive:

"Mâh... Mâh..."

That appeal of hunger, which trails like a chant through the entire horde, has ended up giving a name to the mothers it implores; they are the ones that the whining voices from the depths of the sack begin imploring as soon as the nursling wakes up. It is toward them that the plaint of the weaned brat, who does not know how to find food, rises up: "Mâh... Mâh..."

They are the Mah-Mahs.

They lend themselves to that guardian role; not only does each one feed her own baby, chase away the flies and delouse it, but she does not disdain either to help or to nourish another. Hock and Ta, when they were the only two, lent themselves to that communism, and their daughters continue to practice it without repugnance. They take pleasure in contemplating the frolics of the brood. When their gazes linger over the melee of little round limbs beating the air, one could believe that their eyes become soft and that over their rude, bleak faces, the promise spreads of what will one day become the womanly smile.

But that gentleness is not constant; crises run through it, especially in the early months of maternity. In that period, the young mothers show themselves to be intractable, and with their aversion for the other sex, they combine a particular irritability with regard to their child. They cannot tolerate a male approaching it, much less touching it; if one takes the risk, they fly into a fury, uttering shrill screeches, and bite; if, unfortunately, one succeeds in picking it up, if only momentarily, they throw themselves on the abductor, and as soon as they recover possession of the little creature, their anger turns against it; they seem to execrate it.

In one of those fits of dementia, which occurred during a halt, one of Hock's daughters strangled her new-born; for a long time, she remained stupid before the limp cadaver.

In spite of the vehemence of the protection with which the mothers surround their babies, they have no veritable love for them. As soon as they are no longer suckling, they begin to lose interest in them; when they can walk on their own, they detach themselves further; when they see them start to run, they experience a kind of rancor against them, as if they have been exploited, or deserted. From then on, they scarcely count, and are soon confounded within the host of their peers; among that turbulent rabble, the former Mah-Mah can no longer recognize, without an effort, the one that emerged from her.

LVI. Children

Descendants of Hock or Ta, they resemble one another like chicks of different broods; in the former as in the latter there are the same gestures, the same appetites, the same impulsive reflexes, the same receptivity to what is happening around them; incessantly, without discernment, they move and they eat; their mind eats via the eyes, as their body does via the stomach.

What they absorb most fully is the example of their elders. The little girls imitate the women; the little boys ape their big brothers. The former play at carrying sacks on their backs full of leaves, or pretend to give the breast to a piece of wood; the latter brandish sticks, beating bushes as they go past. As soon as the path becomes wider they immediately grip their branch by one of its ends, and attempt to give it a gyratory movement by rotating their arms, like the Chief's club. Those gymnastics are accompanied with menacing grimaces, which seem to them to be an indispensable accessory of virility. Although they are not yet conscious of their sex, an instinct informs them of their future role, and inducts in them at an early age in the gestures of battle and murder.

These games the children play have a primordial importance. In the epoch when humanity is making its debut, by imitation, the infants, who are debutants and imitators themselves, appear as the veritable prototype of human being. For those who were dormant in the cells of the race the day before, the normal pasture is that which, like them, emerges immediately from the race: the milk of the teat and the essence of ideas. As soon as they are born they find within themselves certain inveterate instructions, like that of sucking the teat; as soon as they open their eyes they find around them the model of the most recent practices. The task is incumbent on them of consecrating those new customs and transforming them into rites; it is to their power of assimilation that societies will owe their permanent habits and ideas; they are the expert preservers, the fixators of acquired notions, the guardians of beliefs, and, in consequence, religions. They attach civilizations making progress to their past. Without the resistance of children, who do not want to lose anything of what is delivered to them, humane presumptuousness and nervousness would have led the world to anarchy.

Children are the brake of humankind.

When they reach maturity and agitate, they encounter within themselves the very memory of the species; without any doubt, that backward force will hamper the course of progress, but it will also attenuate the effects of the devastating ferocity that leads humans to devastate everything, and which they readily turn against one another for want of any other victim, to destroy their work in embryo and to crush the future by virtue of rancor against the past.

LVII. The Sling and the Ax

At about the age of twelve, Ta's eldest son made an in-genious discovery. As always, he made it by chance. His club, already heavy, had just split at the end, as a result of striking rocks and tree trunks. To punish it for that defection, he slammed it into the ground furiously, holding it vertically, and the split widened: a stone had become wedged in it, and re-mained stuck. Immediately, the little man's anger was trans-formed into hilarity; with malevolent laughter he mocked the captive stone; he teased it with his index finger and encour-aged the wood to cling hard.

The amusement of torturing his prisoner was beginning to fade away when the horde came into a clearing. He twirled the club with a movement of his wrist and the stone flew away. If it had fallen straight down, in accordance with the custom of its peers, that would have been tolerable, but when it went upwards, as if trying to escape, that was a provocation that got a poor welcome. The boy followed it with his eyes, frowning, and saw it fall into the moss. He ran after it, and leapt upon it, palms open, as if upon a rat, in order to prevent it from fleeing again.

When he had put it back in place, he looked at it, shaking his head with an authoritarian expression, and menacing growls emerged from his throat. He was suspicious, though; a new escape seemed to him to be imminent; he kept watch on the enemy from the corner of his eye. In order to tame it fur-ther and prove its defeat, he leaned on it, and made use of his club as if it were a walking stick. The cleft of the divided wood above and below the flint became plastered with clay.

Escape now if you can!

With the first whirl, the stone, heavier by virtue of the clay, fled with increased violence.

The boy stood there open-mouthed. What he had done, with that coup, was discovered the principle of the sling. He had no suspicion of it and did not give it another thought; another concern was preoccupying him: his prisoner had just made fun of him again! He searched for it in the grass, with the stubbornness of a beast that will not give in, and subjected it to the grip again. The grip of the cleft, enlarged by his efforts, became increasingly slack, and the stone kept slipping out; it even profited from a distraction to quit him definitively.

The next day, when he woke up, the memory of his successive defeats returned to his mind; as he was hungry, he became enraged. Immediately, he went to look for another stone, larger and heavier: a fragment of flint pleased him by virtue of its dimensions and its cutting edges. In order to imprison it more solidly, he first employed a handful of clay, which he kneaded in the fissure, like the one the day before. In order to do better still and perfect his work, he looked around in quest of an idea, an example. As was his fashion, he sought advice from things. Suddenly, he saw a tangled creeper, and his eye lit up; he knew, having suffered there, how resistant those ligatures were that so perfidiously wound around a limb. Would they wind around a stone as well?

By looping fibers around he succeeded in fixing his shard of flint at the extremity of the club. Triumphantly, he lifted the swollen assembly, and weighed it at the end of his arm, slightly astonished and even vaguely anxious to observe that the sly stone was making itself heavier at the end of a club than in the hollow of a hand; did that eccentricity, obviously intentional, not conceal some further treason? He would see about that! He brandished the weapon overhead and brought it down against a tree trunk.

The stone bit into the bark and stayed there; humans possessed the ax.

A fragile weapon still, and very precarious; nevertheless, everyone wanted to have one. All the clubs were ornamented with a cutting stone, except Daâh's; his pride consented to imitate the beasts without admitting it, but affected to scorn the inventions of the brats.

177

For the vines that broke too easily, someone thought of substituting a strip of hide that was hanging from his fur and served to retain that piece of fur on his back. Leather ligatures were immediately adopted.

The flint persisted nevertheless in escaping frequently, but when that notion was admitted, they took as much pleasure in that game as the other. Sometimes they amused themselves making the stone fly, helping it to do so, making it into a bird, in wanting it to fly; they became proud of its flight. Sometimes, on the contrary, they took pride in is firm adherence to the shaft, of its vigor in entering into the wound of a tree or an animal. What laughter there was for a rabbit cut in two by a slicing impact! What a feast, too, in honor of an Eagle that was watching from the edge of the cliff and was driven away from its summit by a hail of stones!

They progressed gaily, and that dwarf, which had just arrived stark naked among the colossi of the Pleistocene forest, the Human male, becoming more expert every day in the art of killing, was already announcing what he would become: the prince of exterminators.

LVIII. The Destruction Machine

Considered in the ensemble of the preglacial fauna, and by comparison with the other forest mammals, humans are manifest from the very start as nasty beasts—twice over, because they present all the characteristics of what we call a pest, and also of what we would call a vicious animal. In the first place, they have a need to destroy, and in the second, a taste for causing suffering, adding insult to injury.

Those two tendencies are revealed in humans with an acuity that is already unhealthy, and whose equivalent is found nowhere else. They are not yet insane, and will not be for a long time, but they are vertiginous; modern jurists would declare them irresponsible, since all their malevolent actions are imposed upon them as consequences of their physiological condition.

The hypertrophy of the nervous system, which is already and immediately found in the race in the state of an acquired characteristic, and whose supreme achievement will be to turn a cerebellum into a cerebral brain is only denounced provisionally by a morbid activity: an activity that is necessarily double, since the primate in question possesses both motor nerves and sensitive nerves. The exasperation of the former suggests to humans a continual mobility; the exasperation of the others endows them with an excessive impressionability.

From the former, they will obtain that incessant order of movement and action, whatever the value of the action or the consequence of the gesture might be; it hardly matters what will result from the movement, provided that the movement occurs and something follows in turn. Now, as every manifestation of activity inevitably leads to a destruction, the maximum harm will necessarily correspond to the extreme of motility, and the most active of the animals will be, by the same token, the most harmful.

That is human beings. Being perpetually agitated they are the most accomplished machines of destruction. Automatically, mechanically, without being aware of it, by the mere fact of living and functioning, they break, they smash, they put to death; all along their route, they perpetuate a carnage of flowers, leaves, buds, and defenseless creatures; everything that is within arm's reach is uprooted, torn apart and crushed; animal or vegetable, they massacre it, in order to occupy themselves; and in order to carry out that massacre, they impose supplementary fatigues upon themselves without regret.

They have no need, in order to destroy, of hatred or anger; the murderous gesture is triggered involuntarily; to bring into play one of the levers that kill, it is sufficient to attract its attention: a kick at the stem of a mushroom because it stands up; a blow of a club on a vine because it hangs down; a stamp of the heel upon a toad because it is passing by! They do not pick flowers in order to look at them or delight in their perfume, but in order to crush them and extract a juice that oozes and is sticky; only when they have thoroughly pulverized the object and reduced it to pulp do they sniff the fresh odor of vegetable death on their stout fingers.

During a halt, when they are weary, the mechanical play of all hands consists of tearing up leaves and plants; it is a form of repose; everyone takes charge of devastating a circle around them. Ferns and grasses are generally the first to be executed; their attitude recommends them to the choice of the ravager; one takes the stem by the base in a tight fist and with an upward gesture one strips it, gazing with dazed eyes at the bundle of debris that forms within the funnel of the thumb and index finger. Sometimes, with a symmetrical maneuver, one operates with both fists at once, and the double pendulum goes up and down, and then repeats, until the surrounding area is clear. Then, springs of moss are turn up, one after another. One massacres whatever one can, negligently, and finds in that a stupefied pleasure.

A keener pleasure is found in killing consciously; then the murder is not simply the outcome of a motility exercised at hazard but the satisfaction of an appetite; it is still the nervous system working spontaneously, but there is a motivation, on this occasion, that enters into function. It, too, is in the process of inauguration, and it, too, makes its debut as it can; while awaiting the ages in which that evolved malady will have utilizable manifestations—intelligence, affectivity, altruism, a taste for arts or poisons, etc.—the morbid need for vibration is still in its first phase, and practices only one excess: cruelty.

LIX. The Invention of Pain

Having eaten and slept, they amuse themselves.

They form a circle, on all fours, heads toward the center, faces toward the ground; the round balls of their heads immobilize, one beside another, their arched backs bulge under the rain, and from the neck to the loins, like a prolongation of their manes, a train of stiff hairs bristles on their meager spines. Sometimes, a frisson shakes their streaming shoulders, but the downpour is not the cause; they do not feel it. It is an internal emotion that harasses them: a force agitating within them, new and nascent, stimulated by what is agitating before them. It is exercised by the receipt of a shock that comes from outside and propagates through their entire being. They are electrified. They are watching suffering.

It is the first circus. In the center, a wounded hare is writhing, and finishing dying; its eyes are distended with horror and it is emitting screams, like those of a child carried off by a Tiger. The spectators, leaning over that agony, are panting; it enters them through the eyes and the ears; they drink it in, they savor it, it stirs their entrails. When the patient forgets to suffer, they wake it up by planting thorns in its head or belly, in its corneas or in its feet, in order that it will quiver and howl: whoever extracts a fine scream enjoys himself more than the others.

Sometimes, a human face looms up above the circle; it has dilated nostrils, intoxicated eyes, and it pivots on the neck with viperine slowness, questing around as if in search of another life to tear apart. When two gazes meet, then, the troubled blackness of the pupils lights up with disquieting gleams; the lips draw back from teeth ready to bite; fingers clench as if for a strangulation; madness hovers.

Whether it is a matter of their fellow or a weaker animal, they find an acute voluptuousness in causing suffering. It is strange, as if they were almost sympathetically moved by the spectacle of a pain that they are not experiencing, and which they are, on the contrary, enjoying imposing, or aggravating to the extent of torture. When the suffering of another is the result of an accident, it touches them and they feel it in themselves; when it is their work, it intoxicates them.

The unhealthy excitement that the spectacle of dolor provokes in them is already a particularity of the species; no other animal devotes itself as they do to the intoxication of torture. A number of felines are cruel, but not in that voluptuous and passionate fashion. There is a vast difference between Human cruelty and that of the Tiger. The Tiger amuses its claws on a prey, and the prey suffers, but it does not seem to have the intention of causing suffering; it possesses a mechanical plaything from which takes pleasure in extracting twitches and contortions; if the functioning of that mechanism is accompanied by suffering, the feline does not deign to take any notice of the fact, and is probably not even aware of it.

In brief, the Tiger plays with its prey, whereas the Human plays with the pain; the former is activating a mechanism, the latter a sensibility; what delights the Tiger in its impassivity is the movement produced, but what excites the Human is the sensitivity, the motivating cause.

Humans understand; they know; and they prove it. In the beasts they torture it is the pain they seek; they aim to obtain a familiar vibration, about which they are curious, and which they imagine at the same time as they provoke it; it reverberates in their mind when they procure it in their victim. In that appearance is the admixture of intelligence, of which it is the sole trigger.

They have just invented that game, hitherto unknown on earth: the Culture of Pain. It is the initial discovery of human genius. To enter into a relationship with the ambient world, they put pain to work; their already intelligent hyperesthesia makes the human being the animal expert in cruelty; it is via cruelty that their moral relationships with creatures of their own kind and others are inaugurated.

It also seems that the commencement in question is inevitable. From the moment that Nature in progress has been able to engender a being capable of taking an interest in something other than itself, and since, finally, amid the brutality of the world, a mental attention has become capable of arresting on others, it is necessary, at the very least, that an external object should come along to provoke that still-latent faculty in its inner being; it is necessary to awaken it and induce it to labor. How? What can awaken that dormant curiosity? What is it in a foreign existence that the individual will deign to contemplate, if not that which, above all else, interests it in its own existence.

What vibration on the part of another can resonate more clearly in one's own depths than the one that represents the most intense emotion of one's own flesh? Pain is incontestably the sharpest, as well as the most ancient, of animal sensations: destined to warn the living being of external or internal danger, it necessarily appears at the very beginning of sensitive life; the first notions that the zoophyte has of its existence come to it through pain.

Generator of perceptions, educator of nerves, pain is the dawn and awakening of everything, far anterior to pleasure, since the former is and the latter is not a utility essential to the conservation of the individual.

LX. The Culture of Pain

The primordial importance that pain has in the history of
organisms invites us, logically enough, to suppose that it will
attract the first gaze of the nascent mind. In animal egotism,
pain alone was capable of introducing an imagined commotion, and it is by virtue of pain that the egotism in question
learned to exteriorize itself. Before a patient whose nerves are
being twisted, the nerves of the spectator quiver; for the first
time, a creature is able to vibrate in unison with another.

That reversibility of egotism, which the Greeks so justly
call "sympathy," comes to link the individual that is suffering
to the one watching it suffer, by revealing to the one that the
other is similar to himself; by the same procedure, it will eventually inform him that the other is his kin. Without pain, humans would probably have taken far longer to perceive that
similarity and that relationship; thanks to pain, they obtained a
taste for watching suffering and being moved by it, and then,
as a corollary, in creating it, and even in warding it off.

Thus, the impressionability of humans to the pain of others gave rise within them to a double phenomenon: cruelty and
pity. Exactly like cruelty, pity will be a human prolongation of
pain and fear; both of them have the same origin, the suffering
of another, and he same cradle, human being. But those two
manifestations of an intellectualized neuropathy did not appear
in the race with the same urgency; pity only developed second; it does not have, like cruelty, the violent attractions appropriate to primitive beings.

In fact, their extreme mobility turns them away from
contemplation and toward action. Pity is essentially a spectator
and cruelty an actor.

Pity is passive and neutral; it submits, it assists, it remains parallel to the evil, it counts for nothing in terms of action; it is, in fact, undoubtedly the displeasure of its inertia that
will eventually suggest the idea of intervening ingeniously in

the drama, by striving to attenuate effects and even to combat causes.

Cruelty, by contrast, is active from the outset; it does not follow, like pity, it leads; it is creative, and knows it; it enjoys it; the nervous vibration that it has before its eyes is the product of its intention, the proof of its efficacy. By virtue of all that, it flatters the pride of force, it excites to action, and above all to the repetition of action, overexcites by virtue of functioning and accelerates to the point of provoking a vertigo, an intoxication, in the operator; it carries within itself the morbid seeds of an excess; from the outset, it presents all the elements necessary to the constitution of a vice, and will later become one.

But hairy humankind will have a long road to travel in the depths of the woods, and a long sojourn to make in the depths of caves, before reaching a state of civilization that will permit the full blossoming of the ferocity to which it is susceptible, and which no other species will be able to equal. To reach that stage, it will be necessary for the perfectible race, moving from progress to progress, to refine itself by education, sufficiently for savage humans at least to become barbaric humans. Only then will their sensibility and imagination, enriched by experience, conclude in the ingenuity thanks to which we have been able to extract the maximum rendition from pain.

In brief, culture is lacking; human beings are revealing themselves as a monster unique in nature, but only in terms of their exceptional curiosity for sensations: their ferocity is making its debut, and being tried out; naïve and inexpert, it is only an art in its bud. The future artist, so avid to see vibration and cause vibration, will demonstrate a capability of taking an interest in his peers; while waiting for him to think of helping them, he already knows how to animate them by means of pain; pity is in embryo, and infantile cruelty remains the unique form of nascent altruism.

LXI. The Rights of the Weak

The rights of the strong impose themselves so naturally that no one imagines finding them contestable. The only right the weak have is to perish, and they know it; when the strong content themselves with robbing them, instead of killing them at the same time, it is because the strong are showing them mercy.

In those conditions, the idea of property cannot arise. Every object belongs provisionally to the individual making use of it, and only until someone stronger decides to take it; then weak individuals must choose, and quickly, between their own conservation and that of the object; as their own skin is dearer to them than a bearskin, they concede; when they resist, they are beaten, and they have asked for it. If the two contenders are equal in strength, they fight.

Now it frequently happens that something possessed by one individual attracts the gaze of another, and that the latter immediately begins to desire it ardently, simply because he has observed it in use. His need to imitate is envenomed by a jealous appetite; his desire to enjoy it is ignited, and he takes possession of it. He is not stealing, he is conquering; the one who is dispossessed may growl with anger and regret the object, but he cannot deem himself to have been wronged. As for the taker, he installs himself proudly in his victory, with a joy all the keener because the pleasure of victory his supplemented by the voluptuousness of inflicting harm. If he is dispossessed in his turn, he will see nothing abnormal in it, if he is not strong enough to prevent it.

One day, however, something strange happened.

At a bend in a ravine, the Chief perceived a man. He rushed at him, uttering his battle cry, but the other did not stand up either to fight or run away. He waited, almost recumbent, with a terrified expression. He was seen to make an effort to get up, painfully, and then fall to his knees again, with his head in his hands. Daâh was still moving forward; the horde, running behind him, was howling to excite him to murder; the Chief's warrior soul was inflated by that familial clamor. Already, the club was whirling.

But the sick man, his arms still extended, slowly raised his face: a poor face with blue-tinted orbits, tortured by winkles, with eyes that were so humble, accepting, imploring...

The club remained in mid-air.

The horde, forming a bewildered circle, was no longer shouting. They looked alternately at Daâh's face and that of the dying man. No one knew why the club had not come down; all of them were astonished, and no one would have disapproved of its fall. They stood there, motionless, eyes wide, like creatures suddenly halted by darkness.

In that sudden night, groping with all their souls, they strove to discover themselves; and those embryonic humans, stupefied to find lurking in the depths of their obscure consciousness the tiny glimmer of a sentiment that their intelligence could not comprehend. They glimpsed the rights of the weak.

LXII. Morality

Their morality was to live, and nothing more. Of good and evil they had not the most imperceptible idea.

A babe in arms or a dog, ignorant as they might be of the duty that awaits them, are at least capable of understanding it, because the notion of the rule is latent within them, and they are only ready to adopt it because they have been educated to it for centuries. Humans, however, who are only just beginning to group together, and, in consequence, find themselves for the first time in a condition to establish a connection between their individual interests and those of others, are unaided in confrontation with that problem by any ancestral experience.

The utility of reciprocal concessions, without which the community cannot prosper, is not apparent to anyone. It will first be necessary to discover it, and afterwards to invent the means of providing it; when the possibility is finally demonstrated, it will still be necessary for generations to pass and succeed one another before the recognized utility can succeed in achieving the importance of a primordial necessity. Only then will it assume the character of an absolute, which is the essence of duty; only then will the times be inaugurated when that restriction, by dint of being recorded and reiterated from one generation to the next, ends up constituting a second nature in the species, an inveterate law. The children coming into the world will find it already within them, and the sum of those efforts, intervening in the course of the ages to discipline the race, will be affirmed in the individual with the authority of a religion that no one any longer disputes.

Philosophers have been able to imagine a primitive humankind endowed with all the virtuous candors;[11] of the moral

---

[11] The reference is to Jean-Jacques Rousseau and his notion of the primal innocence in which human societies lived, in his

value of that virginity we are informed on a daily basis by the phenomena of regression manifest among the degenerates of the present day. The violations of the rule that we designate by the names of crimes and vices are merely reminiscences of a time when animal egotism had all the rights, and practiced them without objection, provided that it had the strength; in the same way, what we call virtue is the ennoblement of the privations that the social estate has gradually been able to impose on individual egotism.

At this eventful moment when a human family has just been constituted, the needs of the individual do not yet show themselves in opposition to those of the group; the mode of existence is too uncomplicated for conflicts to be produced, except accidentally, between one creature and another; the common interest only exists as the sum of individual interests. The latter can incorporate one another because they are exactly similar, but they remain indifferent to one another; they are, vigorously, a matter of every man for himself; that is all there is; and it is justice, for the time being, that the law of the individual holds sway over that of the group. The wellbeing of the collective does not count as yet; a problem arises, too serious for others to be able to balance it out; what is presently at stake is the life or death of the human species. The number of humans is too tiny, and the fate of the race, in the midst of the enemies that assail it, is too precarious, its future too dubious, for any question to arise other that this one: will the species succeed, or not, in implanting itself on the planet?

In fact, that vital question is reducible to the issue of whether the unities threatened by so many perils will escape them to perpetuate the species. In these conditions, the individual, being so rare, becomes more precious than anything else; by safeguarding one's own body, one conserves the seed and hope; in slaking one's appetites of hunger and amour, one

---

opinion, before being corrupted by civilization. Haraucourt's argument is constructed with denial of that supposed delusion in mind.

is ensuring the conquest of future times; the fate of the race is incarnate in oneself, united with oneself. The success of the generations to come, or not to come, depends on whether one's egotism is triumphant or vanquished. The individual is the depository of destiny, the reservoir of the future, the egg, and the egotism of the individual is sacred. Nothing demands the sacrifice of the individual's life or desires; on the contrary, if one does not allow oneself to be killed, if one eats, if one reproduces, one has fulfilled all of one's duty to the species.

The principle of duties is not and never has been anything but the benefit of the common cause; in whatever epoch, even when the group or its members are unconscious of the ends to which they are inclined, innate obligations only ever have one single aim: general salvation. And it is for that reason that, at least for a time, the mission of that young humanity, its virtue, its duty—which is the supreme law of its mores which we call its morality—will, logically, be the inverse of what we will one day designate by the same name of morality.

LXIII. Amour

Endure and perpetuate oneself: that is the whole of their morality; they know nothing but life, with the imperious mission to transmit it, without even suspecting that they are giving it; of amour they know nothing but the gestures, because they have found in their cells that science bequeathed by others; and the prescribed gestures are accomplished in the ritual manner. But sexual union, which is a need in them, does not appear to them as a pleasure or a game, since the possibilities of its realization have become constant and facile.

It was different in the epoch when Daâh lived alone; his adolescence knew bitter desire, which was the consequence of a privation that constituted normality for him in the condition of exile; then, the solitary individual, a hunter of females as well as a hunter of meat, coupled as he fought, as a dominator, a vanquisher; two appetites, hunger for the subsistence of his individuality, and lust for the subsistence of the species, threw him brutality on to flesh; in amour as in feasting, he was a beast of prey.

The children of the horde, however, are ignorant of that misery; they no longer have the time to learn it; desire, as soon as it is born, is satisfied, and does not sharpen; familial promiscuity has suppressed anxiety, and it anticipates the impatience of males by procuring them immediate pasture; at the opportune moment, one sex is always there, present for the satisfaction of the other.

To the facilities procured by number, the contagion of example is added. It is rare, in fact, that the spectacle of a coupling does not provoke a similar desire in others and a similar act; the genetic sensibility has always found a powerful motor in visual suggestion, and it is logical that these primitives should be supremely impressionable to the influence of images, since nothing exists in their minds except by that route. Apart from those whom the example will excite to imitation, no one takes any notice of these copulations; the sight of a young male in coitus with a young female is less interesting than two athletes competing, because the phases and the conclusion in the former are known in advance.

Like any other exercise, this one is practiced in broad daylight, during the halt. At night, one sleeps; the tree in the bosom of which the horde will shelter is ill-suited to vigorous actions. Amour will only become nocturnal when humans have conquered the caves, where everyone lies down pell-mell on a bed of plants and hides, and also when the morality of the clan has invented scruples that suggest the idea of concealment; before social laws that will be applied to restrict abuses and raise barriers against desire, more urgent laws are imposed, which prescribe amour instead of proscribing it. The small number of humans only demands, for the time being, their multiplication; nature is hasty and urgent; instinct alone rules, and the function is exercised without material or mental obstacles.

Polyandrous and polygamous, all females belong to all males, and all males to all females; communism is the rule; it is the time of original chaos. Nothing opposes incest and everything requires it. Their kinship does not trouble them because they have no suspicion of it; if they were aware of it, nothing would denounce to them that the community of blood in question might embody a prohibition of one game rather than any other. They therefore hold, like animals, to the simplest notions.

One vice announces itself, however, and that is a tendency to abuse; these primitives show themselves, like the monkeys, strongly inclined to indulgence, toward which the exceptional development of their nervousness encourages them; they devote themselves to it with a frequency unjustified by the needs of reproduction; lascivious as they are cruel, by virtue of an overabundance of nerves, they expend themselves, already surpassing the dictates of nature. Erections tyrannize them; they are already slaves to them, defenseless against

193

temptation. Their amours have no season; the whole year is good for them.

The initiative always comes from the male; the female does not provoke it as yet. It might seem logical that her more sickly impressionability ought to dispose her more than the male to sexual pleasure, but for the moment, that is not the case. One might say that, being the very organ of fecundity, she finds in the depths of her flesh a kind of physiological consciousness that is informed as to what is and is not useful to the predestined goals; outside of the times when conjunction might be efficacious, she experiences a repugnance whose causes she does not discern but whose effect is manifest: she flees, she hides, she resists, at least initially; she is not concerned to put a higher price on her consent, but she is afraid, without knowing why and perhaps in spite of herself; an innate apprehension invites her to defend herself.

Virgins, much more than women already proven by amour, expend in combat all the energy of a real fear, and that reticence of the flesh, as instinctive as it is legitimate, as the first appearance of the sentiment that will subsequently be idealized to the point of engendering feminine chastity and coquetry.

The male does not triumph without difficulty; he only succeeds when the heat of the struggle has ended up awakening in the opposite sex a desire analogous to his own. Moreover, the vigor and duration of the contest are inconstant; they vary in accordance with the subject, more or less rebellious, the moment, more or less opportune, and the aggressor. A female who refuses herself to one male easily yields to another, but it is rare, even when she is willing, for her not to protest momentarily, and no less rare, even when she runs away to start with, for her not to end up surrendering.

In the males, too, preferences are sometimes manifest, although they are exceptional, temporary and by no means exclusive. The attraction that draws one of the young males, with a marked predilection, toward one of the young females does not prevent him from using others on occasion; more often than not it is proximity that guides his choice, and to-day's choice does not influence tomorrow's.

It also sometimes happens that two adult males are more especially interested in the same female; each of them experiences a visible irritation as soon as she falls into the other's hands; the witness growls, comes running and substitutes himself if he is the stronger, growls and resigns himself if he is the weaker; but a state of aversion persists, and without knowing exactly why, the two rivals willingly fight, on the slightest pretext, especially in spring, and slightly more if they are of different races. Then the hostility passes as quickly as it arose.

As for the amorous parades that will one day mask and embellish the brutalities of the work, they are only fashionable in certain insects and a few birds. Inferior species, which date from an age already remote, have had the leisure, in two or three thousand centuries, to attain a state of civilization that they will no longer surpass. On high and down below, in the branches of the trees and the grasses of the clearings, winged males dance around females, turn cartwheels, inflate their plumage, prance, and trill throaty songs intended to seduce...

A human stops in the middle of a puddle to watch the frolics of the brilliant bird from a distance, but is too young to comprehend them, and he laughs, amused to see the luxury of tenderness deployed that will later fill the lives of his own kind.

LXIV. Modesty

Those that are watched in action, whatever they are doing, are animated in their tasks; the gaze of their brethren excites them. On the other hand, it never embarrasses them; none of life's actions seem to require more than any other to be concealed. All animal needs are manifest with equal simplicity, and are equally satisfactory; in the absence of any convention, nothing incites anyone to hide their appetites or their emotions, and no hypocrisy encumbers relationships.

By means of certain signs, however, the announcement of what will become modesty can already be discerned, and even the various forms that it will eventually affect.

The first manifestations of those phenomena go back to the days when Daâh lived alone. At all times he understood the dangers of certain postures required by his organic functions; he has recognized the need at those dangerous moments, when it would be awkward to defend himself, to protect himself from a surprise attack; in order to cover his behind, he always looks for the rampart of a rock or a tree trunk; he never commits himself until he has checked that no gaze is spying on him, and for as long as the critical pose lasts, his anxious eyes keep watch on the surroundings. Similarly, he hides his excreta, which might denounce his passage and guide an enemy.

This scatological prudence, which is imposed on a daily basis, could not take long to constitute an inveterate habit and become a rule—with the reservation, however, that the requirement for dissimulation only exists in the context of encountering an eventual enemy, and does not concern familiar individuals from whom there is nothing to fear.

An analogous suspicion concerns the act of sexual intercourse; that, too, and more than any other, exposes one to the dangers of a surprise and puts life in peril; more than any other, it necessitates the choice of a safe place. Never, in the times of his solitude, did Daâh knock down a spouse without first checking the surroundings, and his eye remained alert.

That anguish is attenuated somewhat for his sons, who know that they are protected by numbers; an alarm call will be uttered by others. On the other hand, communal existence has engendered a new inconvenience, less serious but unpleasant: the young males, in letting themselves be seen, risk exciting an envious individual and being dispossessed by him; the females have no similar dread. The circumspection that presently imposes itself on males thus has a less pressing character so far as the females are concerned; genital modesty was originally a virile prerogative rather than a feminine one, and the centuries have not effaced all vestiges of that initial state.

Another reason, even more imperious, soon incites males to hide an organ too vulnerable to blows; many beasts attack there, knowing it to be a vulnerable spot; several were wounded by dogs, horses or humans. Branches are also to be feared, and creepers, and thorns; as they plunge into the undergrowth, the young males veil their nether regions with their free hand, as the young women protect their breasts; the modest gesture of Venus is shared by both sexes.

In spite of these measures, accidents were repeated until the day when the ingenious son of Ta, irritated by a wound, found in his anger the idea of binding the bear-cub skin covering his back around his loins—and that was the first armor. All the sons imitated him, but the daughters, for whom that precaution had less utility, did not adopt it.

That invention had social consequences; it gave rise to the notion of property. Until then, the male only possessed his offensive weapon, which never quit him and became part of him; henceforth, he has a defensive weapon, less inherent to his person, but which it is good to conserve; no one takes his club from him, but someone might steal his loincloth. Practical sense is inaugurated, with the vices corollary to it, and they will develop together; opportunity will multiply them.

In fact, the hunter who has taken it into his head to protect one part of his body will not take long to armor others.

The hides that were not appreciated greatly while they were only offering protection against the rain will gain a major interest now that it is known that they might serve a purpose in combat; in the warm forest, they are not disputed to any great extent, but their merit will become more obvious as climates become cooler in the next period.

The best furs will also belong to the strongest, the women will only have them if any remain; they will dress themselves in rags abandoned by combatants who have found better ones—and that regime, to which the egotism of the male will restrict them for several thousand years, will harden them so well against the cold that they will permanently retain the faculty of living in a state of semi-nudity.

LXV. Esthetics

In a landscape, they see the brambles, because they scratch, the branches, because they block the way, and the undergrowth, because it might conceal an enemy. In the presence of an obstruction, the only question to be decided is whether it is better to go across or around it. In what measure will it procure fatigue, prey and danger? That is all. If it promises to be practicable and to provide nutrition, visages will expand; if it is difficult to penetrate and threatens to conceal wild beasts, faces become sullen. One likes it if it is brighter, fears it if it is more obscure.

They are radically insensitive to the beauty of forms. The contours of an object, whatever it is, constitute a reality that nothing distinguishes from any other; all aspects of matter are recorded indifferently. No one has any idea of comparing what they are with what they are not, and concluding, by virtue of that imaginary juxtaposition, the admiration of a beauty. They cannot group on their retinas the objects juxtaposed there to reconstitute the whole that they have before them, and discern the harmony therein; things appear to them in isolation, always independent of one another, and fix attention in an exclusive fashion that prevents any relationship between them being observed.

The grandiose spectacles of nature can impress them with terror, anguish or vertigo, but it is the morbidity of their nerves that is struck, and their minds do not perceive the majesty inherent in them. The magic of blossoming and nascence does not interest them; they do not see it. The grace of a curving vine does not exist for them. Birdsong does not possess any charm; they only represent it as the provocation of an ungraspable prey; the voice of frogs is more beautiful, since it promises a meal.

Their esthetic sensibility is limited to the horror of darkness, the apprehension of the penumbra and a violent liking for anything shiny. All reflections attract them, except that of water, which is too frequent to warrant their taking notice of it. Around a piece of quartz that scintillates in the flank of a rock, they jostle one another; if one of them succeeds in prying loose that splendor, he turns it over and over in his stout fingers, sniffs it, bites it and ends up throwing it into the mud, for no desire is durable; someone else immediately picks it up. On the iridescent nacre of a shell, they lean in a group, marveling at the changing light, their eyes sparkling with joy; when the heads come up again, a glorious laughter expands the faces. Why?

They only notice certain colors. Green, brown and gray, to which they are too accustomed by the trees, the mud and the clouds, might as well not exist; they are confounded in an indifference that has become, at length, incapable of observation. Blue provokes their attention more because it only shows itself rarely through gaps in the sky. In truth, they only gaze with pleasure at bright yellow and red—especially red—which solicit the eye by the brutality of their glare. One could say that they like them, insofar as they are curious, and those two colors exert a prestige on the eye that conceals some mystery; they run toward them with a particular urgency, which is not completely explained by the crudity of the hues.

It suffices for a child to dive into a thicket, where he has glimpsed a scarlet flower, for other infants, or even older children, to launch themselves forward to dispute its possession; the one who succeeds in picking it adopts a triumphant attitude, and contemplates the flamboyant petals at arm's length. He seems to be searching for something, or rummaging in his memory to recover a fleeting memory. The immobility of his irises, under frowning eyebrows, expresses the effort of attention that one has before a face glimpsed once, a long time ago, which one is trying to recognize.

What, then, are they remembering? In a few millennia, barbaric peoples will have a reason for cherishing the splendor of crimsons, incarnadines and oranges, which evoke fire, but these people have never seen it. Could it be that they are recalling it without knowing it, because their ancestors, in the times of the Pliocene and the dry forest, watched conifers struck by lightning blazes? Might the fearful admiration of those distant ancestors have left a memory in the race that will not perish?

Perhaps they are searching now, for the great living red and yellow flower. Although they no longer know that it exists, perhaps it is that of which they dream, because they lack it and have need of it. Perhaps it is to its conquest that the children hurl themselves when they encounter a rutilant corolla, a fragment of mica that lights up, a piece of nacre that glitters.

Was it also to the conquest in question that Daâh rushed when he nearly perished in pursuit of the fire follet, and toward the same conquest that they march, following the road indicated by the Suns?

LXVI. The Mute

Whereas Daâh was formed in solitude, with so much difficulty and slowness, his children, born in a group and living
together, are animated by a less concentrated and more complicated life, less bleak and more productive. The more they
exteriorize, the more they acquire a taste for it. Their curiosity
and their appetite for vibration, combined with their surprising
faculty of assimilation, renders them the most apt of all to
profit from grouping and not to allow any of its possible benefits to be lost.

Not only do each one's discoveries immediately enrich
everyone, but the mental labor operated in the brain of one has
an almost instantaneous repercussion in all the neighboring
skulls. As if the surrounding movement were provoking an
identical movement in those machines of sensation, they excite one another by means of their internal agitation; like piles
that one brings closer together, they electrify one another mutually; the number of heads multiplies the lent forces in each
of them. Eyes get used to looking at eyes; no longer being
exclusively occupied, like Daâh's, in scanning the material
world, they learn to observe the unreal world of ideas, and
pupils already know how to see, in the depths of pupils, the
wellsprings of thought rising up like water seething in a troubled spring.

They glimpse it; it is there; they sense something alive
that is trying to emerge; they want it; in order to grasp it, they
do what they can, and, as born hunters, they apply to its conquest the means that they employ against the prey that similarly hides in holes. Sometimes, two beings, face to face, enigmas to one another, look at one another intently; they seem to
be searching, via the bay of the pupils, the depths of their
heads; on the two masks, impatience contracts the muscles;
the eyebrows agitate, the nostrils distend, the lips draw back

and little guttural cries, which resemble plaints, are exhaled from the depths of their throats.

Their tongues try to modulate in passing the air that flows under the palate; the sounds, before becoming words, make a music of sharp and changing notes; the voices that would like to talk only succeed in singing. As if they were obscurely conscious of a possibility that escapes them, they exert themselves in a vague effort, in quest of a means of expression they do not know, but of which they have a presentiment; before knowing that it will exist, they divine it by virtue of the need that they have, and they suffer from not having it.

Daâh believed that he did not lack anything, as long as he could howl in imitation of the wild beasts, which have no speech. In spite of his cries, however, Daâh was silent; they were mute.

Certainly, they like human eyes, but even more, they like the sound of the human voice. It is dearer to them than anything else; more than anything else, it procures them an impression of security; even though they are not very helpful and do not expect anything of one another, they comfort one another nevertheless, by the mutual awareness of their presence and the guarantee that the reassuring sound of the voice gives them. A cry of terror in the night frightens them by contagion, but tranquilizes them by the same token, by proving to them that they are not alone.

Nothing causes them as much anguish as the weight of silence; it stifles and crushes; it is worse and more redoubtable than obscurity, because it affirms isolation more fully. In the darkness, one can hide, crouch down, make oneself forget the peril, and cling warmly to oneself; in the silence, there is no refuge from the panic of the darkness that one bears within oneself; it makes one understand death!

And of the horror that our ancestors had in the forest, we find the vestiges in the desolation of the deaf, more abandoned than the blind.

LXVII. The Spider

At the moment of the halt, Daâh has his back against a tree trunk; old Ta has just sat down beside him. They are both exhausted, and their lassitude brings them together; it is one of those bad moments when they feel throughout their being the weight of the discouragement accumulated by so many efforts, always similar, which never change anything at all. That plaintive reverie is merely a fatigue of their bodies, interpreted by their brains. Sometimes, the female turns to the male, as if to search in his pupils for the direction of his mind.

Suddenly, she pushes him, in order to show him, close at hand, a Wasp that is caught in a Spider's web, and struggling in its toils. He laughs. The Spider comes. The couple both interest themselves in the spectacle, but the woman and the man are not discovering the same things. Ta senses in her nerves the panic of the animal that is about to be devoured, and Daâh the triumph of the one that is about to eat.

He watches the play of the feet that extend swiftly toward the prey and retire prudently; he observes the result of the maneuvers; he conceives the idea of a trap, which he thinks convenient and enviable; he is jealous of the hunter's shrewd ingenuity, which permits it to wait for its prey without danger, instead of pursuing endlessly, forever...

He thinks about himself: the teeming envy germinates within him. To envy is almost to seek. Does the imitator of the world perceive in the depths of his understanding a possibility of one day doing as well as the arachnid?

The Wasp is dead. The Spider with the large belly has sucked out its entrails. Now it is repairing its web, and Ta leans over the work. She has never before examined in that fashion the light thing that oscillates and trembles, the threads that radiate and the threads that intersect. She sees the network reform, and before the agility of the little creature that can weave a veil, she laughs in her turn. Her laughter is already an admiration—but her eyes, soon fatigued, are lifted toward the trees again; the vines that are interlaced from branch to branch above her head resemble the threads of the web. She tears one away, and another, and a third; she stretches them gravely; very attentively, she begins to connect them, like the spider.

She does not know how to tie a knot; her fingers become entangled in the sticky stems that slide and twist. She soon becomes impatient; she is already clenching her jaws...

It is over. She growls with anger; she screws up the vines in the hollows of her palms and throws them into the mud.

Meanwhile, the spider has completed its task; the web is restored; the holes have disappeared. But Ta is no longer admiring anything; she looks with a malevolent eye at the work accomplished; she does not know that the Spider has been exercising its art for thousands of centuries; she is only aware of her own impotence; she rages. Her arm extends, she breaks the web, and everything has disappeared, the creature along with its work.

The woman resumes her pose and her immobility, her arms wrapped around her knees. Her vengeful gesture has calmed her down, but her languor persists; again, her gaze rises up toward the foliage, where it loses itself, along with her vague thought. The memory of her failure returns at the sight of the vines. Then she lowers her head toward her hand, which she examines for a long time. She waggles the stout fingers. She thinks.

Daâh understands her, and immediately commences the same gestures; he opens his right hand and his left; he closes them, turns them over, displaying the back and the palm, folds the articulations, straightens out the phalanges.

Stupidly and sadly, he contemplates that tool, which will be the instrument of his genius.

LXVIII. Pathology

Humans are, to a greater extent than any other, adaptable animals; they have proved that by succeeding in living in a world in which everything cooperates in their annihilation: their nudity, their small number; the weakness of their natural weapons, the multiplicity of beasts that eat them, the variation of tropical and glacial climates that they have been able to traverse by turns, while other species, seemingly more solidly endowed, have been obliged to emigrate or perish.

Of maladies, in particular, they have no shortage. The extreme humidity of the climate, the constant rain that falls by day and night, the lack of shelter, garments and fire, fatally determine an early rheumatic diathesis. The abundance of marshes and the profusion of insects also propagate paludal fevers.

Perpetual mastication having inflamed the gums, they are red. In many cases, the teeth have become detached. Bellies dilate. The most frequent troubles afflict the digestive tract; a total absence of foresight ensures that, by turns, they eat too much, or no longer eat, or eat no matter what, in accordance with the seasons. A carnal alimentation of strong meat, swallowed raw and in excess, alternates with long fasts, and periods of famine in which they fall back on the fungi that abound in the drenched forest, tempting hunger and provoking stomach aches and poisonings.

From these accidents they never obtain any practical education; they only receive an impression of mystery. When a livid individual with contracted features, naked under the rain, writhes in the mud, they form a circle around him; no other circumstance of life can fix their attention for such a long time. Rendered stable for once, they move internally; emotion, the distant generator of thought, labors them; thus apparently stopped, they are almost thinking.

They assist one another by the simple fact if remaining side by side and extending their souls toward a single goal; mute but unanimous, they are already a crowd, and all together, with a common certainty, they imagine the absurd; like Daâh: no one doubts that the patient is the prey of an invisible animal. That imagination was the first acquisition of their genius, and, puerile as it seems to us, it is not so stupid, since the progress of science has tended to bring it back; furthermore, it was the only one permitted to them.

The overburdening of their nerves also exposes them to troubles that are especially manifest in the children and the women. Convulsions are frequent among the former; as for the latter, overwhelmed by fear, fatigued from puberty by successive pregnancies of whose cause they are ignorant, they die young, or at least younger than the males. For old age was then a condition that did not have time to appear, since any decrepitude of the individual immediately made the invalid a laggard, vanquished and comestible.

LXIX. Patriarchy

Daâh was not yet decrepit, but a singular fatigue was beginning to weigh upon him, and astonished him. His limbs, less supple, refused certain gestures, which made him cry out in pain. Sometimes, he had difficulty drawing himself up to his full height. Several of his sons were more upright than him, stronger, and especially more agile.

He remained convinced nevertheless that all of them, big and small, had only survived because of him, and continued to owe everything to him; their birth was virtually the only thing with which he thought he had no connection, but if he had no inkling that a line parentage attached him, as a man, to the produce of the women, he was, on the contrary, perfectly well aware of the link of dependency that attached that crowd of protégés to their protector. His ignorance of his paternity did not, therefore, diminish the sentiment that he conceived of his paternal authority.

Of that he was jealous. He did not permit anyone the attitudes of a chief, and no one had any pretention to them; even the males were only rarely reluctant to obey him or to imitate him, having been subject since their earliest infancy to a training whose habits were prolonged into their maturity.

In spite of that deference, he only tolerated those fully-grown sons impatiently, and their valor or vigor displeased him increasingly as he felt his own strength diminishing. When one of them had felled some large item of prey, he abstained from taking part in their dances, but he pretended only to be standing aside out of disdain. Wedged against a tree trunk, he watched the horde caper around the beast, and he would not have admitted either to anyone else or to himself that any physical reason compelled him to adopt that noble attitude.

For analogous reasons, Hock and Ta, less proudly dissimulated, also dispensed with gamboling; they came to crouch at his feet in their lassitude, one to the right and the other to the left, and the trio waited impassively for the feast, with the result that he gradually deluded himself as to the initial causes of his abstention and ended up believing in the necessity of his contemplative role. He was presiding; he was officiating.

At the same time as he took on a quasi-sacerdotal role, the ceremony that was accomplished before his eyes increasingly took on a ritual character, and the future patriarch was prophesied in the father.

LXX. The Rights of the Chief

One day, Hock's eighteenth grandson, who was then in his fifteenth year, killed his first Bear. He was proud; he struck his torso, showing his club to his brothers and sisters, and they all quivered with joy. But Daâh did not experience any. Standing a few paces away, his brows furrowed over his narrow eyes, and he gazed without moving.

The brown beast was lying on its side and its mouth was bleeding onto the grass. The adolescent, one foot posed upon it, was laughing; all around, the naked family was pressing; the smallest were wriggling in between the longer legs in order to get a closer look. Backs were bent and raised, waving arms extended from the mass, and heads rolled; that swarm of russet or rosy flesh moved its living brightness in the green shadow of a fig tree, and the beaming face of the victor dominated them all.

At that moment, Daâh felt a strange languor in his chest and more heaviness in his limbs, more fatigue than he had ever had after expending himself in a rude combat. Still without pleasure, he watched the contortions and mimes of the round-dance; by their gestures, the dancers announced its defeat and death to the Bear, as if it were unaware of them, and as if it were still capable of hearing their mockery and suffering in consequence.

You won't prance anymore! You won't eat any more little humans!

Some mimed trampling the children and young women beneath their feet and chewing the backs of their necks; others threw themselves on the ground in the prop of the cadaver, in order to be trampled, and let their tongues hang out.

That's what you look like now!

The triumphant victor urinated on the Bear's head, in the midst of laughter, and again, he made his chest resonate with blows of his fist, to affirm his prowess.

Daâh could no longer stand it. He came forward. A disdainful moue inflated his large mouth. Shaking his head, he pointed an index finger at the dead beast, and with the other hand, whose palm was spread at the height of his nipples, he indicated that the prey belonged to a small species. Then, in his turn, he hammered his torso, and, hoisting himself up on tiptoe, he raised his right hand as he could, expressing in that fashion that he had killed a colossal monster, a true King of the Caverns, and he showed his right hand: "Ta!" and showed his left: "Ta!" because he had known that victory twice.

After which he returned majestically to the trunk of the fig tree, satisfied that he had humiliated his rival.

The latter growled because someone wanted to diminish his merit; until the end of the dance, he sulked; at times he turned a rancorous gaze toward the Chief and shook his fists. With one bound he hurled himself upon the beast and tore out the eye.

"Mâh!"

He showed it to everyone, and burst out laughing, and held it high above his open mouth, in his fingertips, preparing to swallow it. Before that assault on the privilege of the master, faces gaped in fear.

Daâh, lashed by the insult, had roared; already, he was in the center of the group. He seized the insulter by the midriff, and the bear's eye rolled in the mud. With a vigor multiplied tenfold by rage, the father shook his grandson as he would have shaken a tree in order to uproot it; the other gasped and bit the skin of his scalp through the thicket of hair.

They collapsed together, the younger underneath, crushed by the mass of his adversary and stunned by the impact. Daâh took advantage of that to get hold of his neck with both hands. As he got to his feet he lifted him off the ground and whirled him at arm's length; then, relaxing his grip, he launched him into the distance, above the heads of the admiring horde.

The young man got to his feet. Without even looking at his relatives, he departed, forever.

In the middle of the circle, Daâh was panting; his torso swelled with pride. Slowly, he turned his head to the right and the left to show himself to everyone. Serene henceforth, because he had just proved that he was still the strongest, he picked up the muddy eye and swallowed it.

LXXI. The Edge of the World

It is now more than thirty years, and perhaps forty, that Daâh and his women have always moved forward, in the direction of the Suns. They have no notion of time; they only know day and night. They have vaguely observed the alternation of the seasons, which alternately render existence a little more or less hard, but those variations have not been sufficiently sensible to strike their minds; all days are alike under the indefinitely veiled sky; from one end of the year to the other, the thunder beats time for the moments. When the leaves fall from the branches, they know that they will soon be getting more fearful and hungrier, since the nights will be longer and prey rarer; they know that beyond the trees there are other trees, which are similar, with similar costumes of green and brown, which they will shed and put on again; everything recommences; they know the endless monotony of a march whose goal is always receding.

They have nothing more to learn about the world; they have recorded all its resemblances, and that interminable renewal of the same forms: Oak and Beech, Oak and Birch, and more Birch and Oak, one Cloud followed by another Cloud; the water flowing in the river, and the Hippopotamuses on the bank, the pools with the Damsel-flies, and the Oak with the Birch...

They know what it is important to know about all of them: the Fig tree is good; the Walnut and the Chestnut are also sympathetic to humans and prove it by the fruits that they offer and the shelter they provide. The Fir-tree, by contrast, is treacherous, unwilling to tolerate anyone climbing it and vengeful; when one asks it for shelter in case of pursuit it breaks a limb for the pleasure of throwing prey to the predator circling its trunk. The best of all is the Oak; it is the ideal friend, providing acorns, the most solid clubs and the most reliable shelter; one sleeps better in its black branches than in

213

those of any other tree, confidently; places to lie down are broad and numerous; the entire horde can take refuge there; thanks to the Oak they are close to one another, and less fearful by night; the Oak has understood that and gives a benevolent welcome to the fright of poor humans; as strong as the Elephant, it is tutelary and familial; they love it and venerate it.

Several weeks ago, however, the forest they know so well changed its character; the species of trees, less varied and less densely crowned, provided less obstructed paths; between the rigid trunks of Pines and Firs the ferns bent down in docile fashion as the humans pass by, caressing their torsos. That amenity of the vegetal world pleased the humans, who were not accustomed to being so well received. An odor of resin pricked their nostrils cheerfully; the sandy soil no longer stuck to the feet; herbivores became rare, but also predators; pinecones were abundant and squirrels scattered. There were days of relative quietude.

Ultimately, the forest ended.

The soft Ferns have been succeeded by an inextricable thicket of gorse; that is a kind of forest, too, a wretched forest only a little taller than a man, but dense and spiteful, the leaves of which bear thorns, and which does not want anyone to go through it. It claws furiously at everything that passes, and does not let go of its prey. No game lives there, except for mocking birds that fly away as one approaches; the only nourishment to be found consists of pods of tiny black seeds. But the Chief will not consent to turn back; breaking a passage with his club, he goes forward. The horde follows, coarse hides bloodied by grazes. The children do not even cry any more.

That march lasted two days.

Then, there was a carpet of brown heather underfoot, with innumerable mounds under which they killed moles, which they ate without skinning them, they were so hungry. On the whole of that plain, they could no longer perceive a single tree. Nothing but Clouds! The humans had arrived in the land of Clouds; high up, in front, behind, all around, they were hastening toward the region from which the Suns and the Humans come. Their flight passed overhead like an advice to retrace their steps, and over that land devoid of shelter the wind blew with a vehemence that they had never known under the trees of the forest.

The Chief has understood that this region defends itself, like all the others; the land does not want humans any more than any other; it, too, repels them, with all the weapons and all the strength it has; after having starved them it lacerated them yesterday in order to eat them, and today it has them chased by the Wind. But Daâh will not give in! Upon the invisible adversary that seizes him by the torso and shoves him backwards he rains blows of his club, and rages at being unable to see his enemy. In order to prove that he is not afraid of it, he imitates it:

"Vouh! Vouh!"

He is obliged to lower his head, like a buffalo, in order to advance. The women and children follow on all fours, disheveled and blinded by the tempest that stings their eyes; when they pass their tongues over their lips they taste salt, which astonishes them.

Daâh raises his head and stands there, amazed. Facing him, the horizon is extended beneath the sky with a rigidity that has been seen nowhere else. To the right and the left, enormous rocks loom up, and between them, in a kind of hole, there is something vast, uniform and bare, which seems to be moving without changing its location, and which extends...

Daâh tries to comprehend. Anguish grips his throat. The immensity of the expanse weighs upon his loins. Too much space, too much sky, emptiness, the hectically racing clouds, that flat desert in which everything is astir, and the pitiless band that stripes the unknown, fill him with a fear that fixes him in place. Predators frighten him less; they are perils of his own size. The vaults of the forest are not there for him; he has never been so small and so alone.

However, a raucous sound of quarreling voices reaches him, and he divines a battle in the hollow at the foot of the rocks. Mouths are barking and howling there: are they biting one another, tearing one another apart? Who? He does not know those voices. He will go find out, but alone.

"Ta!"

He stops the horde behind him; lying face down, he moves to the edge of the heath; he crawls into the shelter of a rock and then, abruptly, stands up again.

Daâh is confronted by the Sea.

A sacred horror penetrates him. All his strength has melted away at a stroke. Daâh feels that he is like the dead. He no longer exists. Troubled and rapid, his entire past goes through his head. For as long as he has been marching, he has been marching in vain! The impenetrable has stopped him; nothingness has appeared to him. The great soul of mystery takes hold of his little nascent soul and stifles it.

For the first time, the Human has received the impression of Infinity.

LXXII. Low Tide

Immediately, Daâh and his children accommodated themselves to this new region. After the rude shock of their encounter with the Sea, the emotion calmed down; after an hour, the Ocean was summarily recorded.

It was the autumn equinox, and the tide had just reached its full height. The fury of the breaking waves lost its prestige by admitting its impotence; they soon perceived that the formidable beast was unable to emerge from its lair, and that it was roaring in vain; it rolled with ease enormous blocks that the entire horde could not displace by the thickness of a leaf, and it was obvious that it would be capable of throwing a Hippopotamus as a child throws a chestnut, but the prey that it tries to seize remain safe as long as they remain a mere two paces away from its reach; they could even throw stones at it without it succeeding to avenge itself; at the most, it spits; they spat on it in order to mock it, and they laughed in loud bursts before the monstrous waves.

They thought they had defeated it when it withdrew. They followed it. The saltiness of the water no longer astonished anyone. In the holes abandoned by the reflux, they found a host of crustaceans and mollusks, and rock fish, the abundance of a new pasture, and joy. Eels, maladroit Serpents, fled under the drying plants, where they killed them with clubs; Crabs appeared like redoubtable Spiders; they recognized Lobsters as giant Scorpions, whose tails clattered in anger, and one of them sliced clean through a woman's thumb with its blue pincers. The Shrimp were the Flies of the sea; the Octopodes with Tigers' eyes, when they bit into them, drooled blackly and wound their tentacles around arms, planting their suckers on the skin of faces. By hammering them with stones they opened up Oysters and Scallops. The entrails and gills of fish were savored with even more delight than their flesh, which lacked blood.

They had a feast, sitting on reefs quilted with wrack, and when their stomachs were full, their mouths continued even so to chew raw fish and amused themselves by spitting out showers of scales, which made them laugh.

Afterwards enormous algae, torn up from the depths, furnished festoons of ribbons, of which one alone was sufficient to encircle a torso with a resplendent adornment.

In the sand of the beaches empty shells gleamed with varied colors, like stone flowers; others resembled teeth doubtless extracted from beasts that the sea had devoured; many had holes. A young female threaded them on to a thin piece of seaweed and then suspended the brilliant necklace around her neck. As a surplus of joy, the pleasures the day were increased by an unusual security provided by the absence of predators.

However, when the waves returned with the rising tide, they swallowed up two young males who had lingered too long on one of the reefs. No one lamented them, for that fatal accident was in the natural order of things.

What surprised them more was to find the two bodies on the shore the following day, almost intact; the Sea, after having nibbled them, had not deigned to eat them.

That disdain seemed offensive. More than one had a strong desire to show the Sea that human children were not repugnant, and that one could eat them without disgust—but Daâh, who knew the world, after his fashion, knew by experience that all gestures are imitated, and he did not want to teach enemies what they did not have the idea of doing. Since the Sea did not know that children are good to eat, let it remain ignorant. Shaking his head to indicate *no*, he frowned at those who wanted to utilize that fresh flesh and, with an authoritarian gesture, ordered them to go and hide their feast on the heath behind a rock.

LXXIII. The Land of the Suns

In any case, a more copious windfall was reserved for them. As they went along the strand, they encountered the corpse of a Whale run aground in a cove. Deposited there by the tempest, doubtless several days before, the flesh was adding a stink to the wind. They were filled with admiration; they had never seen a monster of such dimensions. In that blue mass with the white underbelly they recognized a dead Cloud. Daâh, with a knowing expression, proposed that explanation by pointing at the sky and simulating a fall; no one hesitated to believe him. They circled around the colossus, inspecting it. With great difficulty, a doorway was opened in the thick skin; when it was large enough, the entrails flowed out; they went inside the beast.

They went into it in single file, great and small, tearing off shreds, which they devoured on the spot; the idea of an edible grotto amused them enormously. They gorged themselves on fetid grease; clamors of contentment emerged from the hole; sometimes, a naked individual, all sticky with black blood, emerged in order to breathe in the violent air of the sea.

There were days of idleness, for they stayed there for two days; such a beautiful prey merited the halt.

Another reason also invited them not to hurry; the day before, Ta had only been dragging herself along with difficulty. The rude effort of traversing the forest of gorse had exhausted her last reserves of strength; she had only caught up with the horde in the twilight of the second dusk; she did not want to march any longer. Shivering in the hollow of a rock, she received with a plaintive expression the slices of whale meat that the children brought her; she sucked them without biting into them.

Suddenly, on the third morning, after a more violent pressure, the tempest ceased. In an instant, the firmament cleared and the azure appeared, with a radiant Sun. Little white Clouds fled after the others and vanished. Light inundated everything.

Never before had the Nomads seen a sky so pure; never had the blue persisted for such a long time. Dazzled and open-mouthed, with half-closed eyes, they gazed through their lashes at the splendor that wounded the pupils. The Sea, suddenly blue, glittered; a multitude of little Suns danced on it and crackled, more numerous than mosquitoes on ponds; they played alongside one another, brilliant, pretty and happy, all young; even tinier ones lit up on the tips of damp blades of grass. The humans, bewildered by such a novel spectacle, no longer budged. Not a sound emerged from their throats.

Finally, in the silence, a child cried with pleasure, and then a woman. Almost immediately, Daâh burst out laughing, drawing himself up to his full height, and he beat his torso with mighty blows of his fist, in order to say to his family:

This is the Chief who was able to lead you to the Land of the Suns!

Then, a howl of victory rose from all throats into the light.

LXXIV. The First God

Old Ta, still crouched in the hollow of her rock, has heard that clamor of the delirious horde, rushing to the joy of living, from some distance away. The joy of living is no longer for her; old Ta senses that. An intuition informs her of her impending end. The light that is enthusing the others makes her feel ill. She has put her hand over her eyes to protect them, but gradually, she parts her fingers.

The entire heath, somber before, is enlivened, as if the myriads of corollas had suddenly blossomed. In that sudden light falling from the sky, that entire earth becomes a flower; the russet cereals agitate their stems, and the belated florets of autumn light up mauve and violet petals in the blonde vegetation; facing the sea, so blue, the burned ferns shine in sprays of gold; even on the waves, white bouquets spread out and sway as they advance; the brown granites have become rosy, and those gigantic flowers are lilac shadows vibrating in the placid breeze.

The dying woman widens her eyes now, in order to drink in more of the magnificence of the illuminated sea and the colored land. In order to see and feel more she crawls away from her rock. The light envelops her, the mild air caresses her. To extend all of her body to the benefit of that warmth, she props herself up on her knees, her torso forward, her arms widespread, palms onto the ground. Very slowly, on all fours, she moves.

She dares to raise her face toward the Sun again. In the time required to open and shut her eyes, she has seen it! It is not dull and round like the pale balls that one sometimes perceives in the clouds above the forest. Tressed with bristling points, it projects around it things that squirt and sting; it is like a resplendent rain springing forth and striping the surrounding sky. She has surely seen the rays the she believes she can hear. They go:

221

"Dzi! Dzi!"

She feels them stinging her skin; she admires the way that they shine on the hairs of her arms and thighs. They are alive. They penetrate into her utmost depths. Their warmth circulates in her veins and reanimates her; she feels radiant, like the sun; she believes that she is carrying it within her; her being expands. While the others, in the distance, continue to howl their inebriation, she excites herself in order to savor that supreme benefit more. Gravely, she gazes into space, with all her might. The world is becoming beautiful just as she is about to quit it, but she can see it, and all of her agonizing life in concentrated in her pupils.

Immobilized, she contemplates the universe; she is the first spectator.

She no longer dares to raise her eyes toward the splendor that is sizzling at the zenith, but she can still hear it.

"Dzi!"

She listens. Waves are breaking gently on the beach, lisping softly. In the harmony of the light, she discerns the harmony of sounds. The voices of the horde only reach her now as a distant murmur; they are drowning in the great All.

The universal vibration cradles Ta's soul, which dissolves and floats; she dreams; ideas that rare still nebulous are disengaged deep within her; with the clairvoyance of those who are about to die, she watches them rise.

She sees herself. She is very tiny, in the midst of an immense light; she is alone, and always has been. She is being released. Everything is abandoning her, even life. No one is paying any attention to her. She observes that without bitterness; she expects no more, of others or of herself...

Now, in her misery, help has come from someone: a force that is sent to her expands and warms her. She feels assisted, and she knows by whom. From the depths of her distress, she loves that which loves her; gratitude rises within her.

"Dzi!"

The Sun is good. She raises eyes toward it that give thanks. But the benefactor will not tolerate being looked in the face. Quickly, she has closed her eyes again, and, in order to receive the radiance in her heart, she strives to raise her upper body; she pushed the earth with her palms, her knees dig in. Finally sitting on her heels, she extends her arms toward the star; she offers her hairy breast to it. She implores it to vivify her a little, a little more.

She prays.

"Dzi... Dzi..."

Divinity is conceived; a woman has just given birth to the first human god.

Dzi of light, beneficent Dzi, protector of life, father of the world...

Soon, the Sun will be God.

LXXV. The Vanquished God

From the rising tide, however, a gust of wind suddenly blew, and Ta looked ahead, anxiously.

From the dull background in the distance, the storm is advancing once again over the Sea. The violet-tinted water is traversed by glaucous frissons, and is degrading all the way from the edge of the sky to the edge of the land; a somber band, extended over the horizon, is broadening under the mass of Clouds that is descending toward her, as if their weight were dragging them down. The Wind is a mere breath. The breaking waves are no longer foaming over the rocks. A sly silence extends over the motionless waters, seemingly emerging from the sea. The Sun has disappeared. A bright hole is diminishing in the distance. The Sea and the sky unite, and are only one.

Then, suddenly, a wave leaps up in the rocks, slapping the air. A wan gleam, which comes from nowhere, wanders as if seeking to flee. It has only lasted a moment. A squall, tearing the totality of the dark cloud, scatters shreds of cloud. The Sea, in a moment, becomes pale, and the entirety of the visible world, the waves, the coast and the heath, disappears at a stroke in the universal Rain.

It falls, intensely; the wind curls it up; its columns, swollen and twisted, like funnels, run toward the land, and their curves snake among the inlets and the reefs. Under that recommencing flood, the moribund woman extends her back; crawling on all fours, backwards, she returns to her shelter. She does not even grumble; she is docile and resigned; since birth, she has been accustomed to obeying forces, without wondering whether things would be better if they were otherwise, without comparing what is with what might be.

Returned beneath her rock, she gazes into the distance bleakly. Rocky islets suspended in the mist float out there, like great birds the color of mud. She remembers having seen them a little while ago like flowers; a desolation descends upon her, as vast as the rain and as heavy as the sea; the good Sun, which paid heed to her, has been vanquished and eaten; her hope dies of the same blow; nothing will protect her any longer; she renounces and abandons herself. She wedges her spine against the granite. She consents to die.

But life is still stubborn, and the rude ancestor does not die.

LXXVI. The White Flies

The torrents of the downpour fell for two days. The horde, which found ample food along the strand, waited patiently. All in all, life was good, since they only had to suffer without having to tremble; the absence of predators constituted a new pleasure, which they enjoyed even though it suggested a kind of malaise, equally new. The unanimity of large beasts in not wanting to dwell in the region was somewhat disquieting; it resembled a warning; it gave an impression of exile, and the humans, in whom the sense of animal solidarity still had the force of an instinct, were suspicious. The young males, especially, more bellicose and more nomadic, began to get bored with not fighting and remaining in the same place.

Hock scarcely quit old Ta, and every evening, Daâh returned to shelter with them; the horde imitated him. As one single rock could not be sufficient to shelter them all, three groups were formed, a short distance from one another, in the hollows of three refuges. Under the granite ceiling, they had cleared away the sandy soil without difficulty; by night, they piled into the moist holes.

Suddenly, the wind veered, blowing from the north; all day long, a furious breath whipped the sea and skimmed the heath; the rain stopped. The dying woman's teeth chattered and she tightened the pelt of a horse around her, which gusts of wind tried to tear away from her; burning with fever and thirst, she crawled on her belly to a puddle in order to gulp a little muddy water.

The night was glacial; the wind only slackened as morning approached.

There was then a very strange dawn, scarcely bright, and an entirely new sky; instead of the voluminous clouds, which ordinarily pursued one another, a green-tinted mass stagnated in immobility.

The thunder fell silent; a mutism succeeded its perpetual rumbling, which numbed the heath and even the sea. The weight of an invisible burden oppressed their chests; a lassitude devoid of a cause made their limbs heavy; their faces became bleak in the penumbra without anyone knowing why.

That semi-darkness lasted for another two days. Then tiny white things began to descend from the opaque sky.

Rare at first, and then multitudinous, they came silently, like dead Flies; gradually, but very quickly, they became so numerous that they filled the air; nothing of the world could any longer be seen.

Stupidly bewildered, the humans gazed at that pale and mute invasion, which they had never seen. On their arms, their hands, their shoulders and all over their bodies, those incomprehensible flies settled gently, and vanished...

They had the impression of an impenetrable force tightening around them, enclosing them in a circle forever. In that grayness, frightened silhouettes were seen, which raised their arms, running as if in search of a way out; they generated fear in their turn, so much did they seem no longer to be real human beings but shadows. No matter how close they were, they seemed to be distant; their cries of terror were stifled by the avalanche.

Panic took hold of the horde. They started to flee in all directions.

The Snow fell until dusk, and it fell throughout the night; the following day, it continued.

It took possession of the world for centuries.

LXXVII. The White Land

The naked humans gathered under the three rocks, uniquely attentive to protecting themselves from the cold and reassuring one another by huddling together, remained curled up and silent. Massed and entangled, skin against skin, tightening scraps of fur over them, they displayed nothing but a cluster of haggard and bushy faces, issuing from a thicket of fleeces, with round eyes and lips parted in terror. Their flared nostrils sniffed the mystery of the surroundings. Of their perpetual mobility, nothing remained to those creatures but an anxious swiveling of the head on the pivot of the neck, as if they were searching relentlessly for the open gap through which they might escape toward life.

They scented death everywhere. From dusk to dawn and from dawn to dusk the white ground extended with an irreducible exactitude, and they watched it rise. An even plain spread out coldly, livid in the vicinity, dull in the distance. Anyone who tried to set foot on it sank into it thigh-deep. In spite of the hunger that was beginning to torture their stomachs, no one dared venture forth into the hazards of that world, which no longer had any form. The memory of the Whale run aground on the shore was no longer capable of giving them courage. One hungry individual, however, wanted to go toward that meat regardless; he never came back.

The certainty of a definitive impotence was increasingly affirmed; slowly, it was disengaged from the universal menace; slowly, it fell in dense flakes, to enter into the depths of souls. The horror that penetrated them all, at the mere thought of leaving the group and isolating themselves in that desert, even in order to find something to eat, became an obsession, and the obsession became a thought.

To think is to pause; a mind moving in a moving body, the human being who moved so much was not apt to reflect until the day when he paused in one place and on one idea.

Immobilized under that rock and by the ambient death of everything, and besieged by it, they perceived a truth, without which their race would inevitably have perished. It fell upon them with the snow: humans must not isolate themselves, under pain of death, and their resistance, as well as their strength will result uniquely from the association of their forces.

That rational idea was not suddenly inspired in them by the atrocity of the present moment; their whole existence had prepared it within them by an accumulation of examples. Furthermore, the violent influence of one soul was exercised on theirs.

Better than anyone, in fact, and a long time before the rest, the dying woman had understood; it was in her that the revelation first occurred, and she helped the others to think because she thought. In the center of the group, shaken by the horrors of a peril that she saw probable and imminent, she was the nucleus of the idea.

They're going to leave! Ta will be ALONE!

The consequences of solitude displayed themselves to her, in precise scenes that she discerned with the lucidity of an intelligence morbidly exasperated by fear, and the entire horde, around her, thought like her, a little less clearly, but no less egotistically.

To all of them, the region which they had previously thought magnificent and benign, was revealed to be uninhabitable. They execrated it. Its very splendor had been nothing but a trap to attract prey.

The eyes of Serpents summon Birds, and that deadly country has appealed to humans with its bright Sun, shining like an eye. It has made them come, in order to eat them with its white mouth, which is closing upon them! They are going to die!

Unless someone saves them, if anyone can, if they can still be saved...

Ta senses the idea that is floating and laboring in all those beings. The conclusion is still belated in them when the dying woman is already sure

They are going to leave, and Ta will remain here all alone. They are going to leave if a Sun does not come back...

LXXVIII. The Eye of the World

From the depths of her distress she thinks about the Sun that helped her, in kindly fashion; by returning to the sky, perhaps it would retain the Nomads? She disengages her arms from the furs; with an almost intuitive gesture, she extends her arms toward the place where she saw the resplendent Benefactor.

Astonished, the others watch her do it; she sees their gazes converging on her face, and in her turn, she fixes her ardent pupils on theirs; she contemplates them avidly; she plunges into them with a frenzy. Soon, she can no longer see them, the eyes of humans! They have gone, like the One in the sky. An affinity appears to her between the eye that perceives the light and the one that pours it. She loves them together, she regrets them together, and she assimilates them.

Dzi, Eye of the World!

Better to implore it, she moves out of the shelter, her knees in the snow. She evokes it with all her might. With all her mind, which extends, she searches for a means of aiding the god Sun to return to her, of obliging it to return.

Eye that shines, great friendly Eye, you who prevent solitude and denounce dangers, you who make one less afraid at the same time as one is warmer...!

She adjures it mentally. In the desperate effort of the dying woman, who is seeking a means of exciting the protector, an idea springs forth! Ta remembers that examples are always imitated; she knows that; she has had proof of it so many times! That memory, suddenly, has leapt into her head, and her idea, which bears within it the seed of future magic, is already the embryo of the naïve hope that will dream of exciting the forces of nature by means of an example offered to them.

"Dzi..."

231

She murmurs the sacred name. At the same time, with the tip of her index finger, she designs in the snow the roundness of an eye; in the center, she pricks the dot of a pupil.

Over her shoulder, curious faces lean. They examine. They seek to divine. Mute gazes meet and interrogate one another. Except for the dying woman, however, no one can understand, as yet. It is too soon for those who are alive; they can look with all their soul at the snow over which the old woman's finger has moved, but all they can see is a streak, and a hole.

They sense, however, that something strange is happening. An ambiguous anxiety oppresses them; a kind of respect intimidates them; without moving, they observe the back of the ancestor, whose two hands are now trembling toward the sky; in their turn, they raise their heads to try to follow the direction of the gaze that is scrutinizing space, fascinating a god.

LXXIX. The Accursed Land

In vain the dying woman extended her arms toward the zenith; no Sun appeared.

Suddenly, behind the veil of raw flakes, something stirred. A gray form appeared: a human, buried waist-deep in the snow, gesticulated. To test the ground, Daâh had crawled outside the shelter, and marched as far as the next rock; he had come back. He had his club in his hand, as in the forest.

Ta understood immediately why he was carrying his club.

He stopped in front of the group,

"Heûh!" he said.

His voice was irritated; his guttural exclamation was accompanied by a grimace of hatred and disgust. At the same time, he had spread out his arms, and he turned his face alternately to the right and the left to show the horror of the region, everywhere.

The human cluster, which approved, growled "Heûh!" And all the faces contracted in a grimace similar to his.

Daâh was satisfied by that assent. Immediately, he pointed his index finger in the direction of the sea, which could be heard growling very faintly, and toward it too he howled:

"Heûh!"

"Heûh!" replied the men, angrily.

"Heûh!" repeated the women.

Even the children, from the depths of their throats, uttered the cry of aversion, thin and shrill. No one wanted that region any longer!

Then, the Chief indicated, in the opposite direction, the region from which they had come; with his arms curved around his skull, he evoked the rounded form of a vault, toward which he raised a marveled gaze, and everyone, at the same time, remembered the big trees.

"Ta!" he said.

The dying woman understood full well that he was not talking about her, but the forest. *That is where we must go!* The Chief's statement, this time, was as clear as an order. Everyone approved. Voices clamored:

"Ta!"

Let's go back to the trees!

Like a brood of larvae that suddenly begin to wriggle, limbs and torsos were disengaged from the heap. In the blink of an eye, they were all on their feet. The departure had been decided.

But the children yelped fearfully when they were pushed toward that cold whiteness. With a brutal fist, Daâh seized one and threw him out of the shelter. The little naked being rolled and stood up again; then, with bewilderment, they saw that he barely sank into the layer of snow, which the previous night had hardened. Was that plan less impracticable than they thought, then? Since Daâh had been able to go from one rock to another, since the white thing had not swallowed the child, was marching not impossible?

A vast gale of laugher saluted the brat, who was capering, and the boldest rushed gaily into the snow.

LXXX. The Adieu

The ancestor contemplated them in silence. The thought of retaining them or imploring them never even occurred to her, and the idea of abandonment was not very precise in anyone. They were going away, nothing more. If someone stayed behind, at their own risk, that was no one's business but hers. They had acquired, just now, a fugitive notion of the interest that humans had in not separating, but that notion did not implicitly entail that of familial solidarity. In any case, the memory was already distant. They were no longer thinking about anything but the forest, and that evocation was delightful; they were going to revive and march, and they were already on the move. There was no longer any room in their souls for anything but the joy of living and moving.

They did not even perceive the efforts that the dying woman was making to resume her place in the shelter of the rock. Moving backwards, she frayed a passage, brushing their legs with hers, but no one paid any heed to her. Only when she had arrived at her destination did they notice her, because of her immobility, which contrasted with the agitation of everyone else. Leaning back against the rock, curled up, her neck between her shoulders and her chin on her knees, she drew the pelt of a horse around her, and her teeth chattered; her little eyes, in the depths of sunken orbits, had the fixity of a shiny stone; her visage expressed the distress of an animal on the lookout for an inevitable blow, waiting for it.

Before the depressed attitude of old woman, they were content simply not to envy her place. It happened, however, that some of them paraded a grave lingering glance over her, in which there was sadness, and perhaps pity. But none of her children or grandchildren thought that they might take her with them. She alone had that furtive thought, when her last-born passed in front of her. He was now a tall and solid male; she gazed at him slowly, and she remembered.

I carried you on my back when you were tiny!

That thought only lasts as long as a fleeting memory; Ta does not dwell on it. She knows full well that women carry their new-borns and men their clubs, nothing more. In the forest of gorse, they would no longer be able to drag her; they would leave her among the thorns; it is better here. She does not reason, but the images file past, and she refuses them. She accepts her fate; by virtue of having compared it momentarily with a fate that seems worse, she even feels better; she will wait. She is ready. She draws the horse-hide more narrowly around her loins, which are shivering.

The horde is about to leave.

It is at that moment that Hock comes to sit down next to her, as if to say adieu; with an abrupt surge, she arrives, and she sticks her shoulder against that of the abandoned; then, lowering her head and twisting her neck, in order to look the other in the face at close range, she looks her in the eyes, and she laughs.

For the last time, Ta feels the warmth of a human presence penetrating her body.

Daâh, standing in front of the two grandmothers, contemplated them with an attentive, almost severe, expression; while examining them, he searched for something in himself, a very distant memory...

Finally, he understood: the group of the two women reminded him of the days of their youth, when the horde did not yet exist, and when, coming back from hunting, he discovered the two companions side by side, under a tree, exactly as they presented themselves here, under the rock.

In order to remember better, he screwed up his eyelids and clenched his teeth. What he perceived in the depths of his memory was undoubtedly agreeable to rediscover, for it made him laugh.

Immediately, Hock and Ta, who were already remembering, understood what he was thinking. Hock started laughing again, vehemently, shaking her bald head in front of the dying woman's face. The latter no longer had enough strength to imitate them, but they saw a blissful crease in her face, and two gleams of gaiety in her pupils.

Daâh was no longer laughing, however, and he remained standing, hesitant to give the order to depart; even though the gesture was decided, he delayed making it; he experienced a vague malaise, an embarrassment, difficulty that he could not explain, a sudden timidity, perhaps a shame.

He fixed his hard and anxious gaze on the old woman's eyes; then, again, he extended his arm in the direction of the necessary forest, and in a voice that was soft, in spite of his intention, he said:

"Ta!"

The moribund nodded her head up and down, to approve the departure.

Then he turned his back and started marching.

Hock got up and followed him.

The whole horde followed, without looking back.

Then the veil of snow fell between the abandoned woman and those who were going away.

LXXXI. The Abandoned

The last silhouettes, becoming paler and paler, faded away; the last muffled voices fall silent.

Now Ta is alone.

In order still to sense a presence, she draws her folded thighs against her breast with both hands, and hunches her back in order to drive her chin deeper between her knees. She listens; there is no longer anything in the air but the distant sound of the sea, whose waves are breaking. She gazes; there is nothing around her any longer but the movement of the falling snow.

She hurls into the desert a cry for help that is prolonged and interminable, like those of little children, and her voice comes back to her, returned by a rock. She will never hear another human voice again. She will never see their eyes again...

She raises her own eyes toward the place where the Sun shone, but everything is gray. She lowers them toward the place where she drew the Eye of the World a little while ago, but footprints have erased the drawing and the snow is effacing the footprints. The flakes, one after another, are piling up and filling in the holes. The plain is becoming uniform again.

Once again, in order to hear the sound of a human voice one last time, she cries out to the echo.

The snow falls.

LXXXII. The Couple

No one remembered Ta any longer.

The horde had returned, with difficulty, to the forest. Several of its members had been left behind on the way, buried in holes in the snow. The Chief always kept going, always in the lead, but with a more evident slowness and an increasing fatigue.

He was not old, but forty-eight years of marching beneath the rain and incessant battles had brought him to the end of his tether. No white hairs glistened in his fleece, but his entire body was striped with scars and his entire face creased by wrinkles. His teeth, after having chewed for fifteen hours a day for half a century, had been worn away almost to the jaws, like those of an old horse, and his heart, at times, ceased beating in his chest. Then, he choked; sometimes, he even collapsed; as soon as he recovered consciousness, he suffered less from the pain than the humiliation, and those who tried to help him irritated him no less than the malevolent animal hidden in his chest; he pushed them away, taking responsibility for punishing it on his own, with blows of his fist.

In fact, it was prodigious that he had lasted for so long. He was even conscious of that, and took no small pride in the fact of having seen so many sons and daughters of all ages disappear while he remained standing, unscathed; he concluded that he was admirable. Candidly, he considered himself to be incomparable, and was not far from admitting for himself the benefit of an exceptional immortality; at the very least, he was proud of having remained, without having any idea of mourning those who had not.

He did not refuse to grant a portion of that esteem to the companion who had been able to resist as he had; a little more than before, that life appeared to him as his work, since it had only continued thanks to him, and it was still his own strength that he admired therein.

As for Hock, she thought exactly as he did: as she felt her weakness increasing, the need for assistance and a confidence made of accumulated memories attached her more narrowly to the protector of her youth; although he was less and less capable of defending others, she did not feel secure except in his presence. She did not readily consent to leave his side. As soon as she lost sight of him she moaned and trotted on her old legs, arms forward, in order to catch up with him. That was, at any rate, much easier than before, because he rarely went out on hunting expeditions.

Sometimes, although he was close by, she bleated his name in a soft voice, purely to remind him of her existence.

"Daâh..."

He growled, not without gentleness:

"Hock..."

He had certainly noticed that increasing assiduity. He was flattered by it, encouraged it and lent himself to it, finding therein a compensation for the negligence that was beginning to become manifest among the young females and males, who were less attentive to his person. The continued presence of Hock became necessary to him; more than that, he was anxious about her as never before.

Sometimes he called to her, spontaneously:

"Hock..."

Immediately, she replied:

"Daâh..."

And, like a dog, she was very proud that someone had thought of her.

Thus, they arrived together, she by virtue of humility and he by virtue of pride, at the same point: the sentiment of decrepitude on her part, and the refusal on his to believe in a diminution, led them to a common need to unite together, and they finally became a couple.

LXXXIII. Time Past

Since the epoch in which the obstacle of the Sea had obliged the Nomads to retrace their steps, the horde had been marching for three years in the forest. As before, they lived on fruits, roots and meat; as before, they slept in the trees.

But how things had changed!

Under the cover of the branches, the humidity became cold. From year to year the temperature declined. The first frissons of the glacial period were descending from the distant Alps, entering the underwood and making the leaves, the beasts and the humans shiver. Until then, they had scarcely known two seasons, an autumn and a spring, but from the fourth year onwards, a perpetual winter set in. The rain only fell rarely, but snow was daily. Thunder growled with less frequency in the clouds, but a uniformly dull sky displayed itself above the region without budging. The north-east wind dispersed that oppressive veil more often, and the daylight displayed the azure and the night the stars, but no one any longer rejoiced in that, because that thorny wind tore at the skin and the nights were glacial; sleep became impossible for naked humans isolated in a fork in the branches.

They began to search for shelters in order to pile themselves up there and keep warm, as they had done beside the Sea. They disputed with predators for their lairs, and between themselves they fought over furs. The notion of property, for which the invention of the masculine loincloth had prepared them, became more entrenched in their heads. To conquer the garment they lacked and to protect the one they possessed, the strong became more ferocious and the weak more cunning.

At the same time, the climate exercised a direct influence on the nerves, and subsequently on souls; every time the wind blew from the east, the spirit of the horde took on a more aggressive and more intolerant character; quarrels became more numerous, and degenerated into battles more surely. The women were even more subject to that irritant influence than the men; they shouted and bit one another. One day, two of them were seen to seize their new-borns by the ankles, in the guise of clubs, and strike one another with the infants' skulls.

As best they could, however, they adapted to the new conditions of life; the young, having scarcely retained any memory of their childhood, gave no thought to comparing the appearance of the world to its anterior state. The old suffered more; Hock and Daâh especially sometimes recalled the days of their youth, which seemed to them to have been better. Many joys were no longer for them. They contemplated the games of amour and battles gravely. Nothing tempted them anymore. The snow annoyed them. When it began to fall more thickly and the cold penetrated their bones, they sometimes looked one another in the eye, and one or the other, with a sad and weary inflection, murmured:

"Heûh..."

Then, both of them shook their heads. Their large hands spread out from their bodies to fall back on their hairy thighs, in a discouraged fashion, and the first couple thought:

Everything was much better in our day...

LXXXIV. The Crack

In the vague hope of rediscovering the land of his youth and perhaps the vigor of old, Daâh turned his back on the region of the west and led his troop away. When they arrived at the edge of a forest and he perceived in the distance the dark blue of another forest, he pointed to the horizon and said:

"Ta!"

They eventually reached a mountainous country. The summits were white with snow. They went around them, following the foothills of the range, and followed rivers upstream. They crossed over torrents and forded streams.

One evening, they emerged onto the edge of a plateau; the enormous river flowed down below, and hills covered with meager vegetation descended toward it in gentle slopes. They sheltered there. In the morning, they set out on the march again, and were about to go back into the woods when the sky was suddenly rent by a mad wind that twisted the clouds; in a matter of moments, the azure was clear; then the atmosphere immobilized in amazement. The trees, which the squalls had been twisting a little while before, were no longer moving; even the reeds on the banks ceased signaling with their long leaves. The Elephants lifted their trunks straight up, as if to interrogate space.

That bizarre calm had lasted for several minutes when the thunder began to rumble feebly; that was a familiar noise and no one bothered to remark that it contrasted with the purity of the sky. A few of them, however, burst out laughing, for they thought they had heard that noise with their feet, and not with their ears, as usual. Some of them bent down toward the ground and sniffed it curiously.

Their attention was quickly deflected by a stranger spectacle.

"Ta! Ta!"

He pointed at the plain and the hills; a frantic life was suddenly unleashed there; from all sides, they saw beasts running; they emerged from lairs, from thickets and from marshes; they arrived down below—and so many, so very many! It was as if the country, over immense extents, had suddenly got rid of all its inhabitants, in order to send them away pell-mell. The Rhinoceroses had quit their banks, and the placid Elephants were running at a gallop; Bears were shambling along, chased by Deer; Lions were running away before herds of Horses, or in the midst of them; Bison and Wolves were plunging into the path of Tigers, and Ostriches running on the heels of Hyenas. Not a single cry emerged from those suddenly emerged crowds. Herbivores and carnivores took no notice of one another; hunger no longer existed, nor murder, and the universal stampede hollowed out long parallel trails through the brush; even the Eagles were taking off in order to soar in the air high above the earth.

Before what common enemy were they fleeing in that fashion, in that alarming fraternity? The Humans marveled at the extraordinary flight, and they laughed; cheerful young males tried to throw themselves into the path of predators in order to mock them for their lack of courage; they uttered cries, brandishing their clubs; others crept toward prey; several ran down the hillside and went as far as the bank; women, by contrast, gripped by the panic of the animals, fled toward the forest.

They did not have time to reach it. A formidable crack shook the region; a crevice opened up along the plateau, vomiting mud, sand and fumes; a mountain tipped over and slipped down; another emerged from the river; the furious water climbed the hills, a rising torrent; sudden darkness had enveloped the world; lightning-bolts sprang from the earth; others streaked the sky; thunderstruck eagles fell from the clouds.

The floods went down again, with their cargo of cadavers; the dead were discarded together, animal and vegetable alike, amid the humus and the broken rocks.

The horde had lost several members, most of whom had perished by virtue of imprudence. Undoubtedly, they could not have escaped the disaster if they had tried, but nothing had informed them of the imminent catastrophe, although the other animals, less intelligent but more alert, had been able to recognize the approach of the earthquake.

Is it the case, then, that the latter possessed organs of information that humans do not have, or no longer have, receptive apparatus that has remained in a rudimentary state in them, or which has regressed, atrophied by the excessive growth of a neighboring organ? Has human intellect developed to the detriment of other faculties, while multiple families developing in parallel have enriched themselves with equally precious faculties? That which they will gain on the one hand, they are beginning to lose on the other. More apt to reflect on what they carry within them, they are perhaps already less able to perceive what is happening around them.

Many species demonstrate to humans how vast the world of sensations is that escapes them; to one, the sense of smell denounces what is odorless to humans; in another, the ear vibrates to the sound of mute things; another registers light where the human retina can only see darkness, and colors exist whose notion is forbidden to them that are probably permitted to several. At several leagues distance the effluvia of sex advertise to an insect in order that he might fly toward his bride; birds that orient themselves above continents and seas are able to fly straight toward their goal. Of the thinking faculty of which humans will be so proud, others are deprived, just as humans are deprived of their aptitudes; they consider their own to be supremely noble and of primordial utility; they are not wrong, since it has led them to the conquest of the world, but the others doubtless hold their own in the highest esteem, and cherish their privilege as Daâh is beginning to venerate his.

LXXXV. The Region of Fire

Elsewhere! Elsewhere! Far from the region where the Earth moves like the Sea and eats humans! They were in haste to be somewhere else.

"Ta! Ta!"

They climbed up and came back down. These new regions were strangely uneven.

Then they perceived, in the distance, mountains that did not resemble others: mountains without forests, only whitened by the snow at the base and on the sides, their summits remained dark, with a ruddy light, and a round cloud swayed at their crest; there were several of them, all similar in form, and each one had its glow, and each its cloud. The prodigy was amusing.

"Ta!" said the Chief.

The troop marched enthusiastically. Fond of novelty, the humans were excited in running toward that conquest; voices rose up at intervals to utter the encouraging cry:

"Ta!"

When night fell, the spectacle became more extraordinary still; in the heart of the darkness, the top of the nearest mountain became red and yellow, as if a Sun were setting there; Stars leapt up and fell back; vivid gleams snaked around the crest; the sky above was tinted red, and the neighboring slopes were illuminated. Glimmers, brightening at times, reached as far as the horde; at the tips of branches, leaves were seen suddenly to shine; the children and women laughed as they admired their hands, sunlit in the middle of the night. They could not wait for daylight to return so that they could set out en route again and get closer to the marvel.

Daâh, however, was suspicious of it.

What is this new beast? Might it not be a mother of young Suns?

He remembered having nearly perished, swallowed by the marsh, when he had tried to catch a Bird-of-Light. Several other males were also anxious. As usual, however, curiosity was stronger than apprehension, and as soon as dawn broke, they set off again gaily to get closer to the mountain.

It sent forth gusts of warm wind that gave pleasure to the skin. However, a singular odor stung the throat, and menacing voices were growling on the heights.

Into what new danger are we going?

Daâh was thinking along those lines, frowning. He went even so. The horde followed without protest, but fear was laboring their souls.

Suddenly, a louder growl burst forth. They all fled, seeking shelter. On the edge of a little wood, they hid in order to observe.

For an entire fortnight they prowled around the mountain. It fascinated them; a sharp desire to know prevented them from leaving; fright prevented them from climbing. They went around the slopes, climbing one slope and returning to their departure point. Gradually, they became accustomed to the monster. One morning, two adolescents ventured closer to it. Daâh saw the two silhouettes standing on a ridge that he had not dared attain. He growled with spite and clenched his teeth. Gripping his club, he surged forward.

"Haâh! Han!"

His battle cry roused the host. Men, women and children all ran; a trail of heroic clamors extended behind him, and the ascent commenced. When they were half way, the ground became hard underfoot; not a single plant, not a single blade of grass grew there. All along the route, there were bizarrely twisted protrusions of black rock, like unraveled entrails.

Then they entered a fog bristling with motionless forms like stone Bears, rearing up for battle. The Chief brought down his club on one of them to demonstrate that he was not afraid of anything, but he was obliged to stop there for a long moment, for the beast hidden inside him recommenced biting his heart.

LXXXVI. The Torch

He set forth again, determined not to allow any dread or fatigue to show in front of the young men. But the rude climb exhausted him. He leaned on his club and breathed deeply. He was obliged to stop several times more. He compressed his torso with his hand and waited, bent double. Then he straightened up. Refusing to give in, he cried, angrily:

"Ta!"

He set off again, still in the lead. Soon, the slope became steeper. A gravel of scoria as trenchant as flints slipped at every step. A cold wind was whistling at ground level, whipping around and carrying white clouds. The noise up above was taking on a more frightful violence from one minute to the next. Brown clouds were being exhaled in bursts, illuminated by flashes. Enormous blocks of stone were flying through the air to fall here and there, amid the black pebbles. The horde was reluctant to continue climbing, but the stubborn ancestor howled:

"Ta!"

He continued the ascent. No one followed him, except Hock, who was whimpering behind him, tugging on the flap of his bearskin to hold him back. He turned round, irritated by that surplus of fatigue, threatening. The woman let go. Soon, she saw him stop again, breathing heavily, his head bowed, his palm applied to his left nipple. He set off yet again. Docilely, she followed him. Young men followed in their turn. The majority of the women and children stayed where they were.

The Chief emerged onto a kind of terrace, which hardly sloped at all. The ground, covered with bluish blisters, resumed the aspect of spilled entrails and became hot under the thick pads of their feet. In places, puffs of thin clouds were emerging from that strange ground. An unfamiliar bitter odor caused the nostrils to grimace and stung the throat.

Over his entire body, from bottom to top, Daâh perceived the friction of a caress, as warm as the contact of some creature that was rubbing itself gently against his skin. He searched around him for that living creature, but saw nothing, except that the long hairs of his legs and abdomen were standing up vertically. Perplexed, but tenacious he wanted to go on regardless.

Suddenly, he jumped; a sharp pain had entered into the soles of his feet. No reptile was there, nor claw, tooth or bramble. The ground alone, and completely bare, was sinking those painful points into his flesh. Every time he put one of his feet down, the same inexplicable suffering obliged him to jump.

Hock, twenty paces behind him, watched him dance and was bewildered.

He retreated. Before he did so, furious with that aggressive ground, he struck it with a blow of his club. Then, very distinctly, he heard the plaint of a hoarse voice fleeing into the depths of the soil. At the same time, however, the black tip of the club gave birth to a small cloud: a yellow-tinted cloud, which swelled, and, scarcely born, rose vertically toward the sky. At the same time, Daâh saw a minuscule red Sun shining in the wood of the club.

Gripped by amazement, he sniffed it and coughed. He was suffocating. The heat around him was becoming stifling. Sweat ran down his brow. The fear of the unknown entered further into his soul. In order to see whether some new prodigy was about to assail him from one side or another, he inspected the surroundings.

"Heûh!"

Some distance away to the left, he had just discovered the enemy. Between the rounded walls of its grotto, an enormous red Serpent was emerging slowly from the ground, swelling up and becoming hump-backed, lifting itself up and lowering itself down again, respiring as it advanced, red everywhere, red and turning brown in the distance, for it was prolonging itself indefinitely and the head could not be seen.

Daâh fled and went back toward Hock.

"Heûh!" he said, in a low voice, so as not to attract the attention of the formidable monster.

She was trembling, and for a second time she tugged at the man in order to draw him away. She became even more frightened when she saw him, pale and with his eyes closed, put both hands, interlaced, to his heart, extend his neck, panting, and collapse. He opened his mouth in the fashion of a fish thrown on to the grass.

She spread the broad fingers that he had flattened on his torso, and in order to tame the interior beast, she started hammering his ribs.

Finally, Daâh opened his eyes again. His eyelids fluttered over his dazzled pupils. Turning his head in all directions, he looked around, making an effort to remember and comprehend. Then he perceived the group of young males down below, hesitant to rejoin him. The idea that they might come to defend him and attack the Red Serpent from which he had recoiled, in his stead, revolted his pride. He stood up and picked up his weapon. He shoved Hock aside with his elbows, and escaped from her, in order to run toward the giant reptile.

He no longer felt the ground biting his feet. He arrived, the club raised, and when he brought down his blow on the torrent of incandescent lava, sparks splashed him.

"Haâh! Han!"

Three times, he struck. The club had caught fire and was ablaze.

Having proved his courage, he went back down toward his family, without running. In his right hand, held high, he was brandishing his club in the air, enplumed by a flame that he took to be the blood of the wounded monster.

Daâh brought back fire.

LXXXVII. Toward Destiny

On seeing him come back with that red life at the tip of his club, women fled; a panic drew the horde over the slopes of the volcano.

Daâh continued to descend at his calm pace.

Behind him, the sun was setting; a glacial wind swept the side of the mountain.

Suddenly, everyone wanted to see the monster that the Ancestor was bringing.

He was surrounded.

One of the young males having decided to touch the ardent club with his own, he caught fire. Others, imitating him, ignited their clubs. When they burned their hands, it was necessary to drop them on the ground.

Of some they made a pile. Flames danced above it. A fine heat emerge. They sat around it. Red reflections illuminated their laughing faces from below. In the descending dusk, the first Family formed a circle around the first Hearth.

It was at that moment that Daâh fell unconscious. The beast that was eating him bit him for the last time, and he died.

The next day, when the horde woke up, they demanded to depart, because they were hungry.

Hock refused to accompany them.

She sat down tranquilly beside the immobile body, and, in the morning light, the Humans who were carrying away the Fire departed, toward destiny.

SF & FANTASY

Adolphe Alhaiza. *Cybele*

Alphonse Allais. *The Adventures of Captain Cap*

Henri Allorge. *The Great Cataclysm*

Guy d'Armen. *Doc Ardan: The City of Gold and Lepers*

G.-J. Arnaud. *The Ice Company*

Charles Asselineau. *The Double Life*

Henri Austruy. *The Eupantophone; The Olotelepan; The Petitpaon Era*

Cyprien Bérard. *The Vampire Lord Ruthwen*

S. Henry Berthoud. *Martyrs of Science*

Aloysius Bertrand. *Gaspard de la Nuit*

Richard Bessière. *The Gardens of the Apocalypse; The Masters of Silence*

Albert Bleunard. *Ever Smaller*

Félix Bodin. *The Novel of the Future*

Louis Boussenard. *Monsieur Synthesis*

Alphonse Brown. *City of Glass; The Conquest of the Air*

Emile Calvet. *In a Thousand Years*

André Caroff. *The Terror of Madame Atomos; Miss Atomos; The Return of Madame Atomos; The Mistake of Madame Atomos; The Monsters of Madame Atomos; The Revenge of Madame Atomos; The Resurrection of Madame Atomos; The Mark of Madame Atomos; The Spheres of Madame Atomos*

Félicien Champsaur. *The Human Arrow; Ouha, King of the Apes; Pharaoh's Wife*

Didier de Chousy. *Ignis*

Jules Clarétie. *Obsession*

Michel Corday. *The Eternal Flame*

André Couvreur. *The Necessary Evil*; *Caresco, Superman; The Exploits of Professor Tornada* (3 vols.)

Captain Danrit. *Undersea Odyssey*

C. I. Defontenay. *Star (Psi Cassiopeia)*

Charles Derennes. *The People of the Pole*

Georges Dodds (anthologist). *The Missing Link*

Charles Dodeman. *The Silent Bomb*

Harry Dickson. *The Heir of Dracula; Harry Dickson vs. The Spider*

Jules Dornay. *Lord Ruthven Begins*

Alfred Driou. *The Adventures of a Parisian Aeronaut*

Sâr Dubnotal *vs. Jack the Ripper*
Alexandre Dumas. *The Return of Lord Ruthven*
Renée Dunan. *Baal*
J.-C. Dunyach. *The Night Orchid; The Thieves of Silence*
Henri Duvernois. *The Man Who Found Himself*
Achille Eyraud. *Voyage to Venus*
Henri Falk. *The Age of Lead*
Paul Féval. *Anne of the Isles; Knightshade; Revenants; Vampire City;*
The Vampire Countess; The Wandering Jew's Daughter
Paul Féval, *fils. Felifax, the Tiger-Man*
Charles de Fieux. *Lamékis*
Louis Forest. *Someone is Stealing Children in Paris*
Arnould Galopin. *Doctor Omega*; *Doctor Omega and the*
Shadowmen (anthology)
Judith Gautier. *Isoline and the Serpent-Flower*
H. Gayar. *The Marvelous Adventures of Serge Myrandhal on Mars*
Léon Gozlan. *The Vampire of the Val-de-Grâce*
G.L. Gick. *Harry Dickson and the Werewolf of Rutherford Grange*
Edmond Haraucourt. *Illusions of Immortality*
Nathalie Henneberg. *The Green Gods*
Eugène Hennebert. *The Enchanted City*
V. Hugo, P. Foucher & P. Meurice. *The Hunchback of Notre-Dame*
Romain d'Huissier. *Hexagon: Dark Matter*
Jules Janin. *The Magnetized Corpse*
Michel Jeury. *Chronolysis*
Gustave Kahn. *The Tale of Gold and Silence*
Gérard Klein. *The Mote in Time's Eye*
Fernand Kolney. *Love in 5000 Years*
Paul Lacroix. *Danse Macabre*
Louis-Guillaume de La Follie. *The Unpretentious Philosopher*
Jean de La Hire. *Enter the Nyctalope; The Nyctalope on Mars; The*
Nyctalope vs. Lucifer; The Nyctalope Steps In; Night of the
Nyctalope; Return of the Nyctalope; The Fiery Wheel
Etienne-Léon de Lamothe-Langon. *The Virgin Vampire*
André Laurie. *Spiridon*
Gabriel de Lautrec. *The Vengeance of the Oval Portrait*
Alain le Drimeur. *The Future City*
Georges Le Faure & Henri de Graffigny. *The Extraordinary Adven-*
tures of a Russian Scientist Across the Solar System (2 vols.)

Gustave Le Rouge. *The Mysterious Doctor Cornelius* (3 vols.); *The Vampires of Mars; The Dominion of the World* (w/Gustave Guitton) (4 vols.)

Jules Lermina. *Mysteryville; Panic in Paris; To-Ho and the Gold Destroyers; The Secret of Zippeliu; The Battle of Strasbourg*

André Lichtenberger. *The Centaurs; The Children of the Crab*

Jean-Marc & Randy Lofficier. *Edgar Allan Poe on Mars; The Katrina Protocol; Pacifica; Robonocchio; Return of the Nyctalope;* (anthologists) *Tales of the Shadowmen 1-10*

Xavier Mauméjean. *The League of Heroes*

Joseph Méry. *The Tower of Destiny*

Hippolyte Mettais. *The Year 5865; Paris Before the Deluge*

Louise Michel. *The Human Microbes; The New World*

Tony Moilin. *Paris in the Year 2000*

José Moselli. *Illa's End*

John-Antoine Nau. *Enemy Force*

Marie Nizet. *Captain Vampire*

C. Nodier, A. Beraud & Toussaint-Merle. *Frankenstein*

Henri de Parville. *An Inhabitant of the Planet Mars*

Gaston de Pawlowski. *Journey to the Land of the 4th Dimension*

Georges Pellerin. *The World in 2000 Years*

Ernest Pérochon. *The Frenetic People*

Pierre Pelot. *The Child Who Walked on the Sky*

J. Polidori, C. Nodier, E. Scribe. *Lord Ruthven the Vampire*

P.-A. Ponson du Terrail. *The Vampire and the Devil's Son; The Immortal Woman*

Edgar Quinet. *Ahasuerus; The Enchanter Merlin*

Henri de Régnier. *A Surfeit of Mirrors*

Maurice Renard. *The Blue Peril; Doctor Lerne; The Doctored Man; A Man Among the Microbes; The Master of Light*

Jean Richepin. *The Wing; The Crazy Corner*

Albert Robida. *The Adventures of Saturnin Farandoul; The Clock of the Centuries; Chalet in the Sky; The Electric Life*

J.-H. Rosny Aîné. *Helgvor of the Blue River; The Givreuse Enigma; The Mysterious Force; The Navigators of Space; Vamireh; The World of the Variants; The Young Vampire*

Marcel Rouff. *Journey to the Inverted World*

Léonie Rouzade. *The World Turned Upside Down*

Han Ryner. *The Superhumans; The Human Ant*

Pierre de Selenes: *An Unknown World*

Angelo de Sorr. *The Vampires of London*

Brian Stableford. *The New Faust at the Tragicomique;The Empire of the Necromancers (The Shadow of Frankenstein; Frankenstein and the Vampire Countess; Frankenstein in London); Sherlock Holmes & The Vampires of Eternity; The Stones of Camelot; The Wayward Muse.* (anthologist) *News from the Moon; The Germans on Venus; The Supreme Progress; The World Above the World; Nemoville; Investigations of the Future; The Conqueror of Death*
Jacques Spitz. *The Eye of Purgatory*
Kurt Steiner. *Ortog*
Eugène Thébault. *Radio-Terror*
C.-F. Tiphaigne de La Roche. *Amilec*
Louis Ulbach. *Prince Bonifacio*
Théo Varlet. *The Golden Rock. The Xenobiotic Invasion; The Castaways of Eros; Timeslip Troopers* (w/André Blandin); *The Martian Epic* (w/Octave Joncquel)
Paul Vibert. *The Mysterious Fluid*
Villiers de l'Isle-Adam. *The Scaffold; The Vampire Soul*
Philippe Ward. *Artahe ; The Song of Montségur* (w/Sylvie Miller) *Manhattan Ghost* (w/Mickael Laguerre)

MYSTERIES & THRILLERS

M. Allain & P. Souvestre. *The Daughter of Fantômas*
A. Anicet-Bourgeois, Lucien Dabril. *Rocambole*
A. Bernède. *Belphegor*; *Judex* (w/Louis Feuillade); *The Return of Judex* (w/Louis Feuillade); *The Shadow of Judex*
A. Bisson & G. Livet. *Nick Carter vs. Fantômas*
V. Darlay & H. de Gorsse. *Arsène Lupin vs. Sherlock Holmes: The Stage Play*
Séamas Duffy. *Sherlock Holmes in Paris*
Paul Féval. *Gentlemen of the Night; John Devil; The Black Coats ('Salem Street; The Invisible Weapon; The Parisian Jungle; The Companions of the Treasure; Heart of Steel; The Cadet Gang; The Sword-Swallower)*
Emile Gaboriau. *Monsieur Lecoq*
Goron & Emile Gautier. *Spawn of the Penitentiary*
Rick Lai. *Shadows of the Opera: Retribution in Blood; Sisters of the Shadows: The Curse of Cagliostro*
Steve Leadley. *Sherlock Holmes: The Circle of Blood*
Maurice Leblanc. *Arsène Lupin vs. Countess Cagliostro; Arsène Lupin vs. Sherlock Holmes (The Blonde Phantom; The Hollow Nee-*

dle); *The Many Faces of Arsène Lupin; The Island of the Thirty Coffins*
Gaston Leroux. *Chéri-Bibi; The Phantom of the Opera; Rouletabille & the Mystery of the Yellow Room; Rouletabille at Krupp's*
Richard Marsh. *The Complete Adventures of Judith Lee*
William Patrick Maynard. *The Terror of Fu Manchu; The Destiny of Fu Manchu*
Frank J. Morlock. *Sherlock Holmes: The Grand Horizontals; Sherlock Holmes vs Jack the Ripper*
Jean Petithuguenin. *The Adventures of Ethel King*
Antonin Reschal. *The Adventures of Miss Boston*
P. de Wattyne & Y. Walter. *Sherlock Holmes vs. Fantômas*
David White. *Fantômas in America*
Pierre Yrondy. *The Adventures of Thérèse Arnaud*

SCREENPLAYS

Mike Baron. *The Iron Triangle*
Emma Bull & Will Shetterly. *Nightspeeder; War for the Oaks*
Gerry Conway & Roy Thomas. *Doc Dynamo*
Steve Englehart. *Majorca*
James Hudnall. *The Devastator*
Jean-Marc & Randy Lofficier. *Royal Flush*
J.-M. & R. Lofficier & Marc Agapit. *Despair*
J.-M. & R. Lofficier & Joël Houssin. *City*
Andrew Paquette. *Peripheral Vision*
Robert L. Robinson, Jr. *Judex*
R. Thomas, J. Hendler & L. Sprague de Camp. *Rivers of Time*

NON-FICTION

Stephen R. Bissette. *Blur 1-5. Green Mountain Cinema 1; Teen Angels*
Win Scott Eckert. *Crossovers* (2 vols.)
Jean-Marc & Randy Lofficier. *Shadowmen* (2 vols.)
Randy Lofficier. *Over Here*

ART BOOKS

Jean-Pierre Normand. *Science Fiction Illustrations*

Raven Okeefe. *Raven's L'il Critters; Rave's Faves*
Randy Lofficier & Raven Okeefe. *If Your Possum Go Daylight...*
Daniele Serra. *Illusions*
     Randy Lofficier. *Over Here*

HEXAGON COMICS

Franco Frescura & Luciano Bernasconi. *Wampus*
Franco Frescura & Giorgio Trevisan. *CLASH*
L. Bernasconi, J.-M. Lofficier & Juan Roncagliolo. *Phenix*
Claude Legrand, J.-M. Lofficier & L. Bernasconi. *Kabur*
Franco Oneta. *Zembla*
L. Buffolente, Lofficier & J.-J. Dzialowski. *Strangers: Homicron*
Danilo Grossi. *Strangers: Jaydee*
Claude Legrand & Luciano Bernasconi. *Strangers: Starlock*
Thierry Mornet & Juan Roncagliolo. *Guardian of the Republic*
J.-M. Lofficier, M. Garcia, F. Blanco & J. Pima. *Strangers in a Strange Land*